Terrifying Tailgater

One by one, the streetlights went out. And the whirling tower of dark, shot through with a sickly yellow, advanced toward her down the street.

Bree's dog, Sasha, drew his lips back in a snarl, crouched low, and crept toward the apparition. Bree judged the distance between the thing and the safety of her car. Sasha bounded forward. Bree yelled, "Heel!" in sudden terror for her dog, and sprinted down the sidewalk. The tower of oily smoke grew taller, wider, as if gathering itself for a ferocious charge. Bree flung herself at the driver's door, pushed Sasha in ahead of her, and jammed the key into the ignition.

The smoke swirled around the windshield. In the midst of the shifting mass, Bree caught a glimpse of a grinning white face.

She slammed the motor into life, gunned the car forward, and left the mist behind.

ANGEL'S
Advocate

Mary Stanton

BERKLEY PRIME CRIME, NEW YORK

THE BERKLEY PUBLISHING GROUP
Published by the Penguin Group
Penguin Group (USA) Inc.
375 Hudson Street, New York, New York 10014, USA

Penguin Group (Canada), 90 Eglinton Avenue East, Suite 700, Toronto, Ontario M4P 2Y3, Canada
(a division of Pearson Penguin Canada Inc.)
Penguin Books Ltd., 80 Strand, London WC2R 0RL, England
Penguin Group Ireland, 25 St. Stephen's Green, Dublin 2, Ireland (a division of Penguin Books Ltd.)
Penguin Group (Australia), 250 Camberwell Road, Camberwell, Victoria 3124, Australia
(a division of Pearson Australia Group Pty. Ltd.)
Penguin Books India Pvt. Ltd., 11 Community Centre, Panchsheel Park, New Delhi—110 017, India
Penguin Group (NZ), 67 Apollo Drive, Rosedale, North Shore 0632, New Zealand
(a division of Pearson New Zealand Ltd.)
Penguin Books (South Africa) (Pty.) Ltd., 24 Sturdee Avenue, Rosebank, Johannesburg 2196,
South Africa

Penguin Books Ltd., Registered Offices: 80 Strand, London WC2R 0RL, England

ANGEL'S ADVOCATE

A Berkley Prime Crime Book / published by arrangement with the author

PRINTING HISTORY
Berkley Prime Crime mass-market edition / June 2009

ISBN: 978-0-425-22875-3

BERKLEY® PRIME CRIME
Berkley Prime Crime Books are published by The Berkley Publishing Group,
a division of Penguin Group (USA) Inc.,
375 Hudson Street, New York, New York 10014.
BERKLEY® PRIME CRIME and the PRIME CRIME logo are trademarks of Penguin Group
(USA) Inc.

PRINTED IN THE UNITED STATES OF AMERICA

10 9 8 7 6 5 4 3 2 1

For Nathan Stanton Schwartz

One

"This seventeen-year-old high school cheerleader stole one
hundred sixty-five dollars and twenty-six cents from a Girl
Scout?" Most lawyers learned to keep a poker face early
on. Bree was no exception. She sat up a little straighter in
the kitchen chair, but otherwise didn't react. "What happened, exactly?"

Bree's aunt Cissy zigzagged around the kitchen in a
distracted way. "Lindsey—that's the grabber—and a couple of her girlfriends were tootling around the mall parking lot in her daddy's Hummer. She pulled up to the front
entrance, jumped out of the car, pushed the little girl flat,
and grabbed the shoebox that had the money in it. Then
she got back into the Hummer and buzzed off with the
loot." Aunt Cissy rolled her eyes. "There were a couple of
eyewitnesses, including the Girl Scout's mamma. The
teeners thought the whole thing was a hoot. Hung out of
the Hummer's windows, laughing their keisters off."

Cissy was eight years younger than Bree's mother, but
where Francesca Winston-Beaufort was soft, round, and
red-haired, Cecily was blonde and angular. Her sun-
streaked hair was courtesy of Fontina, Savannah's most

popular beautician; her wiry frame owed a lot to the gym on Front Street and weekly games of tennis. Cissy hopped onto the blue tile counter that topped the kitchen island and bounced her heels against the lower cabinet. "Thing was, some kid with a fancy cell phone videoed the whole thing, called up WKYR as quick as lightnin', and you can just bet the sorry mess is going to hit the six o'clock news. Carrie-Alice is just beside herself."

"And Carrie-Alice is Lindsey the cheerleader's mother," Bree said, just to keep the narrative straight. She added a few notes to the yellow pad in front of her. "I don't think I've met Carrie-Alice. She's a close friend?"

"Not all that close," Cissy admitted. "But the police called her right there in the middle of our Thursday afternoon bridge game. Carrie-Alice and I were playin' partners. I was dummy. We were," she added with a broody air, "about to make a small slam. Carrie dropped the cards and pitched a fit. That blew any chance of a slam." She leaped off the counter and onto the floor. "So what was I supposed to do? Just leave her all distraught in the middle of the card room at the club? No, sir. I have a niece, I said, who's probably the best lawyer in Savannah and she can get your Lindsey out of jail quicker than blink."

Bree raised an eyebrow. "Lindsey's in jail?"

"As near as makes no difference. The police took her down to the station on Montgomery after they caught up with her. Impounded the Hummer and for all I know, impounded Lindsey, too." She shook her head. "Well, now, I'm a liar. The kid's back home, come to think on it. Carrie-Alice hared off down after her and I hared off to find you." Her aunt narrowed her bright blue eyes. "I would have met up with you at your office, but damned if I couldn't find it, Bree. And I've lived in Savannah pretty near all my life. Just where *is* Angelus Street?"

"I'd come home for lunch anyway," Bree said evasively. Very few people knew that the only clients who could find 66 Angelus were the dead ones. The law firm of Beaufort & Company had another office on Bay Street for those clients currently among the living, but renovations were still in progress after a deadly fire. Bree offered her usual diversionary fib: "Mamma might have told you the Angelus Street office is temporary until Great-Uncle Franklin's old offices are ready for me to move into. Anyhow, it's much more comfortable here."

"Here" was the family town house overlooking the Savannah River. It sat at the end of a row of rehabbed brick buildings, two stories above the cobblestone-lined River Walk. Bree loved the location. She could clatter down the steps, with their wrought-iron rails, and walk to the brick bulwarks of the centuries-old wharf and her favorite shops in less than three minutes.

"I hardly think you'd want to meet Carrie-Alice in the kitchen instead of a nice professional-looking office," Cissy complained. She shook her head. "Whatever. I guess you can get on out to Carrie-Alice's place on Tybee Island just as easy." She reached over, twirled Bree's yellow pad, and wrote down an address and phone number. "Be best if you followed me there. I've got a late afternoon massage over at the spa."

Bree needed new clients, but she wasn't wild about representing a kid who'd ripped off an eight-year-old Girl Scout. "I'm sure the family lawyer is well equipped to handle something like this. If not, I can give her a referral to an attorney better suited to criminal law than I am. I'll be happy to meet with Carrie-Alice and tell her so. And what's the family name, Aunt Cissy?"

"Chandler."

Now that was interesting. "As in Probert Chandler? The drugstore king?"

"Marlowe's. That's the one. Pots of money, of course,

which is another reason I thought about you right off. It can't be easy starting out all on your own. And it's a case that will get you a lot of attention. I was thinking about a defense, Bree honey. Probert's been dead less than four months and here his little girl is stealing cookie money in broad daylight."

"I heard something about Chandler's death. He wasn't very old. Late fifties, I think?"

"Fifty-eight. Car accident," Cissy said with a shake of her head. "All by his lonesome on Skidaway Road in a rainstorm." She flung her hands wide. "Clearly—*clearly* the child is suffering from some kind of displaced grief."

"Delayed some, too, since it happened four months ago," Bree said. She remembered the accident, now. It had made international news, the way anything Probert Chandler did. Marlowe's Drugstores, Inc., had annual revenues that rivaled the GNP of a small South American nation. Probert Chandler was famous for building the megacorporation up from a nothing drugstore located in Portland, Oregon. That, and for his unpretentious lifestyle. The car he'd been driving when he went off Skidaway Road to glory was a Buick.

Cissy beamed. "This kid's case is just the sort of thing that can put you on the map, lawyer-wise."

Bree tapped her pen against her teeth. She didn't want cases that got her a lot of attention. She had her hands full with the weirdness of her current caseload. The last thing she needed was a spotlight on the activities of Beaufort & Company. On the other hand, at least some of her clients had to be alive and ready to pay reasonable fees. She looked down at her feet, where her dog, Sasha, lay curled up, nose to tail. Somebody had to keep him in kibble and the office rent paid. Not to mention keeping up with the pitifully small salaries of her secretary and paralegal. And that somebody would be her. But she said, "The Chandler family's got lawyers up the wazoo, Aunt Cissy. I don't see what I can bring to the party."

Cissy put her hands on her hips and snorted. "You're kidding me, right? Is this seventeen-year-old teenager going to relate better to you, or some middle-aged, potbellied banker type who's only interested in protecting the family name? You're twenty-eight and gorgeous. You're somebody she can *talk* to, Bree."

Bree made a face.

"And besides, it's something of a challenge, isn't it? It's going to be quite a trick to make this little girl look sympathetic." Bree took a deep breath. Cissy raised both hands and yelled, "Sorry, sorry, sorry! You've got the same look your mamma gets when she's about to give me a lecture on the overprivileged, which she thinks is you, me, and anybody with the least little bit of a trust fund."

"We *are* overprivileged," Bree pointed out. "You, me, Mamma, and Antonia, too." She thought a minute. "I take that back about Antonia." Her little sister lived at the town house on the incredibly feeble wages she made as a tech director at the local repertory theater. Somehow, she managed to pay her half of the living expenses and for acting and singing lessons, too.

"This is why you should take this case on," Cissy said. "This is what I should have said from the beginning. What I really *mean*, Bree, is that this girl needs your help."

Bree nudged her dog with her toe. There were times when her dog was more than a dog to her. "What do you think, Sasha?"

Sasha lifted his head and shoved his nose into the palm of her hand. Bree looked into his amber eyes. He panted happily, tongue lolling, lips drawn back in a doggy grin. Under her steady regard, he glanced away, glanced back, and barked. A wait-and-see sort of bark.

"That's an awfully big dog to keep in here," Cissy

said, her attention momentarily diverted. "Haven't the other owners gotten a little hissy? I thought the covenants didn't allow any pets over forty pounds."

Sasha stood thirty inches at the shoulder and weighed over a hundred and twenty pounds. His broad chest and powerful hindquarters came from his mastiff forebears. The gentleness of his expression and golden coat were all retriever. "Nobody's noticed anything yet," Bree said truthfully. And very probably, nobody would. The dog had a unique ability to make himself scarce when necessary. It was nothing short of . . . angelic. "As for representing this case"—she rubbed her nose—"I think I'll take a pass. This girl sounds like she needs a shrink more than she needs a lawyer."

"Your daddy didn't raise a daughter fool enough to turn down a case from the Chandler family." Cissy slung her tote over her shoulder with a knowing air. "So are you going to come out with me to Tybee Island?" She drew her eyebrows together. A Botox devotee, her forehead never wrinkled. "If you can't find the time to give this little girl a hand, Bree, honey, you need to *make* the time. I suppose you're all booked up this afternoon?" A trust fund baby herself, Cissy had a touching pride in the success of her professionally employed niece.

Bree didn't have to look at her Day-Timer to know that the rest of her afternoon was depressingly free of client appointments. And she knew her aunt Cissy. She was as determined as a bulldozer. She sighed and threw both hands in the air. "Okay. I give. But I'd rather set up an appointment than show up unannounced." She pulled out her cell phone and glanced up at her aunt. "And I don't mean to come over rude, Aunt Cissy, but we'd both be better off if you didn't come with me."

To her mild astonishment, Cissy nodded agreement. "Be embarrassin' for everybody if Carrie-Alice didn't want to hire you after all." She stooped over and kissed Bree on the cheek. "Thank you, darlin'. I'll be off. Will I see you at Plessey this weekend?"

"At Plessey?" Her family's estate was in North Carolina, a good six-hour drive from the Savannah town house. Bree loved her family, but one of the reasons she'd settled in Savannah was because she *was* a six-hour drive from her loving, intrusive relatives. She shut her eyes in sudden recollection. "Hoo. I forgot. Saturday's Guy Fawkes night." For reasons lost in some time around the Civil War, the Winston-Beauforts had a huge party for it, but November fifth fell on a Thursday this year, so her mother had set the party for Halloween weekend. Bree's excuses for staying put were lamer than usual. Everybody knew she was dateless since Payton the Rat dumped her three months ago. "I don't think so, Cissy. I've got a ton of work stacked up." Her aunt's shrewd blue eyes twinkled, and Bree added feebly, "Research."

"I thought that's what your paralegal's for."

"Petru's Russian," Bree said. "Needs a little help with his English now and then."

"Hm," Cissy said. "That'll not cut ice at all with Francesca. But it's on your head and not mine. Go ahead. Stay home. Just don't answer your phone, that's all I can tell you." She rummaged in her large tote, pulled out her compact, and examined herself critically in the little mirror. "I'm wonderin' if I shouldn't step up the Botox a little. What do you think?"

"I like faces that make faces back at me," Bree admitted.

"You think? Wait twenty years. Once you're nudging fifty you get a whole different perspective." She snapped the compact shut, dropped a kiss on Bree's head, and slammed out the back door.

Bree ran her hand over Sasha's neck. It had been several

weeks since she'd rescued him from an animal trap in the
depths of the cemetery that surrounded her office. The
cast had just come off his leg this morning. He'd put on a
healthy amount of weight. His muscles rippled under his
golden coat. Pink, healthy skin replaced the sores that
had covered his hindquarters and chest. "This is another
kind of rescue, dog. So I suppose I could at least give the
poor woman a call. We'll walk back to the office and do
it from there."

Bree put her lunch dishes in the sink, snapped on
Sasha's lead, and set out on the short walk to Angelus.

It was a fine late October day. The high humidity that
plagued Savannah in late spring and summer was gone.
The family town house sat above the warehouses and
naval stores that had been built into the bluffs overlooking the Savannah River these two hundred years past. The
town house was part of a series of converted offices connected to one another and to Bay Street by a series of
wooden bridges and cast-iron arches.

Bree paused at the top of the cobbled ramp leading
down to River Street. Huey's beckoned. So did Savannah
Sweets. Huey's made a great cup of coffee and Savannah
Sweets had the best pralines east of New Orleans. Sasha
nudged her knee in a mildly reproving way.

"You're right. And yes, I'm going to work. And no,
I'm not stopping for pralines." Bree inhaled the scent of
the river, wondering if she caught a faint touch of brine
from the Atlantic three miles to the east. With a sigh, she
turned and headed across East Bay to Mulberry, walked
one block down, turned east, and found herself facing
Georgia's very own all-murderers cemetery and the small
Federal-style house that contained the office of Beaufort
& Company, advocates for those who had died and gone
to Hell (or, often as not, Purgatory).

Somebody, most likely her secretary, Ron Parchese,

since he was the fussiest—and most able-bodied—of her employees, had weeded around the wrought-iron fence and sunken graves and tidied the kudzu from the gravestones. The azaleas, camellias, roses, and rhododendrons that made such a glory of Old Savannah in spring and summer weren't flowering now, of course. But Savannah in autumn had its own peculiar beauty. Silver-gray Spanish moss draped the live oaks like graceful shawls. Hedges of Russian olive, boxwood, and bougainvillea flaunted the full spectrum of greens, from pale celery to near black. It was a lovely spot, if you could ignore the noxious odors from the graves. Bree took a cautious breath. The dank, earthy smell was charged with a horrid undercurrent of decay this afternoon. She narrowed her eyes against the sunlight and looked under the magnolia tree. Was it her imagination, or did a faint smear of poisonous yellow smoke foul the air?

No. She wasn't going to talk herself into a case of the heebie-jeebies. Bree shook her head, walked up the crumbling brick steps to the front door, and let herself in.

"Yoo-hoo!" Ron caroled. "Did you stop for pralines or not?"

"Not," Bree responded. She was in the foyer, and Ron's desk was out of sight around the corner in the living room, at right angles to the brick fireplace. He didn't need to see her to know who it was. He always just . . . knew.

She set her briefcase on the first step of the stairs leading to the second story. Her landlady, an elderly woman with the energy and mischievousness of an eight-year-old, had painted the stairs with a parade of brightly colored Renaissance angels. The figures marched up the treads and disappeared into the shadowy recesses of the second-floor landing, a blaze of gold, red, purple, and royal blue.

Bree caught the odor of strange and exotic flowers and

heard the faint skittering of paws on wood floors. Lavinia must be up there, tending to her "littlies."

"I'm not going to stay long," Bree said as she walked into the office area. "Cissy talked me into going out to see a new client on Tybee Island. I'm just going to call . . ." She stopped and looked around. "What happened to Petru's desk? As a matter of fact, what happened to Petru?"

"He's in the kitchen," Ron said primly. "Him *and* his pesky desk."

"He and his pesky desk," Bree said; sloppy grammar sometimes made her itch slightly. "What about him and his desk?"

As usual, Ron was dressed in impeccably ironed chinos, a striped shirt, Countess Mara tie, and loafers without socks. He folded his hands on top of his own desk—also, as usual, furiously neat—and gave her a wounded look.

"When *I* said 'him and his pesky desk,' the clause was the object of the sentence," Bree explained. "When *you* said . . ." She struck her head lightly with the palm of her hand. "Never mind. Just tell me why Petru's moved his stuff into the kitchen."

"Break room." Ron corrected her with an air of mild triumph. "You did say that it's more professional to refer to the living room as the reception area and the kitchen as the break room. And the reason he's in the break room is I couldn't stand one more minute of that Russian's mess. And Bree, he hums to himself when he works."

"So you made him move to the kitchen?"

"I didn't *make* him move. He volunteered." Ron wrinkled his nose. "I may have made a pretty heavy suggestion, though."

Bree had discovered very quickly that working with angels did not guarantee angelic temperaments. Ron liked things pathologically neat. Petru worked best as a little mole, hiding behind teetering stacks of files. And he did hum when he worked, a lugubrious drone that made her think of peasants starving to death in the revolution of 1917. She drew a breath and yelled, "Petru!"

There was a brief pause from beyond the door to the break room, and then the shuffle-thump that told her Petru was walking across the floor with his cane. Her paralegal came into the reception area, stopped, folded his hands over his cane, and peered benignly at her through his thick black beard.

"You moved your desk into the kitch—that is, the break room?"

He shrugged. "Ronald was reacting ke-vite badly to my singing, perchance." Petru's spoken English was heavily accented, and somewhat idiosyncratic. His written English was exemplary. "Also, he kept filing those papers which I did not wish to be filed."

"Because his idea of a filing system is to throw everything all over the floor," Ron said. "Honestly, Bree. Why should I have to put up with that?"

Bree cleared her throat. "Gentlemen," she began.

Petru thumped his cane onto the pine floor. "I am ke-vite happy in the kitchen. It's closer to the coffeepot, for one thing, and it is quieter, for another. I like it."

"You do?"

Petru nodded.

"And Ron?"

"As long as I don't have to stare at his mess or listen to him hum," her secretary said crossly, "it's fine. Just fine. Though I suppose if we don't get a case pretty soon, I won't have anything to file anyhow, so never mind."

"About new cases . . ." Bree settled herself onto the leather couch that faced the fireplace. She cast an involuntary glance at the painting propped on the mantel. It was similar in style and content to Turner's *Slave Ship*: a three-masted schooner surrounded by drowning men struggling in the depths of a roiling sea. It was a horrible subject, and it hung there as a reminder of Beaufort & Company's mission to save those unfortunates, abandoned by fate, who came to them for help. Even though, as Bree had learned with their last case, their clients might not have been the kindest of men and women in life. "Although I'm not sure if this is our case or my case."

Ron looked confused. Petru blinked at her wisely. "You have, perhaps, a question about the scope of our cause? Do we defend the living as well as the dead?"

"Exactly," Bree said.

"That's easy," Ron said promptly. "Souls in the temporal sphere don't need us. There are thousands of real-time lawyers out there."

"Oh, dear," Bree said. "I suppose I'll have to turn this one down, then." She tugged irritably at her ear. "To be blunt about it, it would have been a pretty decent fee, too."

"On the other hand," Ron said, "the living are the pre-dead, so to speak. Souls in transit."

"'Life itself is but the shadow of death, and souls departed but the shadows of the living,'" Petru said. "Sir Thomas expresses it ke-vite well, I think." Ron scowled at him. He scowled back. "Although, of course, he was not thinking of the need to pay the electric bill."

Bree's head began to ache. Whoever Sir Thomas was—More? Could Petru be referring to Thomas More? Anyhow—she'd bet he was a soul departed and not a shadow of death. Petru had an unsettling way of referring to long dead poets and philosophers as though he'd just met them for lunch. For all she knew, maybe he had.

"Which is to say," Petru went on, "that you may take on cases outside the venue of Beaufort & Company. And that we can assist you in the normal way."

"Nonangelic," Ron explained. "No extras, if you know what I mean."

Bree didn't have a clue what Ron meant. She did have a million questions about what her employees did—and where they were—even what they looked like—when they weren't helping her at the office. All of the questions seemed incredibly rude and impossible to ask. She had once asked Lavinia the actual form and function of her "littlies" and received, accompanied by an ominous roll of thunder, a sweet, impenetrable smile in response. She supposed they'd let her know when the time was right. In the interim, she roundly cursed herself for a well-mannered coward and let all of her questions boil around in the back of her mind.

"A paying client?" Ron urged. "Go ahead. Do tell."

"Well, this one's a doozy," she said. She explained, briefly, about the cheerleader, the Hummer, and the victimized Girl Scout.

"Dearie me," Ron said. "What a little witch it is. Lindsey Chandler, you say? I've read about her. Richer than she should be and nasty with it, from all accounts. Bree, you can't pass this one up." He reached forward and waggled his fingers. "You have the phone number? Hand it over. I'll set up an appointment right now."

Two

Più non ti dico e più non ti respondo.
I will tell you no more and I no longer answer you.
—*The Inferno*, Dante

Ten minutes later, Bree drove onto President Street, which would take her to 80 East to Tybee Island. Sasha sat in the passenger seat, head out the window, eyes blissfully closed against the breeze, ears flying in the wind. The Chandler place was on the south end of the island, facing Little Tybee. A pricey neighborhood, but not Old Savannah. The Chandler place was set back from the main road, surrounded by a ficus hedge more than twenty feet high. Ficus was rare in lower Georgia; Bree was willing to bet a large amount of money went each year to replacing frost losses. But it was an elegant hedge, no doubt about it.

The house was a Mizner clone. Like its sister houses in Palm Beach, it had a comfortable elegance all its own. The red tile roof, pink stucco, and elaborate wrought-iron fencing spoke of quiet good taste. The lawn was lush, with that velvety green cropped grass that was as soft as moss to walk on. She caught a glimpse of a pool out back surrounded by brick paving. Well-cared-for teak chairs and tables offered an oasis of comfort around the pool. Amazingly modest when you knew how much the Chandlers were worth. Bree felt a flicker of genuine interest in

Lindsey's behavior, in spite of herself. The family obviously downplayed their huge wealth, which argued for pretty good values, as a rule.

Or maybe not.

She settled Sasha in the front seat of the car, left both windows open, and walked up the brick pathway to the colonnaded front porch. Carrie-Alice Chandler opened the mahogany front door as Bree came up the steps.

"Brianna? I'm Carrie Chandler." She took in Bree with a brief glance and said dryly, "My goodness. You're related to Cissy? You're gorgeous, aren't you?"

As this complimented Bree at her much-loved aunt's expense, she wasn't sure how to respond, so she didn't.

Carrie-Alice was shorter than Bree, but then, many women were; Bree was five-foot-nine in her stocking feet. Bree knew the woman couldn't be more than forty-five, but she looked older. Her face was tired. She hadn't bothered to tint the gray out of her brown hair and she wore foundation that was a slightly lighter color than her actual skin tone. Her lipstick was an old-fashioned matte red. She was dressed neatly, if unimaginatively, in a well-cut linen skirt and cotton twinset in pale pink. A pearl necklace, small pearl earrings, and flat Todd loafers completed a look that was fine for the over-sixty set, but odd in a woman with a teenaged daughter. When Bree thought about it later, she decided it was a defensive way to dress.

Carrie straightened up, as if it were an effort to be courteous, and stood aside to let Bree pass. "Thank you for coming so promptly. Please come in."

Bree followed her through the wide, black-and-white-tiled foyer to the rear of the house. The house had a refrigerated flower smell, like an expensive florist. The furniture consisted of good-quality reproductions. The flooring was narrow-planked oak with faux pegs, a composite wood over subflooring, popular now in expensive homes.

"Would you like to sit in the sunroom or the study?" Carrie paused in the hallway and glanced over her shoulder. The door to her left was halfway open. Bree saw a room arranged with desk, bookshelves, and some very nice watercolors on the walls. The sunroom was straight ahead. The French doors were open to the pool area. A streaked blonde head peeked over the top of one of the recliners.

"Whatever you think best," Bree said politely.

"The study's where Probert used to have his little talks with Lindsey. The sunroom's where she and her little buddies hang out when she isn't harassing innocent Girl Scouts."

"Little talks?" Bree said. The phrase had unpleasant overtones. Involuntarily, she rubbed her arms.

"Lindsey's been a handful since she was a toddler," Carrie said briefly. "I left most of it up to Probert to handle. But of course, now that he's dead, it's up to me, isn't it? The study might give you a home court advantage, that's all." She smiled. It didn't reach her eyes.

"Why don't we let Lindsey decide?" Bree made it a question.

"Fine. She's out by the pool, I think." Carrie walked ahead into the sunroom. "You coming along?"

Bree left her briefcase in the hall and followed Carrie through the large, sun-filled room and out to the pool. The streaked blonde head was gone from the recliner. Except for a tote bag tumbled in a heap on the patio bricks, the area was empty.

"Now where did that child get to?" Carrie murmured fretfully. "She was just here."

Bree scanned the backyard. "Is there another way into the house without going back up front?"

"No." Carrie gestured. The sunporch wrapped around

the entire rear of the house. "She'd have to pass us in the hall to go anywhere."

"Then she must have walked around to the front." The west side of the house was dense with shrubbery. The east side had a fine path of raked gravel and slate steps. Bree set off down the path, rounded the side of the house to the front, and saw a slender blonde figure leaning into her car. Her right elbow swung in and out of the window.

"Lindsey!" Carrie said in exasperation.

Lindsey jerked upright. "Is this your dog?" she demanded. "She's, like, totally awesome." She had a peeled wooden stick in one hand. It looked as if it'd come from one of the willows at the side of the house. Casually, she tossed it onto the ground.

Bree bent and peered into the passenger-side window. Sasha gazed alertly back at her with an "I want out" expression. The remaining tenderness in his hind leg made him sit at an awkward angle and he shifted uncomfortably in the front seat.

"Looks like she hurt her leg," Lindsey said. She wiped her hands down the sides of her jeans, which were skintight, low-slung, and exposed a fair amount of skin from her waistline to her hips. She was too thin, her neck rising from her cropped T-shirt like a baby bird's. She had a butterfly tattoo on her right shoulder, a gold nose stud, and clever, wary blue eyes. The pupils were slightly dilated. Uh-oh, Bree thought.

"He," Bree corrected gently. "And his name is Sasha. As for his leg, he had a cast that just came off. And he's glad of it, aren't you, boy?"

"She wants to come out," Lindsey said helpfully. "You can just see it. She probably wants to pee." Her giggle was high-pitched. She shot a nervous glance at her mother.

"Do you mind?" Bree asked Carrie. She wanted Sasha with her, where she could keep an eye on him.

Carrie shrugged. "Certainly."

Bree opened the passenger door and Sasha hopped to the ground. He inspected Carrie with a courteous wag of his tail. Bree, fearful, ran her hands over his coat, looking for spots where this miserable child might have poked him with a stick.

"We haven't had a dog in the house for ages," Carrie said. "Not since we had to give away our Irish setter."

"Oh?" Bree said. It was her firm belief you could tell a lot about people from their relationship with animals. And she sure didn't like what she'd seen so far. "Why was that?"

"Too nervy," Carrie said briefly. "We couldn't stop him running away from home. Found a nice farm for him to live on in the country."

Sasha looked at Bree.

That's a lie.

"She's beautiful!" Lindsey knelt on the gravel drive and flung her arms around Sasha's neck. "And not a thing like that old neurotic Maxie. You're a nice sane dog, aren't you, girl?" She rubbed Sasha's head with frantic fingers. Sasha bore this with the kind of calm possessed by only very large, self-confident dogs. Lindsey burrowed her head into his neck and cooed.

"She's a 'he,' Lin," Carrie said. "And don't hang around the old boy's neck like that. It's a meddlesome thing for a dog."

Sasha sneezed, and then wriggled out from under Lindsey's grasp.

"See?" Carrie said. "I told you."

Lindsey narrowed her eyes and stared at her mother. Sasha shifted on his feet and growled a little.

Bree waited a moment, to see if this tension was going

to go anywhere, and then said, "Let's go into the house. I'd like to sit down and get to know you better, Lindsey."

"Ma hates dogs in the house."

"I do not," Carrie protested. "I had dogs in your grandmother's house all the time I was growing up."

"In Portland, Oregon," Lindsey chanted. "In a little three-bedroom ranch with a big stupid oak tree in the back."

"That's right," Carrie said without expression.

"It's nicer outside," Lindsey said. She smirked at Bree. "And if you want to sit down and get to know me better, it ought to be a place where I feel comfortable, right?"

"Right," Bree said.

They ended up by the pool, seated around one of the tables sheltered by an umbrella, Sasha curled up at Bree's feet.

"Would you like some iced tea?" Carrie said. "It's a little late in the day for coffee."

Bree declined, with perfunctory thanks, and said, "Do you know who I am, Lindsey?"

"Some kind of lawyer." Lindsey slid down in her seat and tucked her hands around herself. Then she leaped to her feet, scrabbled in her tote bag, and sat back down, this time with a pack of cigarettes and a lighter in hand.

"Cecily Carmichael asked me to look into the incident at the mall on your behalf."

Lindsey blew a plume of smoke into the air and shrugged. "I guess."

"I take that to mean you'd like me to represent you?"

Lindsey shrugged.

"Yes," Carrie said. "We would."

Bree took a notepad from her purse. "I'd like to get a sense of what we're dealing with here. As I understand it, the police have been talking to you about the theft of some Girl Scout money?"

Lindsey dropped the cigarette and ground it out with the toe of her shoe. "It just seemed like a good idea at the time."

"What did?" Bree asked patiently.

"Like, me and Hartley Williams and Madison Bellamy were at the Oglethorpe Mall, okay? Just to, like, check things out. And we were cruising for a parking spot closer to the entrance than, like, Iowa, and Hartley's going through the wallets to count up the cash we had on hand, and there was, like, nada."

"You *all* forgot your wallets?" Bree asked skeptically.

Lindsey snorted. "Madison forgot hers. Hartley and I had our purses, stupid." She shot her mother a look of intense dislike. "I'm on restriction, so I get, like, zero cash a week, and Hartley's stepfather, Stephen, is a real asshole when it comes to, like, allowances and stuff. There just wasn't anything in them. And, honest to God, I could have killed for a double latte. So there was this snotty-nosed kid selling those freakin' cookies, and I remembered how much cash the little buggers collect and we just decided to borrow the cash. Just," she said, "so's we could get a cup of freakin' coffee. I mean, you would have thought we were a bunch of freakin' terrorists, the way this thing's been blown up. Way out of proportion. Way out."

"The charges are assault, battery, and misdemeanor theft," Carrie said without emphasis. "She was arrested by two patrol officers and they took her down to the Montgomery Street courthouse and kept her there until I came by. I talked to a detective there—Sam Hunter, I think his name was." She made a vague motion. "Something like that. I have his card around here somewhere."

"I know Lieutenant Hunter," Bree said, then added, with some surprise, because she hadn't really thought about it before, "he's a fair man." And way too senior an officer to deal with a mere juvenile. She drew a question mark on her yellow pad.

"Whatever." Lindsey pulled her knees up to her chin and lit another cigarette. "They put me in a room with some dyke cop until Mamma came running to the rescue." She reached over and punched her mother's arm, with no affection. "Came through for me again, Ma."

"And the two other girls with you? What happened to them?"

"Those two. My best friends. My former best friends." Lindsey expelled smoke through her nose. "Backed each other up, didn't they? Said it was all my fault." She leaned over and whispered in Bree's ear, "Hartley's dad's a judge, and even though her mom's remarried, he's, like, not about to let his little darling get in trouble with the law."

"I know Judge Williams," Bree said. The judge wouldn't be averse to making a few pointed phone calls, but she doubted he'd resort to outright pressure. She also knew Sam Hunter. He was the last man you could accuse of playing politics. If Lindsey's two buddies had been set free, it was more than likely somebody believable had witnessed the whole sorry episode and that the thing was Lindsey's fault.

Bree sighed. It wasn't her job to judge Lindsey; it was her job to represent her interests as best she could. And if the kid were to confess to something, the confession should be protected by attorney-client privilege. Which meant that before this went any further, Carrie would have to sign an *ad litem* agreement and arrange for a retainer.

But first, Bree would have to agree to represent this brat.

Life was too darn short.

She clasped her hands on the table and leaned forward. "Lindsey, Carrie-Alice, I'd like to make some phone calls on your behalf to see if we can find exactly the right law- yer to handle this case."

"I thought *you* were going to get me out of this," Lind- sey said.

Bree avoided Carrie's eye. "And indeed I will, if I can. What you want from me, Lindsey, is the best advice I can give you." She held up her hand and ticked the points off on her fingers. "First, you're seventeen, is that right? That's underage here in Georgia, and you need an advo- cate who knows the juvenile courts inside and out. That's not me. Second, we're dealing with felonies, here. Minor felonies, to be sure, but we're looking at criminal charges. I'm more at home with torts and the ways to enforce per- formance bonds. Now, I take it you have a law firm that represents the family interests?"

"Stubblefield, Marwick," Carrie said.

Bree didn't roll her eyes, but she wanted to. The firm was notorious for its late-night infomercials soliciting business from the brain-damaged, the handicapped, and elderly people who'd fallen down in supermarkets. And John Stubblefield, the senior partner, was one of the most truly obnoxious men Bree had ever met.

"Stubblefield, Marwick," she said diplomatically, "seem to be more expert in civil law than criminal. But there are several excellent firms here and in Atlanta that can give Lindsey the kind of support she needs."

"So that's it?" Carrie said.

"That's it," Bree said firmly. "If you'll excuse me for a moment, I'll make a few phone calls right now." Bree got up. There was no way she was going to make the calls with the two of them sitting in front of her. But her con- science wouldn't let her totally abandon Aunt Cissy's friend. Once the story hit the evening news, Carrie and her daughter were going to be besieged by local report- ers. The Girl Scout angle was just too cute and the Chandler name too big. They needed an advocate, and fast. "If there's a quiet place where I could get through to some of my friends, I'll try and get you set up with an appointment right away."

Carrie hesitated. "Lindsey's being arraigned, is that the right word?"

Bree nodded.

"She has this arraignment on Monday at ten. This is Thursday. That doesn't leave us a whole lot of time to get somebody new."

"We can always ask for an adjournment," Bree said cheerfully. "Do you mind if I use the office we passed by? I'll be out in just a few minutes."

She didn't exactly run from the scene, but she didn't linger, either. The unhappiness between mother and daughter, the truly scary look in Lindsey's eye, was a genuine miasma, an unhealthy fog in the air. What kind of kid mistreats a dog with a cast on its leg? Or a dog with no cast on its leg, for that matter? Sasha seemed to share her uneasiness. He stuck close by her, ears forward, a ready sentinel.

In the short hallway, she picked up her briefcase and went into Probert Chandler's home office.

Unlike the rest of the house, the den had a perfunctory air, as if furnished from a catalog. A couple of tennis trophies sat on top of the maple credenza. A formal studio photo of Carrie-Alice, in the same pearls and an identical twinset, sat on the desk. There were two kinds of books on the shelves: worn paperback tough-guy adventure stories by people like Vince Flynn, and bound copies of trade magazines with titles like *Today's Pharmacy* and *Drugstore Weekly*. The latest copies were dated four months earlier. A framed, fading color photograph of a much younger Probert Chandler and two other young men sat on the credenza, too. All three were dressed in the really ghastly college kid uniform of the '70s: bell bottoms, embroidered vests, and tight shirts with pointed collars. Bree grinned a little at that. A formal oil portrait hung over the bookcase: Carrie-Alice, Lindsey, and two other kids who had to be an older brother and sister stood around a seated Probert. Probert looked just like Harry Truman, down to the wire-rimmed glasses. An indefinable air of unhappiness emanated from Carrie. But the artist had given Lindsey a healthy pink to her cheeks, and ignored the gauntness at her temples. The portrait was familiar. It must have run in *Time* or *People* magazine at some point in the last few months. Bree contemplated it for a moment. Lindsey's older sister had a matronly air. Her brother looked smug.

A leather executive office chair sat behind the desk. Bree hesitated a moment, but the only other chair in the place was a reproduction wing chair patterned in green and yellow plaid. She sat down, put her briefcase on her lap . . .

The blow came out of nowhere. Directly under her heart. She tried to breathe. Couldn't. Couldn't take in air. Couldn't scream. Could only strike out with both fists . . .

Bree leaped out of the chair and half fell against the desk.

"No," she said.

Sasha sat on his haunches, his eyes wise.

"No!" Bree said again.

And then the horrible, grainy, bad black-and-white movie image of a middle-aged man flickered in front of her. Silent flames bloomed like evil flowers around his feet. His hands reached out to her. Clawed talons pulled at his face, his chest, his hair, and drew him down.

"Help me help me help me . . ."

Probert Chandler.

And then a whisper . . . *"I didn't die in the car . . ."*

"Phooey!" Bree said. "Phooey, phooey, phooey!"

I didn't die in the car.

That's what her first dead soul had claimed—that he hadn't died in the sea. Bree'd taken a lot of risks to prove that—and that he had been unfairly convicted of greed by the Celestial Court.

Marlowe's. Lindsey. Blood. Blood. Blood.

And now Probert Chandler pleaded with her from the midst of these black and vicious flames.

"Fine," Bree said a little bitterly, "this is just *fine.*"

Beaufort & Company had a client after all.

Three

Nothing in his life became him like the leaving of it.
—*Macbeth*, William Shakespeare

"I can't believe my own sister stood up in front of the entire TV viewing population of Savannah and made excuses for that little creep!" Antonia slung her legs over the back of the theater seat in front of them and rolled her eyes. Bree sat next to her in the second row of the Savannah Repertory Theater.

It was six thirty in the evening.

Three hours earlier—twenty minutes after her encounter with Probert Chandler's ghost, and ten minutes after Bree had accepted a five-thousand-dollar retainer from Carrie-Alice—the WKYR news van had pulled into the Chandler driveway. The media circus had lasted all afternoon. Bree chased the last of the reporters away at five thirty, then left the Chandler house and sulky Lindsey. She stopped for takeout from the Park Avenue Market, then drove straight to Savannah Repertory Theater to get some sympathy from her sister.

She'd have been better off soaking her head in a tub of tomato juice.

"You'd get more business hanging around the Chatham County Ambulance garage," Antonia added. "At least you'd get a better class of client."

"Snide," Bree said gloomily. "You're being snide."

The stage was busy with last-minute prep for that evening's production of *The Return of Sherlock Holmes*. Far overhead, a tech fiddled with the lighting over Reichenbach Falls. Antonia broke off to holler: "Too blue! Try a number two gel!" She scribbled in her stage manual for a minute, then said, "Your hair looked great, though. That white-blonde usually doesn't come across all that well on camera."

Bree's hair was long, thick, and silver-blonde. It had been a constant nuisance until she'd taken to braiding it and piling it on top of her head. It was good hair, but good hair didn't mitigate the circumstances one little bit, even in the South. As a matter of fact, it made Bree a lot more recognizable than she wanted to be. Lindsey's escapade had made the six o'clock news, as Bree thought it would. Lindsey was persona non grata in Savannah at the moment, and so was anyone who championed her cause. When Bree'd arrived at the theater, dinner for Antonia in hand, one of the ushers tsked at her in a really irritating way and muttered, "Shame! For shame!"

"Phooey," Bree said. Then, "Don't I get some points for not losing my temper?"

"You didn't bust the reporter in the nose, that's true. But you came across as snippy. Very snippy."

Bree thrust a tuna panini at her sister. "Shut up and eat."

Antonia paused, her sandwich halfway to her mouth, her eyes intent on the stage. "Perfect!" she shouted. Then, "That's a wrap!" She sighed. "Oh, God. Oh, God. There's bound to be a major screwup somewhere. But we've gone over and over it. It's in the lap of the gods, Bree. In the lap of the gods." She bit into the sandwich and chewed frantically.

"It'll be fine," Bree said. "And it's dress rehearsal tonight, not the actual premiere."

"The critics!" Antonia could have been Richard the Third calling for his horse, the despair in her voice was so strident. "The critics!"

"They'll love it. Anyhow, local critics are always really kind when it comes to hometown productions. You could be staging the musical version of *Gilligan's Island* and they'd love it. And how much attention do they pay to the technical part of it any . . ." The look on Antonia's face was chilling. Bree shut herself up.

"I am an employed professional," Antonia said coldly, "and this is professional theater."

"Of course it is."

"It's an Equity production," Antonia continued, her eyes narrowed. "And I'm the assistant technical director. The only thing hometown about it is that it's being produced in the theater's hometown. And the only thing local about the critics . . ."

Bree raised her eyebrows encouragingly.

". . . is that they're local." Antonia relaxed and grinned at her. She reached over and patted Bree's knee. "It sounds like you had an exceptionally lousy day, sister. I am well and truly sorry."

Aside from a certain similarity in their voices, which one of Antonia's sappier boyfriends had described as molten honey, the sisters couldn't have been more unlike. Antonia was small, with her mother's red-gold hair, bright blue eyes, and curvy figure. Bree was tall, slender, with green eyes and that strange, silvery hair. Their temperaments were different, too. Bree had a rare, explosive temper, but generally got through the day with an equable attitude. Antonia was as volatile as vinegar and baking soda.

Bree sighed heavily. "Yeah, well, that's what I get for letting Aunt Cissy in the back door. I should have known better."

"So, you've taken on this lost cause for Aunt Cissy's sake?"

Bree rallied. She'd eaten her own tuna panini in the car, and the protein was kicking in. "I don't know that Lindsey's a lost cause. I'm a pretty decent lawyer when push comes to shove."

"C'mon, Bree. The kid primped for the news cameras like she was on a fashion shoot. Has she expressed any remorse for what she did?"

"Allegedly did," Bree said.

"The fact that the mall security camera caught it all on tape means it's still an alleged crime? Is that some kind of legal thing, flying in the face of the facts?"

The security tape was an undoubted fly in the ointment of Lindsey's defense. Bree snatched a potato chip from Antonia's stash and admitted, "So she did it. And I wouldn't say she's expressed remorse. As such."

"There you are. A brat. I especially loved Cordelia Eastburn's decision to push for the 'full penalty allowed by law.' "

"She's running for reelection," Bree said of the district attorney. "Cordy, that is. I don't think poor Lindsey could be elected dogcatcher at the moment."

"What is the full penalty allowed by the law, anyhow?"

"For assault? Battery? Robbery? And Cordelia's come up with something worse, if you can believe it—menacing with a deadly weapon."

"Lindsey had a gun?" Antonia said in astonishment.

"Nope. She had her daddy's Hummer. Now, you and I might agree that a Hummer's a deadly weapon just from the fact it gets six miles to the gallon in an age when that's a crime against humanity, but Cordy's claiming Lindsey tried to run the little kid down. So on that charge, given Lindsey's age?" Bree bit her lip. "Depends. Could be as much as five years."

"Jeez. In a county lockup. I don't wish that on any-body." Antonia balled up the sandwich wrapping. "I've got to get backstage. Thanks for the food. You coming to the show tonight?"

"I might drop in. I'm meeting Hunter at Isaac's, over on Drayton"—she glanced at her watch—"ten minutes ago."

"Hmm," Antonia said.

"No 'hmm' about it," Bree said crossly. "It's not a date. He's the one that did Lindsey's intake interview. I just have a couple of questions."

"A Savannah police lieutenant did an intake interview for a juvenile?" Antonia furrowed her brow. "As a dedicated *Law & Order* watcher, that doesn't sound like usual police procedure to me."

"Nope." Bree got up and dropped a kiss on her sister's head. "Which is why I offered to buy him a drink. Good luck tonight, sis."

"Aaagh," Antonia said, her attention back on the stage. "Aaagh, aagh, aagh. *Who left that dolly on the apron? Somebody's going to break a leg!*"

Isaac's was a fifteen-minute walk up Drayton from Chippewa Square, where the theater was located, so re-luctantly, Bree decided to drive. Her back and leg muscles ached a little, which was what she deserved, she supposed, for skipping her morning run. She could have used the walk, but Hunter wasn't Southern, and couldn't be de-pended upon to wait for her for long.

She lucked out and found a parking spot less than a block away. Sasha sighed and settled nose to tail in the passenger seat, and she patted him sympathetically. "You want to go on home without me?"

He rolled a golden eye at her.

"They don't let dogs in there, even on the rooftop." She ran expert fingers over his leg. "It'll be a bit of a walk for you, with this leg still a little weak. Tell you what. I won't be long. And I'll bring you a crab cake."

The brick building that housed Isaac's was more than three hundred years old, and had seen a lot of restaurants come and go. Bree climbed the stairs to the rooftop bar, which was almost empty although the evening was mild. Hunter sat at a table with his back to the bar, long legs extended in front of him, nursing a beer. Cops had hard lives, in Bree's experience, and most of them looked older than they were. Hunter's premature aging lay in his expression, which was a little weary, a little watchful, and at the moment, as he watched her approach, somewhat ill-tempered.

"My mamma used to say that if I didn't quit frowning, my face was going to freeze like that," she said cheerfully. "Not to say that a frown doesn't improve your looks, Lieutenant!" She fluttered her eyelashes at him. "I'm a little late, am I? I apologize."

He nodded, then cast a look over his shoulder at the bartender, who came halfway toward the table with an inquiring look.

"Just a spritzer for me," Bree said. "With a lot more soda than white wine, if you please." She smiled at Hunter. "Can I get you another beer?"

"All this charm is in aid of something," Hunter said. "Let me take a wild guess. Lindsey Chandler."

"You saw the six o'clock news."

"Not your usual sort of case, is it, Bree? I thought the Winston-Beauforts specialized in civil law."

"More of a favor for a friend of my aunt's," Bree said. "But this isn't your usual sort of case either, Hunter. According to my sources, you did the intake interview."

"True enough." He shifted back in his chair. He had good shoulders, Bree thought, and an even better chest. It was hard to tell just how much better since she'd never seen him without his leather jacket.

"So, maybe we can exchange a little information?" she said hopefully.

That made him grin, which lightened his face and did in fact make him better looking. "Now, what kind of information have you got about this case that I don't?"

"Not a thing," Bree said promptly. "That was just an opening ploy, to get you off your guard so that you'll lighten up a little. This isn't a big deal. I'm going to try and plead the child out, get her some counseling, maybe. Do my best to make it go away. I'm just wonderin' if there's more to this than meets the eye."

He ran one hand through his hair, which was thick and curling a little with the evening damp. "Like what, for example?"

"Like maybe Probert Chandler?"

"Daddy?"

"Daddy." The bartender placed her drink in front of her, and she took a cautious sip. "I understand he was killed in a single-car crash about four months ago?"

"That's right."

"And, I'm guessin' here, so don't go thinking that you've got a leak in the police barracks, but was there something funny about the crash?"

"Funny how?"

Bree took a deep breath. This was the tricky part. "Like maybe he didn't die in the car?"

Hunter ran his hand over his mouth and didn't say anything for a long moment. Then, "You've got mobile corpses on the brain, maybe? You didn't think Ben Skinner died in the sea, either."

"I don't have anything on the brain other than my own good sense," she said tartly. "And I was right about Skinner, wasn't I? And you're Homicide, Hunter. Senior Homicide, at that. Four months after the man dies in a car crash—which last I heard was Traffic's business, and nobody else's—you're asking his daughter questions about a snatch-and-grab at the mall." She took a larger sip of the spritzer and choked. "Now that would have been a real zinger of a point if I didn't have spit dribblin' down my chin."

Hunter's laugh was reluctant, but genuine. "You've spent some time with the family. What do you think?"

"Not an appealing child," Bree said. "But she's seventeen, and it comes with the territory."

"And you're how old, Beaufort?"

"Twenty-eight," Bree said. "What's that got to do with anything? Oh! Was I sounding wise beyond my years?"

"More like full of yourself," Hunter said unkindly. He sighed. "Go on."

"Wild child, and not playin' at it. She's on the road to some kind of self-destruction, that's for sure. As to why . . ." She frowned. Something about Carrie-Alice's reference to those "little talks" gave her the creeps. "Her mother's disengaged. Gave up a long time ago. The two of them sure don't like each other."

"You sound surprised."

"I suppose I am. My own mother . . ." Bree broke off. She didn't know her own mother. But the mother who'd raised her from a two-day-old infant, Francesca Carmichael Winston-Beaufort, would have died for either one of her daughters. "Francesca wouldn't have given up on me, no matter what." She looked down at the table, suddenly depressed. "What am I talking about? This kind of family dysfunction comes down all the time."

"We were lucky to get good ones," Hunter said easily. "Here's to Mom." He raised his glass. Bree raised her own; the glasses chimed together, and Bree swallowed the last of the spritzer.

"So at first glance we've got the standard American dysfunctional family," Bree said. "Or do we? From all we hear through the media, Probert Chandler was a down-home kind of guy. Let out that he drove a Buick when he wasn't driving Pontiacs. Didn't like the high life. Believed in all those Boy Scout virtues and then some: honesty, thrift, and love of God, country, and his mamma. Mean Lindsey doesn't fit this picture. Carrie-Alice doesn't fit this picture. The Hummer doesn't fit this picture. There's a lot of wriggly little questions under this supposed rock of stability. I'm not at all surprised there was something about the car crash that made you antsy."

Hunter shook his head in feigned admiration. "You're good, Beaufort. But not that good. I didn't say a thing about the car crash."

Bree thought about batting her eyelashes again, and didn't.

Hunter grinned unpleasantly. "How did you express it? You're planning on pleading the child out? You're going to make it go away? I think that's a smart thing to do."

"Look," Bree said, "you know Cordelia Eastburn."

"We all know Cordy Eastburn." Hunter nodded approvingly. "One hell of a prosecutor."

"She's a glory hound," Bree said bluntly. "I love her like a sister, but the woman's got ambition like a hound has ticks. Did you hear her on the six o'clock news? I had the radio on all the way back from Tybee Island, and this woman's out to shiny up her reputation at the expense of this miserable little cheerleader. You would think," Bree said more to herself than to Hunter, "that she'd pick on somebody her own size. Did you hear what Cordy said? Well, did you? She's thinking about adding assault with a deadly weapon to the robbery charges. Says the security tape clearly shows Lindsey menaced that poor little Girl Scout with the Hummer."

"Lindsey seems to be her own worst enemy," Hunter pointed out. "She's a heartbreak waiting to happen. But I can see that's not going to stop you riding to the rescue. You ought to think about stabling your horse, Bree. Nothing good's going to come from this case."

"Cordy's playing to the cameras," Bree said indignantly. "Where's the *fairness* in all this?"

"Fairness. Not only do you need to stable your horse, you need to hang up your sword and shield." Hunter looked at her a long moment. Then he leaned forward and said with an intensity she hadn't seen in him before: "Let it go. Do whatever it is you have to do to keep the kid out of jail this time—and I say *this* time, Bree, because with a kid like that there's going to be a next time and a time after that. But let it go. Chandler skidded on a wet road and ended up on a slab in the morgue. A lot of drunks end up—"

Bree sat up. "He was drunk?"

Hunter clenched his teeth. "He had been at the Miner's Club much of the afternoon. After a round of golf."

"The children of alcoholics . . . ," Bree began, then stopped, pleased. Here was a darned good defense. Except it went against everything the media had presented to the world about Probert Chandler. Harry Truman drunk? Hmm.

"Drop it, Bree. The guy had a bit more to drink than usual, that's true. We checked it out. It wasn't a habit. Maybe if he had been a drinker, he'd've been smarter about driving home while under the influence. As far as you're concerned, Chandler's case is closed." He pointed at her. Bree hated it when people pointed at her. "If I find out you've been screwing around with it, I'm coming down hard. Got that?"

The bartender, a reserved young black man who'd been quietly polishing glasses behind the bar, suddenly raised his voice. "Hey! Shoo out of here, you."

"Guess he doesn't like raised voices any more than

I do," Bree said with deceptive amiability. "Don't let the door hit you on your way out."

Hunter stared over her shoulder. "It's not me he wants out of here. It's your dog."

"My dog?" Bree turned around. Sasha trotted toward her. Some trick of the half-light made his eyes glow a deeper gold than usual. He came up to her and put his head on her knee.

"Hey, Sasha," Hunter said.

Sasha looked up at her, panting slightly.

"You're lookin' for your crab cake," Bree said, conscience-stricken. "I totally forgot."

"Miss?" the bartender said. "That your dog? We can't have no dogs up here. Not allowed."

"Yes, it's my dog, and of course it's not allowed. Sorry, sorry. Come on, Sash. We'll get on home and get you some food." Bree gathered up her purse and got up. Hunter got up, too.

"I'll walk you out."

"You just never mind about that," Bree said sweetly.

Hunter grimaced. "You're going Southern on me."

Bree raised innocent eyebrows.

"It's something I noticed," he said with a grin. "You get your temper up, you get more . . . regional."

"Regional," Bree said. She took a deep breath through her nose.

Beside her, Sasha rumbled a little. Then he nudged his great head against her hip. Bree tamped down her annoyance and reached for a reasonable tone of voice. "Look, Hunter. I *know* there's something wonky about the way Probert Chandler died. And surer than sunshine, if you lie to my face, I'm going to look into it all the harder. So why don't you save both of us a couple of pounds of aggravation and tell me right out? Last time I looked, this kind of information ends up in the public domain anyhow. Unless," she added triumphantly, "the car crash case is still open. Is it?"

Hunter rubbed the back of his neck and sighed. He glanced in the direction of the bartender, who had stopped wiping down the bar with a rag and was frankly listening. He grabbed her arm and directed her to the stairwell. He didn't speak again until they were outside on the pavement. "Where's your car?"

"A block away, down Park."

"Good. I want you to walk to it. Get into it. And go home."

Bree took another deep breath and slowly let it out. Then she said, "You're a pestilential man, Lieutenant. But am I letting that get to me? No. I am not. I am, as you see, calmly and happily headed off to my car. You, on the other hand, are in about as much trouble as you deserve."

"What?"

She jerked her chin toward the restaurant stairs. The bartender stood glowering on the bottom tread. He had his cell phone to his ear. "I've got a five-dollar bill that says he just called 911."

"What?!"

"Because *I* didn't pay for those drinks. And it looks like you didn't, either." She bit back a giggle at the chagrin on his face, then turned and walked down the street to her car. Sasha pressed close to her, his big body so close that she nearly stumbled over him.

"You upset about that crab cake?" She reached down, grabbed his collar, and pulled him to her side. He gazed up at her with an intent, worried expression. Bree drew a breath to tell him to heel, when the stench hit her.

She jerked her head up in alarm. Under the glow of the streetlights, the place was deserted. Her car sat a few hundred yards away. At the far end of the block, an ominous pillar of smoke took shape against the night. It grew, man-high, and the scent of decaying corpses grew stronger. A low growl gathered in Sasha's throat. With her left hand, Bree grabbed her briefcase more tightly and swung it, like a weapon. With her right, she closed her fist around her car keys, so the sharp metal ends of the keys stuck out between her knuckles.

One by one, the streetlights went out. And the whirling tower of dark, shot through with a sickly yellow, advanced toward her down the street.

Sasha drew his lips back in a snarl, crouched low, and crept toward the apparition. Bree judged the distance between the thing and the safety of her car. Sasha bounded forward. Bree yelled, "Heel!" in sudden terror for her dog, and sprinted down the sidewalk. The tower of oily smoke grew taller, wider, as if gathering itself for a ferocious charge. Bree flung herself at the driver's door, pushed Sasha in ahead of her, and slammed and locked it. Wildly, she jammed the key into the ignition.

The smoke swirled around the windshield. In the midst of the shifting mass, Bree caught a glimpse of a grinning white face.

She slammed the motor into life, gunned the car forward, and left the mist behind.

Four

"Who was Probert Chandler? Where did he come from? What was he like as a man? And how did he really die?"

Bree folded her hands on the conference table and looked at each of her employees in turn. It was, she felt, an impressive start to Beaufort & Company's morning meeting. Four of her colleagues were there: Lavinia Mather, her landlady; Petru Lucheta, her paralegal; and Ronald Parchese, her secretary. Sasha lay asleep in the corner.

"Did I ever tell you about the time I walked dogs for a living?" Ron set a tray filled with the coffeepot, a plate of beignets, and four coffee cups in the middle of the conference table and settled into his chair. He was more than usually well dressed this morning: cream-colored linen trousers, a pale blue dress shirt, and a pink and blue rep tie.

"Dog walker? No. It wasn't in your résumé," Bree said. "As a matter of fact, neither was your otherworldly address."

Ron blinked and smiled at her.

Bree sighed. Her dramatic opening comments had fallen flat. She'd practiced the lines in front of the bathroom mirror just that morning, too. She accepted a cup of coffee and took an absentminded sip. "None of you listed angelic employment. But did that get you fired when you finally fessed up? It did not." She pointed at herself with a demure twinkle. "You've got a pretty good boss in me, if you don't mind a little bragging. So I figure I'm owed a little respect. If we can get to the point here, I'd appreciate it."

Ron fussed with the coffeepot. Petru sat with his hands folded over his cane. Lavinia Mather added three teaspoons of sugar to a cup that was mostly cream and regarded them all with bright black eyes.

"There *is* a point," Ron said. "If you'll just let me make it. I was a dog walker, as I said. For about ten seconds. Horrible job. When I was living in New York. Four dogs at a time. A Boston pug, a fox terrier, and two whacking big black Labs. The minute I got those dogs onto the pavement outside the Dakota, they set off in all directions. I about split into four separate parts. That's what this case is like. Four different directions. Well, two anyway."

Bree looked at him with some perplexity. She still hadn't figured out how her angels managed their temporal existence. But every time she asked any one of them about their earthly lives away from the office, all she got were angelically innocent smiles and charming evasions. Like this one.

"Perhaps the robbery and the death of Mr. Chandler are not connected," Petru said. "That is perhaps what Ron is trying to say. We should not concern ourselves with the bumptiousness of teenagers, but rather with the appeal of Mr. Chandler for a reversal of his sentence." His expression behind the thicket of his big black beard was hard to read, but his Russian accent somehow made everything he said sound wise. If Tolstoy had been a paralegal, he would have sounded a lot like Petru.

"Now, I can't agree with that. That chile's behavior comes from something bad in that family," Lavinia said. "And that daddy of hers got called down instead of up when he died 'cause *he* did something bad." She took a huge, appreciative sip of her coffee. "You come right down to it, everything's connected."

Bree rubbed her forehead. She hadn't slept well. The attempted attack on the street last night had unsettled her, even though she'd decided not to bring it up. Plus, she wasn't too sure about the mayonnaise in the tuna panini. Now her dramatic opening failed to inspire her employees to direct and immediate action. Just blabber blabber blabber about dog walking. "I don't know, Lavinia. Do you think that's true? Do you think some people are just born bad? Or that they get made bad?"

"Everybody," Lavinia said firmly, "gets at least a couple of chances to choose."

Which was an answer of a sort, Bree supposed. "Well, we need to find out what kind of choices Probert Chandler made when he was alive, or I won't be able to plead his case now that he's dead."

"What's he in for, anyway?" Ron asked.

"In for?" Bree said blankly.

"You know, Ben Skinner was originally sentenced to three to ten" (not years, but millennia, Bree had learned) "for misdemeanor greed. What's Chandler done?"

"And where's he servin' time?" Lavinia bit into a beignet. "Purgatory or Hell itself?"

"Y'all don't know?" Bree said.

"Gosh," Ron said. "Should we?"

"If you don't know, who does? Wait a minute." She frowned in concentration. "Gabriel Striker told me about the initial charges against Ben Skinner. Who told him?"

Then, because she wasn't really sure she wanted to know the answer to that, she amended her question. "How did Striker find out?"

"I s'pose you should ask him," Lavinia said vaguely.

Bree scowled. Striker was a PI who had been recommended to Bree by her former law school professor Armand Cianquino. Striker's function within the Company, as near as Bree could figure out, was to get in her way. As for the professor, Bree found him mysterious in law school and even more mysterious now. Armand's job seemed to be to point her in the right direction, stand back, and let her fall flat on her face.

Petru tapped his cane on the floor. "No need to bring in Striker. I will check the reports."

"The reports?" Bree said blankly. Then, "Oh! The *reports*." The depositions of all criminal and civil cases, from arraignment to final outcome, were listed in reports filed daily at the courthouse. In municipalities like Chatham County, at any rate. Bree wasn't sure about matters celestial.

"And then, of course, since Chandler has filed a request for an appeal, you will need a copy of the original case. I will obtain that also. Ke-vite routine, dear Bree."

"Of course," Bree said. "Then I suppose those will be located . . . where?"

"On the seventh floor of the courthouse, 'dear Bree,' " Ron said, with a scowl in Petru's direction. "*I* can get those for you this morning."

"*I* am the paralegal," Petru said. "Such is the occupation of same. I will retrieve the files."

"I'm the secretary," Ron said. "Such is the occupation of *me*."

"Cool it, you two." Bree looked at them thoughtfully. "You know," she said, "I think I'd like to do this little chore myself."

"I'd better come with you," Ron said briskly. "If you're new to the process, it can take forever to get copies of the appeal." He winked. "Thank goodness we've got friends in high places."

The Chatham County Courthouse was a newish, rather ugly six-story building made of concrete block painted the color of scrambled eggs. Bree found a parking spot just off Montgomery, opened her purse for inspection by the police officers on guard, and went through the metal detector, Ron at her heels. The hall was crowded with lawyers in suits, policemen in both the brown uniform of the Chatham County Sheriff's Department and the navy blue of the city police, and ordinary citizens. Most looked either bewildered or sad. Nobody looked happy.

Bree stood in front of the bank of elevators, surrounded by three cops; a large lady in flip-flops, baggy pants, and a T-shirt that read *I've got PMS and I've got a gun*; and two young kids making a noticeable effort to be cool. A sign by the elevator listed the function of each of the building's six floors.

Bree and Ron rode to the second floor, where the kids got off; the fifth floor, where the belligerently T-shirted lady got off; and then to the sixth and last floor, where the cops got off. The older cop held the door for her politely— she noticed he didn't seem to register that Ron was in the elevator, too, and she smacked her head with the heel of her hand. "Forgot something!" she said. "Thanks!"

The elevator doors closed and the car kept on going up. The doors swished open to a place Bree had been just once before: the home of the Seventh Circuit of the Celestial Courts.

She'd been too nervous on her previous visit to register much of her surroundings.

Sunlight from a series of skylights in the ceiling flooded the hallway. The floor was of terrazzo tile, and the walls had wainscoting of warmly polished cedar. Or a wood that looked very much like cedar. The air was fresh and spring-like.

Instead of the Great Seal of the State of Georgia, the wall opposite the elevators held a seal lettered CELESTIAL COURTS. She did remember that. The symbol in the center was becoming increasingly familiar: a pair of the Scales of Justice surrounded by angel wings. To the right of the seal was a directory:

Justice Court—*Circle One (Justice Azreal presiding)*

Circuit Court—*Circles Two, Three, and Four (Justice-in-Residence)*

Court of Appeals—*Circles Five, Six, and Seven (St. Peter presiding)*

Appellate Division—*Circles Eight and Nine*

Hall of Records

Clerk of Court (Recording Angels)

Detention

The directional arrow to the Court of Appeals pointed up. The arrow to Detention pointed down. All the other arrows pointed to either the east or the west. Ron touched her arm. "This way."

She followed Ron down the hall to a door marked REC-ORDS. Ron tapped lightly, and then opened it up.

The records room was dim, dark, and cavernous. It took her a moment to adjust to the low light, since the main source of illumination was lanterns. Rows of breast-high pedestal desks ran the length of the space. The floor was paved in stone. The ceilings soared up, a series of vaulted arches. Flaming sconces flared on the walls. The figures huddled over the desks were . . .

"Monks?" Bree said, in a half whisper.

Ron rolled his eyes. "Complete with quill pens and inkwells. Can you believe it? I've been trying to get them to modernize since 1867, the year you temporals invented the typewriter. But am I getting anywhere? Not so's you'd notice. Tradition is everything around here." He walked briskly down the center aisle. Bree had to trot to keep up with him. A few of the cowled figures looked up as they passed; Bree caught a glimpse of eerily bright eyes. And there was a hum of recognition, the words as soft as a dove's murmur. *"Leah's daughter . . . Love the hair . . . Did all right in the Skinner case . . . 'spect to see her moving up one of these days . . ."*

"Ron!" Bree caught at his arm. He stopped and turned. "Did you hear that?" She kept her voice down, despite the urgency she felt. "Somebody said 'Leah's daughter.' That's my mother. The one who gave me up. Ron! Do they know her here?"

Ron smiled at her. The smile suffused his face in light. A feeling of warmth and safety flowed over her like a cozy blanket. Lavinia had smiled at her in just that way. A faint—very faint—rumble of thunder sounded beneath her feet, and then died away. "We'll find the files over here."

Stonewalled again. Or rather, angel-walled.

Ron wound his way briskly around the desks to a chest-high oak bar that ran the length of the far wall. Bree had to stand on her tiptoes to look across its width to the activity. A narrow aisle ran between the bar and the wall, which held hundreds, perhaps thousands, of cubicles. Ron shook his head. "Goldstein modeled it after the library at Alexandria. Never mind the fact that any decent software program could free up this whole space for other stuff."

"What other stuff?" a surly voice demanded. "I ask you. What other stuff would there be? This space is here for *this* stuff."

"It's you, is it?" Ron said unenthusiastically. "Hello, Goldstein."

"If it isn't St. Par-*chay*-se," Goldstein sneered.

"If it isn't St. Luddite," Ron sneered back. "When are you going to computerize, Goldstein?"

Goldstein was short and bald, with a belligerent lower lip and a pair of large, melting brown eyes. He wore his cowl shoved back onto his shoulders, and Bree could see the tip of a feathery wing beneath the folds of fabric around his neck. "When will I computerize? When Hell freezes over!" Goldstein shouted. "Ha! Ha-ha!"

"That joke's older than Adam," Ron muttered.

Goldstein smiled at Bree. "And this, Ronald, is this Leah's daughter?"

"Of course it is," Ron said. "Bree, this is Goldstein. He's section head of Records."

"How do you do?" Bree said. She extended her hand over the counter. Goldstein reached across the boards and shook it gravely.

"Welcome," he said. "I knew and admired your mother. She is sorely missed. Now, how may I assist you?"

Ron's hand on her shoulder forestalled any questions. He said, "We think we have a new client. Probert Chandler. He's filed an appeal. We'd like to see the case file."

"Chandler." Goldstein closed his eyes. "Hmmm. Let me think. Chandler. What jurisdiction?"

"We have no idea," Ron said. "Aren't you cross-referenced by name?"

"The name doesn't help a whole lot," Goldstein grumbled. "Do you know how many millions of Chandlers have lived and died since the Word?" He blinked twice. "Oh, my. I recall it now." He frowned and tsked. "You're going to have your work cut out for you on this one. It's a ninth-circle case."

"Hm," Ron said. "Quite serious, then."

"Quite."

Bree looked a question.

"Nine circles of Hell, nine court jurisdictions," Ron said briefly. "The charges get worse the higher you go. Mr. Skinner, now, he was a circle one, which is your basic misdemeanor greed. This one must be a doozy . . . hand it over, Goldstein."

The records clerk pulled a thick roll of parchment from one of the cubicles and passed it over to Ron, who tucked it under his arm. Goldstein pulled out a fat, leather-bound book, paged through the dusty leaves, placed it flat, and turned it to face Bree. He shoved a quill pen and inkwell set in her direction. "How long will you want it for?"

"Just until we copy it, I guess," Bree said.

"This *is* a copy. Copy number one. We track all the copies, of course. Just sign your name and check the relevant due date."

"A month, then?" Bree hazarded. She grasped the quill pen, signed her name with some difficulty, due to the thickness of the ink, and looked on in amazement as the signature styled itself in perfect Copperplate:

Brianna Winston-Beaufort, Esquire

She hesitated, then checked the *30-day due* column.

"Thank you, Bree." He smiled at her, and that sense of cheery comfort flooded her with calm and warmth. There were advantages to dealing with angels, even testy ones. She doubted that she'd ever need Prozac.

"Think Microsoft in future, Goldstein," Ron said. "It'd save us a trip down here. C'mon, Bree. This is going to be interesting. A ninth-circle case. I can't wait. Shall I take a look?"

Bree turned and swept the huge room with her gaze.

One of the torches in the wall snapped and sputtered. The angels in their monk's habits scribbled away peacefully. Bree breathed in the dusty, library-scented air and said, "I don't know if I can handle anything much more interesting than this."

"La, la," Ron said, unrolling the parchment, reading as he went. "Simony. Profiteering. Hm. That's all seventh-circle stuff. Not nine. Doesn't matter, though. So maybe he did get a raw deal. It's been known to happen, especially if the prosecution's zealous." He shook his head. "If Chandler's appeal isn't reversed, he's going to have an uncomfortable time of it, hereafter. Looks like a worthy case, Bree."

"Let me see." Bree took the paper and scanned the first few paragraphs. The petition was laid out in an elegant Gothic script. "This isn't an appeal. It's a request for a retrial based on evidence not in fact."

"Humph," Goldstein said. "That's what they all say."

Bree looked at him with a slight frown. "Mr. Chandler's disputing the suicide charge. He says he didn't kill himself. He says someone else did.

"He says it's murder."

Five

It was not that legislators, judges and attorneys weren't good and decent human beings—though some certainly were not, Ford thought. The problem was they and their legal forbears had gradually perverted the legal system for the protection of their own profession. Jurisprudence was no longer a moral process. It was a competition in which the competitors—attorneys—created their own rules.

—*The Heat Sand*, Randy Wayne White

"Come on, Cordy," Bree said. "The kid's seventeen years old. Her hormones are running amok. Not only that, there's a lot of case law about the wonky developmental stages of the teenage brain. I can make a pretty good case for diminished responsibility."

Cordelia Eastburn snorted derisively. She was good at it. "The wonky defense? Give me a flippin' break, girlfriend." Cordy's charm and presence reminded a lot of people of Oprah Winfrey. Unlike that smart and genial talk show host, Cordy had a temper to rival an F5 tornado and an unabashed ambition to become the first black female governor of the State of Georgia. Most of the time, she scared Bree to death. The rest of the time, the two of them got along like a house afire. "She's a spoiled rich kid with an attitude. You tell me how that's going to go over with a jury."

"Well, not so hot," Bree admitted. She settled back in the visitor's chair. The district attorney's office occupied a corner suite on the fifth floor of the courthouse. Cordy's Stanford law degree hung over the credenza, surrounded by photos of Cordy with the current governor of Georgia, two former presidents, and two of the Take Back Our Street missions to which she dedicated much of her off-duty time.

On impulse, Bree had stopped to see if she could catch Cordy on the fly. She'd sent Ron back to Angelus to begin researching Probert Chandler's background. The thrifty family man image was at odds with the charges in his original case, and there was a pile of investigating to do. Cordy was in, and agreed to spare Bree a couple of minutes.

She wore what Bree had come to think of as the uniform for professional Savannah women: a dark suit with a skirt that came to below the knees, a silk turtleneck, and low-heeled shoes. Cordy's only concession to frivolity was her earrings, which were large, splendid, and handmade.

Bree looked her right in the eye. "Let's be blunt here. Is this push for a prison sentence because she's a spoiled rich white kid?"

The DA glared at her. Her temper was legendary. Bree was hard put not to sink down in her chair, close her eyes, and stick her fingers in her ears in anticipation of the coming storm. But Cordy controlled herself with an effort, expelled her breath with a sharp "Pah!" and then said, "I'm not going to dignify that with an answer."

"Your current drive to break up the street gangs has the support of a whole lot of people," Bree said. "But you and I both know that the drive's been politicized. And it's not just that small segment of the African American voters who're screaming your cleanup campaign is racially

motivated and that you're an Auntie Tom. A lot of white
liberals are, too. If I were in your shoes, Cordy, you bet
that I'd be taking a kick-butt attitude about this little case,
if only to demonstrate that the law applies equally to
everybody. It's high profile enough to make your point
without you having to defend yourself on the early morning talk shows. So—do I think you're pushing this because she's a spoiled rich white kid? You bet." She leaned
forward and said firmly, "I'm not going to holler about a
rigorous prosecution. You want to push the aggravated
theft charges, that's fine with me. But this business of
threatening bodily harm with the Hummer is a real stretch.
I watched the video of the surveillance tape on the late
night news before I went to bed last night. What I *am* hollering about is your excess of zeal."

Cordy tightened her lips, thought a moment, and said,
"You've got a point." There were a lot of good things
about Cordy; chief among them was that she conceded
with grace and a no-hard-feelings attitude. She chuckled.
"The kid's gonna hang herself the minute she opens her
mouth anyway."

"No kidding," Bree said gloomily. "So we can deal a
little on these charges?"

"Tell you what. The kid allocutes to the crime on camera."

"Cordy!"

"Not negotiable. Sorry. I've got to feed the ravening
herd. The people of this state want to see some groveling.
And I want to see her express a little remorse. But then
we can talk about a community service sentence. Scrubbing public toilets, maybe. Like that model."

"I'll talk to her." Bree extended her hand. "Thanks,
Cordy."

Cordy reached across the desk and took Bree's hand in
both of hers. "I've been hearing a lot about you lately,

Bree. Ever think about joining the good fight down here at the DA's office?"

"Me?" Bree said. "Really?" She could feel herself blushing. She had an enormous respect for the DA's office and the furious focus that Cordy brought to the job.

"Liked the way you stood up to John Stubblefield over that Skinner case."

"If I went into public service, I can't think of anyone I'd rather work for than you," Bree said honestly. "But I've got my hands full at the moment. Maybe in the future . . . I don't know. Let's meet for a drink sometime."

"I've got high blood pressure, and problems with sugar. So I don't drink. But I'll be glad to buy you one, any old time." Cordy grinned at her, released her hand, and stood up. "All right, then. You'll let me know if the kid agrees to the deal?"

"Fast as I can. I'd like to get this one out of the public eye sooner than quick." She followed Cordy to the door. "By the way . . ."

Cordy paused and sighed. "How come there's always a 'by the way'? I give a lot more than I was intending to, let you push me around, and instead of a 'Thank you, Miz Cordy, for all your help' I get a 'by the way'?"

"Probert Chandler?"

"Probert Chand . . ." Bree could almost see the data retrieval going on behind Cordy's eyes. "Okay. Got it. The kid's daddy. DOA on Skidaway Road about four months ago. What about him?"

"Have you heard anything about the resolution of the investigation into the car crash?"

Cordy raised one eyebrow. She had an open, very readable face. "And what should I be hearing?"

"I don't know. That the case is still open, maybe?"

"I can find out, I suppose. Any reason why I should?"

"Just lookin' for every possible exculpatory road."

Cordy shrugged. "Guy was rich. Got himself drunk and misjudged the turn in the road on a wet and stormy night. Just have to praise be he didn't take any of our innocent citizens with him. Now, if you don't mind, Bree, I've got to get along."

"I owe you one, Cordy. Thanks."

"You owe me a lot more than one." She smiled widely—not an angelic smile, by any stretch of the imagination—and stepped aside to let Bree through her office door. "One last thing. If the kid doesn't agree to my terms, she's looking at some jail time for sure. You got that? This is the deal. I'm not open to any further negotiations."

Bree nodded. "You'll be hearing from me. One way or the other."

"So if there is an ongoing investigation into Chandler's death, the DA's office doesn't know a thing about it." Bree sat at the desk in her tiny office. She'd gone straight from the DA back to Angelus Street, flushed with the minor victory. Petru sat in the only other chair the space allowed. Ron perched on the edge of her desk. Lavinia hummed away in the corner, brushing the feather duster over the bookcase under the room's sole window. She looked at her team with affection. "If we can prove it's murder, it mitigates the other charges, don't you think? At least it can help. And poor Mr. Chandler gets to move out of the ninth circle to a far sunnier place, just like that." She snapped her fingers.

"There are the other charges to consider," Petru said gravely. "Simony. Profiteering. I do not believe we can guarantee sunshine. At least not yet."

Bree smiled confidently. "We're going to give it our best shot. Which means all the usual info, guys. Autopsy report, accident report. Interviews with any witnesses.

Just for a start. We don't have a ton of info from our client, to be sure. Just 'Marlowe's. Lindsey. Blood. Blood. Blood.' And, of course, 'I didn't die in the car.' But I think it's safe to assume that this is one case with three connections, not two cases that are unrelated."

Ron nodded. "Got it."

Petru shook his head. "Perhaps."

"Petru, please get me all the background data on Chandler and his company that you can find. Who was he? Where did he come from? Who did he associate with? Anything you can turn up on the Internet. We haven't got a lot to go on. Just his ghost's reference to his business. But any lead's better than no lead."

"*I* have already started a file," Petru said with a rather smug air. "I assumed we would be following the procedures established by our last successful case."

"Well, whoop-dee-do," Ron muttered.

The two angels glared at each other.

Bree paused a moment. This antagonism was new. Finally, she said, "Is there something the two of you need to discuss? With me? With each other?" Neither of her angels looked her in the eye. "No? If not, can we get on with this case?" She locked her hands behind her head and leaned back in her chair. "I think procedures are a good thing, myself," she said. "But we've got to be flexible. Each of us has to be able to take on all kinds of things. Circumstances are going to be different with each new case. I don't need to remind you both that we're a team here, and a pretty specialized team at that. We've got a live client here who's going to need a pretty aggressive defense right here in Savannah, if I can't get her to plead out. And I'm no expert in juvenile cases."

"You sayin' you might need to bring somebody else in to help with this chile's defense?" Lavinia said.

"I hope not. So Petru, I'd like you to start researching

similar cases involving minors, so I can get a better sense of the pitfalls ahead. If you can get the names of the two or three top juvenile specialists here in town, I'd be grateful. And Ron—could you set up meetings with Madison Bellamy, Hartley Williams, and the Girl Scout and her mom? What's her name? Sophie Chavez, that was it. And I'd like a copy of that surveillance tape from the mall." She got to her feet and slung the strap of her briefcase over her shoulder. "I've got to go. I'm going to get Lindsey to agree to allocute, apologize, and get the outward and visible signs of this case out of the way."

Ron rolled his eyes. "Apologize? That kid? When pigs fly, Bree, sweetie. When pigs fly."

Bree frowned. "Why do you say that?"

"You have not seen it yet." Petru sighed heavily and shifted his cane across his knees. "I thought perhaps you had not."

"Seen what? What are you guys talking about?"

"That chile went on Bonnie-Jean Morrissey's talk show and said how'd she do it again, that's what," Lavinia said repressively.

"What?" Bree said. She sat down, slowly. "Bonnie-Jean Morrissey? That's the *Bonny Good Morning* show, right? Lindsey went on the talk show and said she'd do it again? Do what again? Mug a Girl Scout?"

"Yes, indeedy," Ron said. "Said it was a real gas. A hoot. A scream."

"At least it's just a local show," Bree said feebly. Bonnie Morrissey was one of those round, pink-cheeked, silver-haired, extremely pretty women the South seemed to breed like hamsters. She looked like Paula Deen's little sister. Her seven A.M. talk show was gossipy, verging on the scurrilous. "Nobody watches it, though," Bree said confidently. "Cordy hasn't seen it, for instance. She would have said something. She would have said a *lot*."

"Our little princess looked right into the camera and told all the folks at home that she couldn't see what half of the fuss was about. And"—Ron leaned forward, his face solemn—"she's got some modeling contract, she says. Out of L.A. She's headed out west sometime this week to do interviews."

"She's out on remand," Bree said crossly. "What in the name of all that's holy is that idiot child thinking?"

The office phone rang. Lavinia picked it up and said, "Beaufort & Company. If you need he'p, you come to us." She listened a moment. "Uh-huh. Is that right?" Then, softly dismayed, "Isn't that too bad, honey. The courthouse or the jail?"

Bree gritted her teeth.

"Sheriff's office, then. You don't worry, now. Ms. Beaufort'll be along directly." She rested the handset on her thin chest and smiled sunnily at Bree. "Well, I can tell you who *does* watch that morning show, and that's the po-lice. Lindsey's down there right now."

"She's in jail?" Bree clutched her head with both hands. "Damn it all."

Lavinia waved the phone. "You want to talk to Mrs. Chandler?"

"Sure." Bree stretched her hand out, then spoke into the receiver. "Carrie-Alice?"

Carrie-Alice's voice was detached and tired, all at once. "They say she's violated the conditions of her release with that escapade this morning. Did you see it?"

"Did I see it? Not yet. We'll ask the station for a copy." She looked across the desk at Ron and wriggled her eyebrows. He nodded competently and bustled out of the office. "Where are they keeping her?"

Bree had two phone lines into the office—the rep from Southern Bell had managed to convince her that nothing irritated callers more than a busy signal—and the button for the second one lit up. Ron wasn't wasting any time.

"In a holding area with a couple of other juveniles." Carrie-Alice paused, and added doubtfully, "She seems to be safe enough."

Ron glided into her office, a pink While You Were Out phone message slip in one hand. Except that she wasn't out; she was right here. She looked at the scrawled message with some irritation.

Hartley Williams on line 2.

Lindsey's other friend from the mall. Now that was interesting. Bree held her forefinger up in a wait-a-minute gesture and said into the phone, "Do you want me to come down right away, Carrie-Alice?"

"I called George," Carrie-Alice said.

It took Bree a moment to process this. "You mean your son?"

"Yes. He's in Ames. Both my older children are. He works out of the head office. Katherine's in graduate school at Iowa State." She caught herself up. "I'm rambling, sorry. In any event, George will be flying in later today, depending on his schedule. To be frank, I'm not in any hurry to have Lindsey back home until he gets here. If we just let her sit for a bit, would that be a bad thing?"

"It's up to you," Bree said noncommittally. "I wouldn't want her to spend the night there. I'll set the process for the new arraignment in motion. When they give me a date and time I'll make sure and be there. I suppose she's safe enough in the holding pen at the sheriff's office. Where are *you* now?"

"Home," Carrie-Alice said briefly. "The police picked her up a few minutes ago."

The lighted button on the second line went dark. "Then I'll call you when I have a time set to see the juvenile court judge. I'll meet you there, and we can see how successful we are at getting her back home." Bree hung up with a brief good-bye and looked at Ron in dismay. "Hartley Williams was on line two? She just hung up."

The phone beeped discreetly, and Bree picked up and identified herself. The voice on the other end of the line was high-pitched and childish. "This is Hartley Williams," she said rather breathlessly. "I need to speak to Lindsey's lawyer."

"You are," Bree said. "I'm very glad you called me, Miss Williams."

"Oh. Good. I was thinking maybe I should talk to you about what happened out at the mall."

"I think that's a great idea. Would you like to set up a meeting?"

"I tried to find your office," she said petulantly, "but the GPS in my car's all screwed up. Well, it's my step-father's car, which just goes to show. I mean, *everything* about him's screwed up, including his car. So. Anyways. I'm at Savannah Sweets. You know where that is? It's right down on the river."

"Sure," Bree said. "I'll be there in ten minutes."

"And is there, like, anything I have to sign?"

Bree frowned, puzzled. "Sign? Are you looking for representation, Miss Williams? Have you been charged with anything?"

"You mean, like, a crime? No! I haven't done a thing. But you said, like, you could represent me? That'd be very cool. I want to get on the talk shows, like Lin did this morning."

Bree stretched out in her office chair and stared at the ceiling. "I don't do that kind of work, Miss Williams. But I would like a little insight into Lindsey, and I was hoping you could provide some. Are you willing to talk to me under those conditions?"

"Will there be any reporters with you?"

"I'm afraid not. I'll tell you what, I'll spring for a cup of coffee and maybe a praline. How's that sound?"

"Okay, I guess. Could you maybe bring some reporters?"

"No. Sorry. I'll see you in ten minutes, then."

"Better make it twenty. I've got to, like, get my face on and stuff. I just bombed out of the house this morning after watching Bonnie-Jean Morrissey, and I look like, God, I don't know. A total mess."

Bree put the receiver gently into the cradle. "Oh, Lordy," she said to Petru. "Has the younger generation gone completely nuts?"

" 'The young of this city have no respect for tradition.' " Petru's thick black eyebrows drew together. "Cicero, perhaps. But Cicero found the younger Romans to be just as flighty as this Miss Hartley Williams. Things do not change, dear Bree."

Bree looked at her watch. It was less than a five-minute walk to Savannah Sweets. "Did you get your hands on a copy of the surveillance tape? I want to go over it again, just to see how much Miss Hartley Williams contributed to this caper. I'm not sure the television station ran the whole tape."

"I did obtain it. It is stored on my computer."

"Let's take a quick look."

Petru limped out and returned with his laptop. He settled it carefully on her desk, then brought the file up.

The snatch-and-grab didn't take long: two and a half minutes from start to finish. An adorable little girl in the familiar Girl Scout uniform stood just outside Bloomingdale's. She had long, curly dark hair.

"Sophie Chavez," Bree said aloud.

"A charming child," Petru said. "The jury would love this little girl, I think."

The cookies were stacked on a rickety card table. A

middle-aged woman in jeans and a light jacket stopped, examined the cookies, and picked up a box of the peanut butter (Bree's own favorite). The Hummer came down the parking lot. Lindsey leaned out of the driver-side window. A very pretty, athletic-looking girl, whom Bree knew was Madison Bellamy, leaned out of the passenger side. The middle-aged lady gave Sophie Chavez a few bills, received change, and walked on. Sophie put the money in a Skechers shoebox. The Hummer rocked to a halt. Lindsey jumped out. Madison got out the other side, frowning. Lindsey, giggling so hard she couldn't stand up straight, dashed forward, grabbed the shoebox, and danced backwards. Sophie Chavez started to cry. A thin, anxious-looking woman who had been hovering a few yards away dashed up and grabbed Sophie protectively.

"Mrs. Shirley Chavez," Petru said.

Madison turned and began to argue with Lindsey. A third girl, plump, with a thick lower lip, leaned out of the open passenger door, her eyes round with dismay.

"Hartley," Bree murmured.

Sophie, mouth open in what must have been a resounding shriek, ran toward Lindsey. Lindsey whirled, pushed the kid over, and jumped into the Hummer. Hartley withdrew into the depths of the vehicle. Madison ran forward, helped Sophie to her feet, and jumped out of the way as Lindsey gunned the car past her.

"Not menacing," Bree said. "But even so . . ."

The Hummer came to a second, jolting halt—the brakes on the thing must need relining every other week, if Lindsey drove it that way all the time—and Madison climbed back into it.

The image went blank.

"T'cha," Petru said. "KGB potential, that one."

"Lindsey, you mean." Bree leaned back with a sigh.

Petru picked up his laptop. "Did you notice the T-shirts? All three of them were wearing the same T-shirt."

"I did not," Petru admitted.

"Looked like 'Social Club' from what I could make out." Bree shook her head. "Argh. Do you suppose there's a teenage club for muggers?"

⸺⸙⸺

"Savannah Sweethearts Social Club," Hartley said, some twenty minutes later. Then, with an air of reproof: "It's our band."

"Oh," Bree said.

Hartley sucked on her Black Cow milk shake. They sat outside Savannah Sweets at a small table. The Savannah River rolled placidly by. Even in late October, the riverfront here was clogged with tourists.

"Madison even wrote us a song," Hartley said. She was dark-haired and plump, with a pudgy, marshmallow-like prettiness. She sang, in a thin, true soprano: *"Sweethearts send a sentimental sound to the guys, to the chicks, to the people all around. If you'd like another version that'll get you off the ground, it's the singing Sweet Savannahs where the happy can be found."*

The guy at the table next to them—in shorts, white socks, sandals, and a red plastic windbreaker—broke into enthusiastic applause.

Hartley preened. "Isn't that, like, totally cool?"

"Um," Bree said.

"My stepfather manages us." Hartley swished her straw vigorously up and down in her milk shake. "And he is like, *so* into getting us out there and on camera. We've had, like, three or four gigs at other high schools so far this year. I was thinking maybe Bonnie-Jean Morrissey would be, like, over the moon to have us on her show, but

I suppose now that Lindsey's gone and hogged all the air-time, we haven't got a chance."

"You never know," Bree said diplomatically.

"'Course, now that Lin's going to jail, we might get even, like, the networks interested."

For a brief, insane moment, Bree wondered if the Girl Scout cookie heist was a publicity ploy on the part of the Savannah Sweethearts Social Club.

"'Course, Madison doesn't think so. Madison thinks all this publicity is bad for the band."

"Madison sounds pretty sensible," Bree ventured.

Hartley rolled her eyes in scorn. "Huh. Any publicity is good publicity."

Bree took a sip of coffee. "Hartley, I talked to Lindsey for the first time yesterday. She seems bent on self-destruction."

Hartley's eyes grew vague. "Well, you know, she's always been kind of like that."

"Like what?"

"Like you said. I mean, she's got enough money to buy Switzerland and she's, like, got to grab money from this little kid?"

"Exactly." Bree leaned forward. "Can you think of any reason why she might be this way?"

"Genes," Hartley said wisely.

"Genes?"

"Yeah, you know, it's like she's been programmed from birth." Hartley heaved a huge sigh. "We've got genes in science this year." She made it sound like an unwelcome rash.

"Hartley, I'm Lindsey's attorney, which means I'm a pretty safe person to tell things to."

Hartley blinked, as if this actually made sense.

"You guys into any drugs?"

Her lower lip stuck out. "No way! My father's a *judge*, for God's sake."

"What about any other—episodes like this one?"

"You mean stealing stuff?" Hartley scratched her arm-pit unself-consciously. "Well, not me. And not Madison. But Lindsey . . ." She wiggled her hand in a "maybe so" gesture. "But she's nutso, you know. Like, psychotic."

Bree considered this off-the-cuff diagnosis. Then she considered the source. "Can you back that up with any specifics, Hartley?"

Hartley looked into her milk shake. "Not really. Not that I know about, anyways. What you should do is, you should talk to Madison."

"Boyfriends," Bree said, a little helplessly. "Does Lindsey date anyone on a regular basis?"

"Date." Hartley frowned. "Well, there's guys you hook up with, and guys you wouldn't be seen dead with, but date? God. Lin's had, like, nothing but bad luck with guys. You know what you should do? You should talk—"

"—to Madison," Bree said. "Right." She picked up her briefcase and got to her feet. "Hartley, if you think of any-thing, anything at all that's going to help me with Lind-sey's defense, will you call me at this number?" She held out one of her business cards. Hartley took it and squinted at it with absorbed attention.

"Sure thing." She looked up at Bree, her brown eyes sincere. "Anything to, like, help. You know? Because Lindsey's one of my very best friends."

Six

There's small choice in rotten apples.

—*Romeo and Juliet*, William Shakespeare

"What in the world were you thinking? Do you really believe you can get away with spitting in the eye of the law like that? What's all this baloney about Los Angeles? Modeling contracts? You were let out on your own recognizance. You've still got to face these charges. Good grief, girl." Bree was kind, but firm.

Lindsey looked out the car window and shrugged. They were on their way back to the Chandler home on Tybee Island. It'd been a long day, getting Lindsey out of jail and back into her mother's custody, and Bree was getting pretty tired of The Shrug. Quick sound bites of the endless hours of negotiations cycled through Bree's brain.

His Honor Juvenile Court Judge Tyree Washington: "Is there any reason why this court should believe you intend to stay within the confines of your home, Miss Chandler?"

Lindsey: (Shrug.)

District Attorney Cordelia Lucille Eastburn, Esquire: "Your Honor, I demand this unrepentant prisoner be equipped with an ankle bracelet until trial!"

Lindsey: (Shrug.)

Carrie-Alice Chandler: "Lindsey, your father's spinning in his grave at this!"

Lindsey: (Shrug.)

Shirley Chavez, mother of the victim: "Your Honor, my daughter and I forgive Miss Chandler with all our hearts. We have no objection to an at-home remand. We are dropping the charges, Your Honor. No one was hurt, and my Sophie has the money back."

Lindsey: "Screw you."

Motherhood, Bree decided, was something she was going to put off for a long, long time.

"Does it chafe a little?" Bree asked, not without sympathy.

Lindsey looked down at the bracelet circling one tanned, smooth-shaven ankle and shrugged.

"If you shrug one more time," Bree said, "I'm going to scream. And if you tell me to fuck off, I'll stop the car, get my grooming kit out of my gym bag, and wash your mouth out with soap." She took her eyes off the road for a moment and smiled at her. "Just a friendly little warning."

Lindsey rolled her eyes, which made a change from shrugging, but she said, "Whatever."

Bree drove on in silence. Carrie-Alice followed close behind them. Her daughter had refused to get in the Buick with her, and Bree, exasperated to the point of shouting, shoved the girl into her own car and told Carrie-Alice to follow them.

Lindsey chewed gum and stared out the window. An exasperated social worker had confiscated her iPod, and Bree had turned the radio off, but Lindsey bobbed her head back and forth, swaying to some internal music.

"We were lucky that Sophie Chavez's mother didn't want to press charges," Bree said. "Doesn't make a whole lot of difference as far as Cordelia Eastburn's office is concerned, but it sure looks a lot better."

"That busy black bi—," Lindsey began. Bree reached out and closed her hand firmly over Lindsey's mouth. "Not in front of me," Bree said. "Not ever. You got that?"

Lindsey tightened her lips and Bree took her hand away.

"As for Miss Priss Chavez," Lindsey said, as if nothing had happened, "she's not about to rat me out. Scared to, isn't she?"

"Sophie's eight years old," Bree said, astonished. "You're thinking about intimidating an eight-year-old?" She smacked her own forehead lightly. "Silly me. Of course you aren't going to balk at that. I mean, you've already threatened to run her over with a six-thousand-pound urban tank, pushed her to the ground, and stolen her money. Why stop there?"

"Don't be too much more of an idiot. Her mom works at one of our stores. She's not about to lose her job over something like this." She furrowed her brow. "What I don't get is, if she's not going to press charges, how come I still have to go through all this rock and roll? She got the money back, for God's sake."

"You recognized the mother as a Marlowe's employee and figured you could snatch that money and stay out of trouble?" Bree made a point of keeping her hands firmly on the wheel. "You're joking."

Lindsey's shoulders went up in the start of a shrug. She glanced at Bree and took a breath instead. Bree considered advising her client of the difference between civil and criminal law and decided not to waste her breath. Instead, she said, "You're looking at jail time."

"I'm a minor."

"Twelve is a minor. Fourteen is a minor. Seventeen is close enough to legal age to put you in real danger of incarceration. There've been a number of precedents where the court has petitioned to allow seventeen-year-olds to be prosecuted as adults."

Lindsey's eyes widened. "No shit?"

"No shit."

"I think I need a better lawyer."

Bree bit her lip, but couldn't keep the laugh back. "I told you that at the beginning, didn't I?" She pulled up at the Chandler house.

Carrie-Alice had taken her advice, and the place was alive with private security guards. Two of them sauntered toward the car as Bree put it into park; the taller, more apelike one peered into the driver's window. Carrie-Alice pulled alongside Bree's car and sat there, waiting.

"Out," Bree said to Lindsey.

"You aren't coming in?"

"I'm going home."

Lindsey paused, one sandaled foot out the passenger door. "What happens now?"

Had all the hoopla at the courthouse just now gone completely over the child's head? "What happens now is that Cordelia Eastburn has absolutely refused any kind of plea bargain. Either we plead guilty and accept the sentence of the presiding judge, or we go to trial and let a jury decide what happens to you. I've told you this. Your mother's told you this. The decision's been made to go to trial, and I"—Bree took a deep breath—"I am going to put everything I have into coming up with a defense for you that makes some sense."

Lindsey grinned bleakly. "Good luck." She stepped onto the pavement. The two guards stationed themselves one on each side and escorted her up the walkway to the house. Carrie-Alice pulled past Bree to the garages at the east end of the property.

Bree backed into the road, turned around, and went home.

———— ✦ ————

"That poor, poor child," Francesca Beaufort said.

"I don't know, Mamma." Bree tucked her legs under each other and sat cross-legged on the couch. It'd been too much of an effort to stop at the deli to pick up something to eat, so she'd heated up a can of tomato-basil soup at home. She held the soup mug in one hand and her cell phone in the other. The couch faced the small brick fireplace that occupied the end wall of the town house. An ornate mirror that had belonged to her great-uncle Franklin hung over the mantel. It tipped forward slightly, since Bree had hung it on a nail instead of sinking mounts into the wall, and she could see her own reflection. She looked tired and washed out.

Her mother's voice sounded bright and cheerful in her ear. "Only seventeen!"

"She's not an easy kid to like," Bree admitted.

"All the more reason for the pity," her mother said. "Just imagine how awful for them all."

"It does sound as if you have your hands full," her father, Royal, said.

Bree figured he was most likely on the extension in his library. Goodness knew where her mother was calling from. She had stashed extensions all over the place, and Plessey was a big plantation. And her mother hated cell phones.

Her father's voice was full of affection. "If you need any backup, darlin', I can be down there like a shot."

Bree winced. She loved her parents. But it was much easier to love them at the safe distance of the three hundred and fifty miles that separated Savannah from

Raleigh-Durham. "I think I've got things under control, Daddy. But thank you all the same."

"It's all over the news, you know," Francesca said. "Cissy said Carrie-Alice's not all that popular with the folks she knows, so everybody down there's blamin' the poor mother. Although, apparently the girl's a true handful." She sighed. "We've been so lucky with our two, Royal."

"Did Cissy say anything about any rumors of abuse?" Bree said.

Her mother was too old a hand to be shocked at Bree's question, but she paused for an appreciable moment before she said, "No. No, she didn't. And that kind of thing stays underground, dear, as you probably know. But it doesn't stay underground forever. If there'd been anything in the girl's childhood, we'd probably hear about it eventually." She added, reluctantly, "I take it you want me to put out a few little feelers?"

"Physical, emotional, sexual," Bree said. "Whatever you can pick up, Mamma. It's not gossip as such, you know. Well, it is, but it's justifiable gossip, if you see what I mean. I'm going to need all the help I can get. Cissy still thinks of me as a kid, or I'd put the pressure on her to do some digging and spare you. Plus, it'd be putting her in an awkward place to rat on her friends."

"I'll do what I can. I might have something for you when you come on up for the party tomorrow."

"The party." Bree made a face into the phone. Sasha, who'd been peacefully asleep on the other end of the couch, jerked awake and thumped his tail on the cushions.

"Now, Bree, darlin' . . ."

Bree let her mother's light, pretty voice wash over her while she thought seriously about the party. Antonia was tied up with the play. Lindsey should be safe at home over the weekend, guarded by the security detail her mother had hired. And if she left early in the morning, she could get into Plessey around noon. The six-hour drive back on Sunday would be a pain—but better than tackling weekday traffic.

Suddenly, Bree longed for the broad, gentle acres of her old home. The big comfortable kitchen, the cheerful fire in the living room, her old bedroom with the white muslin curtains and the wide-planked pine floors. And no white-faced evil charging at her out of a cloud of dreadful smoke.

"I'll be there, Mamma," she said suddenly.

"And you know how nice it'd be to see—what? You're comin' up?"

"Yes, Mamma. Just for the night, mind. I've got to be back here Sunday night."

"I don't suppose that Tonia . . ."

"Not a chance," Bree said. "The play opened last night. Well, it was the dress rehearsal."

"How were the reviews? Did they mention her at all?"

"The reviews!" Bree made another face into the phone. She'd completely forgotten her promise to see the play tonight. Sasha plodded heavily across the couch cushions and thudded his head into her lap, in sympathy. "I forgot all about reading the reviews! I'm an awful sister, Mamma. She was still in bed when I left for the office, and I haven't had a chance to talk to her all day." She looked at her watch. Seven thirty, and she was as whipped as a dog. "I've got to go. I promised her I'd look in opening night, and I've got, like, two minutes to get there."

"You give her our best."

Bree promised, clicked off the phone, and sprinted into the bathroom. She took the fastest shower of her life, flung on a little black jersey dress that was the most reliable thing she had in her closet, and shot out the door before she remembered Sasha. She skidded to a halt and went to the couch, where he was comfortably sprawled. He opened his golden eyes and looked at her.

"Your dry food's in the lower cabinet."

He blinked.

"Just a bowlful, mind."

He grinned at her, tongue lolling.

She was pretty sure she could trust him to nose open the door and stick to the promise of a single bowlful. There were distinct advantages to a dog with angelic antecedents.

Nothing in Historic Savannah was more than a mile from anything else, which meant that she was in the foyer of the Savannah Rep by five minutes to eight. The remains of a largish crowd drifted into the auditorium. Bree wiggled her fingers at the two ushers standing at the head of the aisle and decided against heading around to the backstage door. Antonia would have her hands full. Beside the older usher was the same guy who'd scowled disapprovingly and muttered "Shame" at her the night before; not only would he discourage her from ducking backstage, he'd probably ignore the informal pass Antonia had scrawled for her and insist on a real ticket. Fortunately, there was nobody in line at the little box office, and Bree got one of the last tickets available. "Practically SRO," the box office attendant said proudly. "Standing room only, you know."

"Seventy-five dollars?" Bree said in dismay. "Seventy-five?"

"Sorry. It's the dress circle. Only thing left."

Bree made it to the front of the house just as the lights dimmed for the first act. The seat was terrific; on the aisle, second row back. Bree sat down with a smile for the usher, and a second, more distantly polite smile for the person in the seat next to her, then did a classic double take. "You!" she said in disgust, as recognition set in.

Payton McAllister gave her a pained look.

Payton the Rat. Of all the people to attend the premiere of a Victorian mystery in which he had zero interest, it had to be the guy that dumped her several months ago when she was still practicing law at her father's firm in Raleigh-Durham.

The last time she'd seen Payton, she'd encouraged Sasha to pee on his shoes. The time before that, she'd tossed him over the restaurant table at Huey's.

He was still gorgeous, though.

Bree scowled at him.

"Yo, Bree. How's it going?"

"Nobody says 'yo' anymore, Payton." Aware that this was the feeblest riposte possible, Bree settled herself into the velvet cushions and stared intently at the stage.

"You're looking great."

"Shh."

The overture began, a sprightly, ominous piece that fit perfectly with the Victorian theme of the play.

"I didn't know you liked Sherlock Holmes."

"Will you shut up? The play's starting." Bree glared at him. "What are you doing here, anyway? The last play you went to voluntarily was the third grade Christmas pageant, and that was only because you played a sheep."

He opened the program and pointed at the actress playing Irene Adler.

"Lorie Stubblefield?" Bree's eyebrows shot up and she giggled. "You're dating Lorie Stubblefield?" The significance of the name hit her. "John Stubblefield's daughter? You're dating the boss's daughter? Payton, you are . . ."

The woman seated behind Bree leaned forward and hissed, *"Shhh!"*

Bree was so annoyed she missed the opening scenes of the play. When she finally focused on the action, it was to admire the deftness of the staging, the really outstanding performance of the actor playing Sherlock Holmes, and the satisfying awfulness of the performance of Lorie Stubblefield. Lorie was pretty enough, but too young for the part and way too vapid to convey the sophistication and depth of "the woman," as Sherlock Holmes always referred to the great Irene Adler. The light from the stage was sufficient to read the program; Bree thumbed through it and was happy to see her suspicions justified: Stubblefield, Marwick was a heavy contributor to the Savannah Rep.

At the interval, she stood up to go find Antonia and at least wave at her, but Payton grabbed her elbow.

"How's about I buy you a glass of wine?"

"No, thank you," Bree said.

"Seriously, I think there's some things we need to talk about. I'll buy you a glass of wine now, and later you can come with us to the cast party. John's holding it at his house on Oglethorpe."

Bree cocked her head and looked at him coolly. "I can't think of anything that we need to talk about, Payton. Except maybe why you don't pack up and leave that sleazy law firm you're working at and get a job with some integrity attached to it. Like maybe campaign manager to elect Attila the Hun to the Georgia legislature."

Payton smirked and gestured at someone over her shoulder. "You remember our senior partner, John Stubblefield." Bree turned. Sure enough, there was the artfully styled white hair, the clean-shaven chin, and the beady blue eyes of John Stubblefield, Esquire, whose TV infomercials, soliciting class action plaintiffs the world over, ran on the airwaves of late night TV in Savannah.

"Miss Winston-Beaufort," Stubblefield said, his eyes cold. He made a mock bow. "Sleazy at your service."

Bree nodded, unsmiling.

"The thing is"—Payton took her arm and led her up the aisle to the foyer—"we may be seeing a lot of each other in the next couple of months, and John wanted me to sort of sit down with you and clear the air."

The penny dropped. Of course. "The Chandler case," Bree said. "Stubblefield represents some of the store's interests? Your firm isn't large enough to handle anything of real corporate importance, Payton."

"The family, however," Payton said smoothly, "is another story altogether. We represent George Chandler's personal interests in Savannah."

Carrie-Alice's son—and Lindsey's brother. Well, Bree thought. Well, well.

"And 'sort of' sit down with me? What's that supposed to mean? Why?" Bree turned to face him, wondering for the hundredth time what she'd seen in those sculpted cheekbones and athlete's body. Lust, that's what it'd been, which just went to show you that lust was rarely a good thing. Behind those good looks was the soul of a sewer rat. "You aren't going to try to warn me off an investigation into Probert's death, are you? The way you tried to keep me out of Ben Skinner's murder investigation?"

Payton's electric blue eyes widened. Their color had charmed Bree, until she'd learned that the deep violet blue owed everything to his contact lenses. "You're looking into Probert's death?" His grip on her arm tightened. "His death was an accident, pure and simple."

Bree cast a swift glance around the crowd. They were surrounded by well-dressed, happy playgoers. At least three of her distant relatives were within hollering distance. She dropped her voice to an angry, ominous whisper. "If you don't let go of my arm right this minute,

I will toss you out the front door and splat onto Magnolia Street."

Payton backed off. Bree calmed down. She had no real control over the fierce, whirlwind power that was occasionally at her command, but Payton didn't know that. The last time he'd provoked her, he'd ended up chin over teakettle on a barroom floor. She knew he wouldn't want to chance that again.

"So what's up with my client?" she said briskly.

"We'd just like to be kept current." Payton rubbed the back of his neck. "And John. That's Mr. Stubblefield, of course. John wants to be sure that any residual feelings over . . . you know . . ."

"Over what?"

"Over my dumping you. He wants to be sure that you're not keeping anything back. Out of spite." He chuckled. "John and I know how women are."

The back of her neck prickled. A slight wind stirred her hair. A tall, silvery shape slid past the corner of her eye. She didn't have to turn to know who it was. Gabriel Striker, private eye and nosy angel who seemed to show up every time she threatened to lose her temper. She kept her head with an effort, since Gabriel's presence meant everyone in the foyer was at risk if she lost it. "You couldn't possibly be implying that I'd withhold information critical to the well-being of my client."

Payton shifted from one foot to the other. "I suppose not."

"We'll plan on sending you a weekly progress report."

His shoulders sagged in relief. "Really? That's great. You promise?"

"Don't push it, Payton. You'll get the reports."

The houselights dimmed, and then brightened.

"There's the signal for the interval. You'll want to be going back to your seat." She wiggled her eyebrows.

"Give John my sincere wishes for the state of his health."

Payton looked momentarily puzzled, but turned obediently and disappeared back into the theater.

Bree waited until the foyer was empty, and then went to the corner opposite the box office, where Gabriel leaned negligently against the wall. "So here you are," she said.

He nodded soberly. "Here I am."

Gabriel was tall, with the heavily muscled body of a boxer. He moved like a dancer, lightly and with precision. His eyes were the color of the Savannah River at dawn. "Interesting new case."

"Mr. Chandler's, I suppose you mean, since he's the one that's dead," Bree said. "Yes, isn't it? I haven't had a chance to go through the pleadings yet, but it looks a lot"—she searched for the right word—"*graver* than the Skinner file."

"Armand is a little concerned."

"Really?"

"Really. We'd like to talk it over with you."

"Well, sure," Bree said. "Would Monday morning be okay?"

"Now," Gabriel said.

Bree looked at her watch. Nine thirty, and she had to get up early to get to Plessey.

"It can't wait?"

He shook his head. "The Pendergast graves are empty."

Seven

Can these bones live?
—Ezekiel 37:3

Armand Cianquino lived six miles out of town in a two-hundred-and-fifty-year-old cotton plantation named Melrose. It had been converted to apartments aimed at those people who wanted elegance, seclusion, and the beauty of the Savannah River. The plantation house was a classic example of architecture in the wealthy Old South: two stories high, with wraparound upper and lower verandahs that completely surrounded the building. The main building was well over eight thousand square feet. A wealthy banker had rescued the property from rot, mildew, and decay in the late 1970s and converted each floor of the main house into three spacious apartments. The outlying buildings—former slave quarters and the original kitchen—had been converted into little cottages.

Surrounded by lush gardens of azaleas, roses, and hydrangeas, the sprawling white mansion brooded on the riverbank. Savannah had the reputation of being the most haunted city in America, and Melrose was believed to have its fair share of "haints." Marie-Claire was the cast-off mistress of a late-eighteenth-century river pirate. Like Virginia Woolf, she filled her dress pockets with stones and drowned herself in the river. The other ghost, a son of the original builder, Augustine Melrose, was hanged in 1805 by an outraged populace after a murderous attack on the wife of a fellow planter.

Bree, who had reason enough to believe in the existence of the ghosts of the newly dead, was not as convinced about the presence of either the wailing Marie-Claire or Augustine Melrose's vicious offspring. But she wasn't anxious to run into either one of them. As she drove up the long, semicircular driveway to the front door, the late night mists of a Georgia autumn evening drifted over the lawns and twined around the boles of the cottonwood trees. Spanish moss trailed from live oaks like seaweed floating in an ocean of earthbound clouds. Bree surveyed the Gothic scene somewhat glumly. Then she got out of the car and walked up the shallow front steps to the large basswood front door. It was open. Bree walked into the foyer. The floor was wide-planked pine, polished to a high shine. The air was fragrant with the scent of freesia. A classic Sheraton lowboy stood against the back wall. The large vase on it held fresh flowers, as always. A wide, graceful staircase rose from the center of the foyer up to the second story.

Armand Cianquino's apartment was to her immediate right. She tapped on the door. Gabe Striker opened it, and stepped back to let her in.

"He's in the library."

Bree nodded and followed Gabriel across the living room floor. The paneled door into the library was made from an exotic wood. Rosewood, Bree thought, or perhaps a lacquered cedar. Artfully shaped spinning spheres were carved into the panel, the same shapes that formed the wrought-iron fence surrounding Bree's office at 66 Angelus Street.

Gabriel knocked twice, opened the door, and Bree followed him into the familiar room.

The library was in stark contrast to the spare elegance of Armand Cianquino's living room. A leaded window looked out over the gardens. All four walls were covered with floor-to-ceiling bookshelves. The shelves were crammed with books of all kinds: thick ones, thin ones, old ones bound in dark, crumbling leather, and new ones in shiny covers. Bree glanced at the shelves that had held the professor's set of the hundred-volume *Corpus Juris Ultima*, that body of celestial case law that had first alerted her to the fact that her old law school professor was not quite what he seemed. The books were still there; the set he had sent to the Beaufort & Company offices must be a copy.

A long table occupied the middle of the library. It was loaded with files, more books, a couple of lamps, and a bundle of old material covering most of a long sword. A wire cage sat smack in the middle of the table. The cage door was open, and a large, owl-like bird sat on the perch inside. His beady black eyes regarded Bree with a somewhat baleful air.

"Hello, Archie," she said.

"About time, about time, about *time*," Archie said.

"Hello, Bree." Armand Cianquino rolled his wheelchair into the light. He was a slender man, wholly Chinese, despite his Italianate name. Bree had known him forever, it seemed. She remembered his visits to the house at Plessey when she was small. And, of course, she remembered him from her years at law school. Highly respected (and much feared), he occupied the Religion in Law chair for most of his tenure. Retired from teaching just after Bree had taken her bar exams, he still gave an occasional lecture, wrote an article or two for the *American Bar Journal*, and consulted on international case law, especially those cases that involved religious freedoms. In the short time from retirement to this, he had changed a great deal. His once black hair was now totally white. And something—he had never told Bree exactly what—had put this vital, challenging man into a wheelchair.

He rolled forward into the light, and Bree was dismayed to see that in the few short weeks since she had seen him last, he had aged further still. She laid her hand lightly on his shoulder. "I hope you're keeping well, Professor."

He grimaced slightly and moved his shoulder away from her touch, not in distaste, but in discomfort. "Sit down, Bree."

She drew a carved wooden chair a little way from the table and perched on the edge. Gabriel stood just out of the circle of lamplight, arms folded across his chest.

She spoke into the silence. "I'm glad to see you. We haven't had much of a chance to talk since we settled the Skinner case."

"Successfully handled," Cianquino said. There was a hint of approval in his eyes.

"Thank you." Bree took a breath. "But it would have been a lot smoother going if I'd been better prepared. I'm at a bit of a disadvantage here, Professor. If I could just—"

"Curiosity killed the cat, the cat, the cat," Archie squawked. He snapped his beak greedily. Professor Cianquino held one frail hand up, and the bird subsided into cranky mutterings. "If you could just?" he prompted.

"Well, interview my client properly, for one." Bree plunged on, not sure how far she would get before the professor reminded her of what she'd had to accept at the beginning of this new—and unwelcome—career: she could only learn the ins and outs of this job through experience. He and the other angels in her company were there to guide and protect—not inform.

"You had several conversations with Mr. Skinner, I believe."

"Very spotty," Bree said. "It was like being at the end of a tunnel. I think I solved that case through sheer dumb luck. And I'm running into the same problem with the ghost of Probert Chandler. I can barely understand what he's asking me to do." She hesitated, pretty sure that she didn't want to know the answer to her next question. "Is there a . . . a place where I can sit down and talk to him properly?"

Archie shrieked, as if he'd been burned.

"There is," the professor said dryly, "but it's unlikely that you would return to continue his defense."

"You mean I can get there but I can't get back?"

"Not precisely." The professor thought a moment, his eyes shuttered. "Probert Chandler's keepers would be delighted to keep you with him. You would be an enormous asset."

She recalled the black flames and the taloned claws that tore at Probert Chandler's shade and shuddered. "Couldn't Gabriel and maybe Petru and Ron go with me? Kind of like bailiffs? Or security guards?"

"No." He lifted his finger to forestall her next demand. "We're not keeping things from you out of choice," he said testily. "Do you remember how you learned to swim?"

"I . . . huh?" Bree blushed. "Sorry. That was rude. Yes, I surely do. But I don't see . . ." She stopped. The professor lifted his eyebrow. "You'd like me to say? Well, Mamma took me into the water and floated around with me. She held me up until I was able to figure out the strokes."

"There is no one to walk into the water to keep you afloat until you learn the strokes." He made an impatient movement. "Don't you see? You do not. Very well. If there was no one to teach you to swim, how would you learn?"

"I'd wade into the water and paddle around until I figured it out, I suppose."

"And if I were on the shore, shouting instructions?"

"I'd be listening!" Bree said indignantly.

"You would be concentrating on me and not on the task at hand. And, what's more, you might take chances in the expectation that I would jump in and pull you out if you started to drown. You are a prudent and resourceful woman, Bree. And you like to win. You only go ahead when you are reasonably sure of a victory. I cannot prepare you for what lies ahead. It's your decisions, your choices, and your free will that push you forward here. Those decisions must be unhampered by any considerations other than the success of the case and your own survival."

The only possible reply to this was a polite variant of "That sucks," so Bree kept her mouth shut, partly out of respect, but mostly because she'd get something along the lines of "Tough!" as a response, and that'd get her dander up for sure.

"Can I quit?" she said suddenly. "I mean, what if I don't want to do this anymore?"

"There are those that would be delighted if you quit," Cianquino said equably.

Bree thought about the pronoun: "that" as opposed to "who." "That" applied to nonhumans. To things, not people. She thought of the yellow mist that chased her, and what terrifying thing it might conceal. "I see," she said, although she didn't, not quite. "So. Getting a sit-down interview with Probert Chandler is a no-go."

"Your investigative skills are considerable," Cianquino said with his characteristic obliqueness. "I have every confidence that you càn answer the questions revolving around his death, and that you can prepare a spirited and truthful defense. He will get in touch with you when he is able to do so."

"How tough is it? For him to talk to me, I mean? We're dealing with a legal system here, and he seems to have the usual kind of rights. If he's got the right to representation, how come he hasn't got the right to use it?"

"You remember your logic classes and the argument against *argumentum in circulo*?"

Bree squinched her face up. She'd been a hardworking student, but not an inspired one. "That's one in Aristotle's list of flaws in logical argument, and it has something to do with the argument going around in circles."

Gabriel muffled a laugh. Archie flapped his wings, stretched to his full height on his perch, and shrieked, "La-*ment*-able!"

"More or less. Mr. Chandler's awareness of his own mistakes in life keeps him from giving full disclosure to you."

"You mean, that's the static interference I get when I talk to these guys? Their sins, so to speak? Sort of a visual pollution?" She rubbed the back of her neck in frustration. "The only thing he said that could possibly be a clue is that his death was connected somehow with his business. Marlowe's. The static interfered with everything else."

"Static. That's as apt an interpretation as any of what prevents the dead from speaking to us clearly. It is the sense of sin carried within us. All men—and I use the term advisedly, Bree, since it applies to women, too—are error-filled. It is a perquisite of being human. And if he was not human and free of mankind's sins of greater and lesser degree, he wouldn't be in need of a lawyer like yourself."

"'Perquisite,'" Bree said. "That's an odd word to choose."

"A benefit and a boon, human failings," Cianquino said. "As well as a curse and a damnation. As you might say yourself, dear Bree: 'You betcha!'"

Gabe spoke from the shadows behind the desk, a let's-get-on-with-it tone to his voice. "It's close to midnight, Armand. Something urgent has come up. It's why we came to see you."

"And we're nearing All Hallows Eve," Cianquino agreed. "Yes. To the business at hand. You are aware, Bree, that there are those who want to"—he paused and thought for a moment—"disrupt your activities." He smiled. "We are aware of all that happens, you know."

"Yes!" Bree said indignantly. "I am. And it's hardly fair, is it? Somebody on the defendant's side is violating some kind of canon of ethics, aren't they? At least, I presume there is a canon of ethics in celestial matters. I mean, where better? So I'd like to file a complaint against the harassment."

"Do so, by all means," the professor encouraged. "Petru should be able to draw up the necessary Summons and Complaint. But I doubt it will have much effect."

"Those Pendergasts," Lavinia said from the shadows. Bree jumped a little. She hadn't realized Lavinia was in the room. She looked into the corner of the library. Gabriel's tall, silvery form spun next to a short, lavender-tinted whirl of light. "Never did take much account of the law when they was alive. Even less so when they died off."

"Ah, yes. Josiah." The lamplight dimmed, as if a hand had passed over the flame. Cianquino frowned.

"The Pendergasts are an old Savannah family," Bree said. "I was in prep school with one of them. Jennifer."

"Who married that no-good son of Mr. Benjamin Skinner," Lavinia said tartly. "Mm-hm. Josiah was her great-granddaddy. And a real no-good, for certain. Not much out of the ordinary for the times, though, since there were a lot of no-goods walkin' the streets of Savannah back then." Lavinia's shade coalesced into her temporal form and she moved into the light. "My first sight of him,

I'll not forget, not for all the time left in this world and the next. I was a-playing in the Nile with my cousins."

"The Nile?" Bree said.

"The part that's in Africa," the professor answered.

"He took the head off of N'tange with one sweep of his sword, and put the rest of us in chains." Lavinia's voice trailed on the air like soft dark silk. "And I spent the rest of my earthly days near this very place. Melrose. Melrose." She fell silent. "Not too long after I come here, Josiah sold me to Melrose's oldest boy. I didn't see too much of the sunlight for the longest time." She shut her eyes and hummed softly, all the while rocking gently on her feet. "There now," she said to herself, "there now."

Bree's chest was tight. She drew a short, shallow breath.

"Betimes," Lavinia said slowly, "betimes whilst I was living out my days in the dark, Josiah met and married Olivia."

"Olivia," Bree echoed. She'd come across Olivia Pendergast's gravestone in the cemetery that surrounded the house at 66 Angelus Street.

"Olivia didn't take to Josiah and his wickedness. So she run off with a handsome lover. It's on her gravestone, her epitaph. One Chronicles twenty-nine, verse fifteen: 'Our days on earth are as a shadow, and there is none abiding.' Yes'm, Bree, and the rest of that verse was poor Olivia to the life and death. A sojourner and a stranger. A stranger to these parts and a sojourner who didn't get too far with her fancy man before Josiah killed them, too."

"Did he stand trial?" Bree asked.

"He did. And her poor corpse did, too, for a-killin' of the child she was to have borned before she went off with her lover. They hanged Josiah. And they put her corpse in the murderers plot, alongside of his. And there they lie to this day, the revengeful dead."

"Except that they're not lying in their graves the way they're supposed to," Bree said. She looked at Gabriel. "You brought me here because the Pendergast graves are empty."

"And so they are," Lavinia said.

"What's this?" Cianquino said. His eyes, brilliant and black, bored into Lavinia's. "Are you certain, Lavinia?"

"I stand between those graves and this life each mortal day," Lavinia said. "And I know when there's been a harrowing. They've gone. Oh, yes. They've gone."

Bree's imagination whirled with terrible images. Lavinia as a young girl, lying chained in the hold of a slave ship. Lavinia in the hands of Burton Melrose, whose crimes against his female slaves had been so crazed, none of the older histories of Savannah detailed them. She wanted to wrap Lavinia in her arms, but the look on the old woman's face kept her from moving an inch in her direction. Instead, she swallowed hard and asked, "But, where have they gone? Josiah and Olivia?"

"They've been unchained from the pits they lie in," Lavinia said to Armand. "And I do believe they are after my girl. My Bree. I'm here to see what you are going to do about it."

"Cry havoc and let slip the dogs of war!" Archie said, as if it were a suggestion and not a quote.

"Perhaps," Cianquino agreed. He smoothed his chin. "I'll make some inquiries about that, Archie. In the meantime, I'll have to do some research. This doesn't augur well, I must admit. I can only think of one precedent, and it's not a comforting one."

"What doesn't augur well?" Bree demanded. "And what happens when a body leaves a grave? Except that the bodies would have rotted a century ago. So what exactly was in those graves? And what happened to it—them— the bones?"

"The dead exist in a universe parallel to this," Gabriel said. "And the physical Bridge between the two is always closed. You will see them, hear them, perhaps even feel the cold of their presence, but they cannot touch you. Your body crosses it when you die. And your body can't cross back."

"Always closed," Bree said, "this Bridge. That's good."

"It's almost always, though, isn't it?" Lavinia said. "Because they're here now, the two of them. And they are loose."

"Loose," Bree echoed hollowly. She cleared her throat. "And what does that mean, exactly?"

"Always takes her fences head-on," Gabriel said to Cianquino. "Brave as anyone we've ever had in the job." He glanced at her. "You've asked a direct question. You deserve a direct answer. Do you want it?"

"Of course," Bree said. She folded her hands on the table—to stop them from shaking, if truth were told—and looked at each of them in turn.

The professor spoke slowly, as if remembering a past life. "When the Bridge between the spheres is breached, it lets loose a certain amount of true evil into the world. Active cruelty. Deliberate malice. Destruction of a kind that, unchecked, could destroy most of what you and yours hold dear. Those large events that horrify mankind come from massive armies of the Adversary. Pogroms, massacres, genocide. The smaller, more private evils come from those like the Pendergasts, slipping through when the attention of the Guardians is elsewhere."

"So I don't have to save the world this week, at least," Bree said. She was proud that her voice wasn't trembling. Her mind was filled with the horrors of serial killers, torturers, rapists, and mothers who drowned their children.

Professor Cianquino smiled wryly. "Not this week.

Just yourself. And those that are close to you. Take care, Bree."

"And you'll send some help?" Gabriel said.

"I'll send some help."

Eight

"Of all the gin joints in all the world . . ."
—*Casablanca*

"So what do you think?" Antonia flung herself onto the living room floor and gazed up at the ceiling. It was coffered. In a fit of Georgian-inspired artistic fervor, a long dead Winston-Beaufort had commissioned paintings in each of the squares between the moldings, and Antonia looked up at simpering shepherdesses and bilious sheep.

"I think I made a mistake when I decided to go to law school instead of becoming a veterinarian."

"I didn't know you thought about being a vet."

"I didn't think long enough. Or maybe I should have been a chef."

"Get out!" Antonia shouted gleefully. "You'd starve to death without takeout!"

Bree was exhausted and wound tight as a guitar string. She was scared and angry with herself for being scared. Professor Cianquino had promised help. Of what kind, he couldn't say. Except that she would know it when it showed up. She hoped it was soon.

She'd almost cried with relief when she'd pulled into her parking spot outside her town house and seen that Antonia was home. For the next few days, at least, she didn't want to be alone.

"When I said what do you think, I meant about the play, not your career." Antonia flopped over onto her stomach, shoved her fists beneath her chin, and looked at Sasha, who was sprawled next to her. "With all due respect, sister, your career seems to be having a totally negative effect on your outlook on life. Tim Adriansen said you were in the theater tonight for about five seconds and then you bombed on out with some good-looking guy, without so much as a peep about the show. I suppose you hated it so much you couldn't stand it. Or it bored you so much you took off with the first good-looking dude that flexed his pecs at you."

"Isn't Tim the usher that dissed me out for representing Lindsey Chandler? I thought so. You believe him over me? The guy's a sneak, a rat, and a toad. Which brings me to who I was with. The good-looking guy was Payton the Rat. The ticket I bought sat me right next to him and his creepy boss, John Stubblefield. If *you'd* left me a real ticket, I would have sat somewhere else and stayed for the whole thing. Plus I would have saved myself seventy-five bucks."

"Oh, shoot. I'm an awful sister. I'm the worst!" Antonia sat up and ran her hands through her hair, which was pretty frazzled to begin with. "They didn't let you in with the pass I wrote for you? I suppose I should have known better. Was he awful to you? Payton?"

"No more than usual," Bree said. "My main feeling when I see him is total self-disgust. I mean, how could I?"

"He's gorgeous, for one thing," Antonia said. "Not that *I* would have fallen for that, but never mind. Anyhow. I'm sorry. About the ticket, anyway. And about thinking you finked out on me. So, what'd you think? About the play?"

"Wonderful," Bree said promptly. "The best part was the staging, no question."

Antonia grinned. "Seriously?"

"Seriously, the staging was brilliant. You've taught me enough about that stuff so that I know it can make or break a play, or pretty nearly. And you made it. The guy who played Holmes was sensational. But Irene Adler—really, Tonia. Did Stubblefield give the Rep so much money they had to cast her, or what?"

"You think Gordon would cast a play because a backer bribed him? You've been watching too many old Preston Sturges movies. No, Gordon cast her because she's sleeping with him. Also," she added, in a more reasonable tone, "she was the best of a bad lot. I mean, the only other serious actor up for the part was me, and I know I'm way too young. Although I can *play* old, which is more than I can say for Lorie."

"Lorie Stubblefield is sleeping with Gordon, your director?" Bree said with interest.

"Yep."

"She's sleeping with Payton, too."

"Get out!"

"Well, he implied that she was. Maybe it's just another one of Payton's little maneuvers to get under my skin. Although it's so like him. Sucking up to the boss's daughter. Anyhow, I loved the play, I loved your work, and I'm going to bed. I'm wiped out."

"You don't want to go down to Louie's for a pizza? Gordon's probably there, and maybe Lorie, too."

"Antonia, it's almost one o'clock in the morning. I have to get up in five hours to drive home."

"You're going to the Guy Fawkes party?"

"Yes. Although why Mamma just doesn't come out and call it a Halloween party beats me."

"The fifth falls on a Thursday this year, and nobody would come, or not as many as would come on a weekend. Anyhow, I say God bless you for throwing your fair body into the breach. *That's* why they haven't given me much of a hard time about not showing up. You'll be there." She jumped up, grabbed her purse, and patted Bree's knee. "You go on to bed. I'm going down for a pizza. I'm about starved to death."

Bree bit her lip. She was afraid something was going to come out of the mirror. She was afraid to go to sleep. Afraid of her dreams. "You're sure you just don't want to go on to bed?"

"You're kidding! You know about theater hours. During a show I never get to bed before three." She headed toward the kitchen, and Bree stood up. Sasha got up, too, and stood with his head pressed anxiously at her knee.

"Hang on. I changed my mind. I'm coming with you."

Antonia skidded to a halt and stared at her. "You're kidding. You've changed your mind about going home?"

"No, no, no. I've changed my mind about pizza. All I had to eat tonight was some soup."

"But you aren't going to get any sleep."

"I'll be fine." She gave Antonia little shove. "I'm right behind you."

Antonia peered closely at her. "Is something wrong? You look—I don't know—kind of run over."

Bree thought: *Well, let's see. In the past twenty-four hours, I've retained another dead soul as a client, dealt with a kid so screwed up she torments dogs, and discovered that yep, I'm being followed by a pair of corpses who've jumped through the barricades between this world and the next so they can take me on a permanent, highly unpleasant tropical vacation.* Aloud, Bree said, "I need to unwind with a cold glass of wine and a nice cheesy slice of pizza. Forget sleep. I can do that anytime."

In fact, she fell asleep in the corner booth at Huey's. A number of cast members had dropped by, after making a dutiful appearance at the cast party hosted by the Stubblefields. Bree was grateful for their presence, and the noise that accompanied it. She tucked herself into the far end of one of the booths, put her head back, and only woke to Antonia's tug on her hair. "You're drooling," she announced. "I had to explain that you weren't the sister that showed up on TV today defending that Lindsey character, but the idiot sister I keep locked in the closet like Mr. Rochester with his first wife. Everybody," Antonia said with satisfaction, "believed me."

Bree looked blearily at her watch. Four in the morning. She looked down at Sasha, who had positioned himself on the floor at the end of the booth, and said, "What d'ya think? Shall we take off for Plessey right now?"

"Now?" Antonia shrieked. "You've got to be kidding!"

"If I get there early, I'll have time for a nap before the party. Much better than trying to get a couple hours of sleep right now."

And much better than facing whatever awaited her, alone in the dark in her bedroom.

Antonia made her a thermos of strong coffee before she took herself off to her own bed, and Bree found herself driving down I-75 with the sun coming up behind her, and the clear road rolling in front. She was in a cheerful state of mind. Sasha sat strapped in the passenger seat next to her, and the fears of the night before ebbed like water down a drain.

She reached the turnoff for Plessey by ten o'clock, and was so pleased with her progress that she decided to stop for coffee and a bite of doughnut before wading into the maelstrom of her family's affairs. "Time to brush my hair, wash my face, and get oriented, Sasha. Where do you think we should stop—Tim Horton's? Dunkin' Donuts?"

Once off the interstate, she'd slowed to forty-five, so she had time to brake when Sasha pressed his nose to the passenger-side window and barked once.

Here!

"The Saturn Diner?" She squinted at the printed slogan below the neon letters. " 'We run rings around the competition.' Cute. Very cute."

She pulled up in front of the plate glass window. There was one other car in the front lot, an old Ford Dually that looked the worse for wear. She glanced at it again. It looked vaguely familiar.

At the rear of the diner, she could see a few other cars parked up against the dumpster; an older model Chevy and a Toyota that probably belonged to the waitress and the chef.

The glass door to the entrance was plastered with signs for community events: Denville Farm Days, the local Elks pancake dinner, a pumpkin festival sponsored by the local Baptist church. Inside, the large dining area was floored with black and white linoleum squares. A dozen or so red plastic-topped stools stood in front of the counter. A glass-fronted tiered stand held plates of pies and cakes topped with cherries and whipped cream. A fryer smell filled the air: fried chicken, chips, and barbecue. Bree loved diners. She loved the hash brown potatoes, fried peach pies, and grits swimming in butter. The only thing she didn't love was the coffee, which was generally boiled to death and burned to perdition. Bree held the door open and waved at the waitress wiping down a table near the cash register.

"Y'all mind if my dog sits outside this door while I come in for some pie?"

The waitress, fortyish, with pale brown hair tucked back in a ponytail, waved lethargically back. "Hell, honey. Bring him on in. If the sheriff stops by, put on a pair of sunglasses and tell him he's a guide dog."

Bree seated herself at the counter. Despite the pickup in front, the dining room was empty of customers except for her and Sasha. The waitress slapped her rag down, pulled an order pad from her pocket, and put her elbows on the counter. The name Kayla was embroidered in red stitching on the pocket of her checked shirt.

"What'll it be?"

"Iced tea, please. And maybe one of those fried peach pies." Bree smiled at her. "I'm Bree, by the way. And this is Sasha."

"Got it. Bree. And for big boy there?" She nodded at Sasha. "Think we got a blade bone from last night's pot roast in the back."

"He'd love that. Thank you."

Bree resettled herself onto the stool and felt the tension leave her shoulders, neck, and back. She was twenty minutes away from home. A truly sensible person could stay there behind the big wrought-iron gates and phone in her resignation from life in Savannah and 66 Angelus Street. She could get a nice, undemanding job. Maybe like this one, where the only dangers lay in bad-tempered Bubbas wandering in from the beer joints down the road after a rowdy Saturday night. She closed her eyes against the glare of the sunlight through the plate glass windows and thought about nothing in particular for the first time in days.

Suddenly, Sasha jumped to his feet and growled.

"Bree? Is that you?"

Bree jerked upright. The owner of the pickup—it couldn't be anyone else—stood at the end of the bar, a half smile on his face. Bree's heart bumped twice in her chest. "Abel?" she said. "Abel?" Suddenly, she was off the stool and in his arms.

At six-foot-four, to Bree's five-foot-nine, Abel always made her feel small and feminine. She gave herself up to his hard, muscled chest for a long moment, then drew back, suddenly aware of Kayla the waitress, grinning cheekily at them both, and Sasha, who looked perplexed.

"What's it been—five years?" Her voice was husky. She stepped back, blushing, then sank onto the counter stool. She reached for the iced tea and took a long drink, resisting the impulse to pour it over the back of her neck. "Well," she said, "well. It's good to see you, Abel."

He leaned against the counter, thumbs hooked into the belt loops of his jeans. It was the only sign of his own loss of composure. The steady gray eyes were the same. But there was a hint of gray in his black hair—how old was he now? Forty-two or -three, at least. His face was weathered, and his smile just the same.

"You look wonderful," he said.

"Thank you kindly, sir. And you look well. Still opting for the outside jobs, I see." She gestured at his hands. "You're as tan as an old saddle. And those calluses on your hands didn't come from scrawling quadratic equations on the blackboard." She drew her eyebrows together. "It *is* quadratic equations you mathematicians go on and on about, isn't it? Math is so confusin'."

"Now, don't go all Southern sappy on me, Bree. I like my women smart."

"And my hubby tells me my ro-mance novels are so much gush," Kayla said with an exaggerated sigh. "Y'all want your pie now? I hope not. I can listen to this kind of stuff all day."

"Yes. Well." Bree took the peach pie in one hand and the glass of iced tea in the other. She looked around rather wildly for a booth, realized with a start they were all unoccupied, and nodded toward the one farthest from Kayla's ecstatic grin.

"Blueberry for you?" Kayla said to Abel.

"Peach." Bree looked at the pie in her own hand. "He always liked peach."

"Peach coming right up."

Kayla disappeared into the kitchen. Bree followed Abel to the booth. After a long moment, Sasha walked to the glass door at the front of the diner and sat down. He looked back over his shoulder at them.

We should go right now.

"Handsome dog," Abel said.

"Yes, he is. His name is Sasha."

Abel craned his neck to look at the scar on Sasha's hind leg. "Looks like that's just about finished healing."

"The cast came off two days ago." She looked at him. "A spring trap. In the yard of my office building. Remember how you found those guys who were setting the spring traps at Plessey? And beat the tar out of them, too."

He nodded. Abel's job as manager at Plessey had lasted three years. It would have lasted forever if Bree hadn't fallen in love with him. She never knew if he'd felt the same for her, although, in her wilder, Scarlett O'Hara moments, she was sure that if circumstances had been different, if he had been free . . .

Bree cleared her throat. "And Virginia? She's well, I hope?"

"Just fine. Still working at the clinic. She's steadier with a regular paycheck coming in."

Bree was never sure how to approach asking about Virginia's illness. Abel never discussed it, although he was a tender, attentive nurse to his wife. Virginia herself was exhaustively, comprehensively, endlessly focused on it. She had one of the many forms of multiple sclerosis. Sometimes she was wheelchair-bound, and sometimes she wasn't.

"And you? Still finding the classroom too claustrophobic to stick at for long?"

He nodded, but didn't volunteer anything more.

Bree shoved her pie back and forth along the table,

almost overwhelmed with feeling. With a sudden, unwelcome flash of insight, she saw her infatuation with Payton McAllister as a blind and stupid hedge against her love for this tall, brilliant, caring man. She had a flash of amused comfort with herself, though: her affair with Payton was explained at last.

"And you, Bree? I hear you moved on to Savannah." He leaned forward and moved his hand toward her. "You okay? You look a little"—he hesitated—"'careworn' is the word that comes to mind."

"Yes," Bree said. "Yes, I'm fine. Something just occurred to me that should have occurred to me long before." She wanted to laugh and cry, all at once. Instead, she ate a piece of her peach pie, which was as good as she hoped it would be. "And I've opened a practice in Savannah. Uncle Franklin—you remember Uncle Franklin? Of course you do. Just before he died, he added a codicil to his will, leaving his practice to me."

"I didn't realize he still practiced law. I thought he spent most of his career on the bench. Is it interesting, his caseload?"

Bree opened her mouth and closed it. "You could say so," she said thoughtfully. "More interesting than I'd anticipated, that's for sure." The peach pie suddenly tasted like cardboard. She sat back in the booth, exhaustion hitting like a brick. "Whoa. Sorry. Guess the drive down here took more out of me than I thought." She rubbed her hands over her eyes. "And you? We didn't hear much about you when you left Plessey."

"I did some work for the forestry service. And you remember my brother? Charles?"

"I do indeed." It seemed so strange to have this normal, chatty conversation on the surface, while the unspoken conversation underneath roared on like a river in spring spate. "He's much older than you, as I recall. And he's got something to do with horses."

"The Seaton Stud." Abel's face was impassive. "And he did have a great deal to do with horses. But not anymore. He died three weeks ago. I agreed to stay and help Missy out until she can find someone more permanent. Or sell out—she hasn't decided which."

"My gosh. I'm truly sorry to hear that, Abel. I know you two weren't close, but . . ."

"A brother's a brother." He finished the sentence for her with a slight smile.

"That'll be quite a challenge. It's huge, isn't it? The Seaton Stud." Her mouth was dry. She took a sip of the iced tea and choked a little as it tried to go down her throat.

"Four stallions at stud and forty mares in permanent residence. And the number of mares doubles in early spring, of course."

"So Virginia's fine with this? Pulling up stakes again and moving to Savannah?"

Because that's where the Seaton Stud was located.

Five miles west of the office at 66 Angelus Street.

Nine

"I ran into Abel Trask today," Bree said casually. She sat curled up in one of the big wicker chairs that lay scattered across the wide verandah. Francesca perched next to her on the porch swing. Her mother was dressed in her usual fashion when she was at home: a long cotton skirt, a brightly colored tee, and comfortable old loafers. Her bright gold-red hair (recently "refreshed" at a darling new shop in Raleigh, she had informed her daughter) was coiled in a careless way on the top of her head. She wore small gold earrings in the shape of a heart.

Plessey surrounded them both like loving arms. Wisteria vines curled around the porch railings, the leaves a yellowy green. The dried heads of hydrangea clustered among the hedges hugging the brick walls of the house were a creamy beige that only faintly recalled the riotous pink of summer.

The old house stood in the middle of five hundred acres of cotton, and had something of the appearance of an oasis among the wide flat fields. Royal's great-great-grandfather had planted sycamores in the half acre surrounding the house and old outbuildings, and the trees had grown to huge, dignified heights. On this, the last day of October, the last of their leaves provided a minimal shade from the autumnal sun. Two large canvas tents had been erected on the wide front lawn. The whole party area was a hum of activity. White-jacketed waiters set up chairs, smoothed the linens on the two big bars, and fussed with the wooden dance floor that lay open to the sky.

The road was a quarter mile away from the house. Since Bree had last been home, her father had skimmed another coat of blacktop on the long drive, and the lawn on either side had been neatly mowed. She looked down the length of the new tar to the wrought-iron gates, open in welcome, as they always were during the day, and said, "Mamma?"

"Yes. I heard you. Abel Trask." Francesca fiddled with her hair, and said, suddenly, "You're looking thin." Her mother nudged the porch floor with her toe and set the swing going. "Have another one of those shrimp thingies."

Bree took another tiny shrimp sandwich from the plate on the wicker table at her elbow. Sasha's ears went up and he cocked his head at her engagingly. Bree gave him her sandwich.

"How is he? Abel Trask."

"Fine, or so it seemed. Hasn't changed much. He has a little gray in his hair."

"That woman," Francesca said with an audible snap of her teeth, "would put gray in the hair of the Kaiser."

Bree wondered if she should ask why the Kaiser, and not, say, some Episcopalian saint, but decided against it. Her mother's thought processes were a continual delight to her family, but rarely logical.

"Virginia," Bree said. "He said she's doing pretty well."

"Virginia. Yes, indeed." Francesca lay back in the swing and stared at the porch ceiling. She looked so much like

Antonia at that moment! "There are very few things harder than living with long-term illness," Francesca said. "So I should shut my mouth and hope for glory." She sat up and fixed her brilliant blue eyes on her oldest daughter. "The two of you have much to say to each other?"

"Not much," Bree said. "He's moving to Savannah, I hear."

"Yes. That nice big brother of his, Charles, that was his name. Well, Charles up and got himself kicked to death by a horse last week. Stands to reason that Abel would step in to help out Missy Trask. That's what—"

"—brothers are for, yes, Mamma. Kicked to death? That's not a usual thing."

"I should hope not." Francesca rubbed her nose, which was small and pert, like the rest of her. "Maybe he wasn't kicked to death. Maybe he broke his neck going over a fence. Cubbing's started," she added, not all that irrelevantly, since if he had been riding to hounds, Charles Trask very well could have fallen to his death. "Anyhow, yes, we heard. Word like that gets around, of course." She rocked violently, and then stopped the swing's motion with a sudden stamp of her foot. "Your father and I always liked him. Abel Trask."

A short silence fell.

Francesca had never questioned Abel's abrupt resignation. And after he'd gone, his name never came up in family conversations. It was as if he'd never existed. But Bree remembered that in the weeks after he'd left, her mother had engaged in a sudden flurry of activity: hauling Bree to Charleston to visit one of Bree's best friends; a series of unwelcome, but pretty, gifts of clothes, shoes, and purses.

If her mother didn't want to discuss it then, she surely wouldn't now. Bree gave it up. "Has word gotten around about my wild child client, Mamma?"

"Lindsey?" Her mother's face cleared into a smile. "Well, now, we haven't heard much. The Chandlers weren't Southern originally, you know. They came from the Midwest someplace." She waved vaguely. "Ohio? Is that right?"

"Iowa, I think," Bree said. "Ames, to be precise."

"Anyway, you know what it's like, their not being local, I mean."

Bree knew. Her mother was openhearted and open-handed. But even she tended to close ranks to outsiders.

"Besides, they were just the most tight-assed people."

"Mamma!" Bree couldn't help but laugh, although a little shocked.

"That was truly vulgar, wasn't it? I do apologize. But the man was stingy, Bree. He had a stingy heart. You know how much he gave to the Overseas Orphans Fund when Bea Forester asked for a donation? Fifty dollars. Fifty dollars! And the man had an income bigger than the annual revenues of Southern Rhodesia. Or so your father says." Her face brightened to the glow she kept for Royal Winston-Beaufort and nobody else. "And here he is. You can ask him about those Chandlers yourself, Bree."

Royal came around the side of the house, walked up the verandah steps, and settled himself into a wicker chair with a sigh. He reached over and gave Bree's hand a gentle squeeze. "How's my best girl?"

"Just fine, Daddy."

Royal Beaufort was tall and thin, with a long, horsey face and a deceptively gentle manner. "Glad you could make it up, darlin'. Looks like we're going to have ourselves a real party here tonight. Wouldn't want you to miss it. Now, that sister of yours . . ."

"She's just desolated she can't make it," Bree said promptly. "But she can't run out on her play."

"I suppose she can't." He sat back and folded his hands

over his lean stomach. "So, you're looking a little worn-out, child, since I saw you last."

"You saw me last a few weeks ago, and not much has changed since," Bree said a little tartly.

"You finished up that Skinner case okay?"

"No problems at all. I gave two depositions in evidence. And I got a check from the client."

"Prompt payers are a blessing," her father said piously. He winked at her. "So I guess you won't need a check to tide you over."

"No, Daddy, I surely won't." Bree felt a familiar surge of chagrin, annoyance, and exasperated love. "I'm doing just fine."

The front door opened, and General's dark head peeked out onto the porch. "Can I get y'all something? A whiskey soda, Mr. Royal?" He let the screen door shut gently behind him. "And it's Bree! How's by you, my girl? We haven't seen you this age."

Bree jumped up and gave General a brief, warm hug. She couldn't remember a time when the old man hadn't been an important part of their lives. "I'm just home for the weekend, General, but I sure am glad to be here."

"I musta been out back with them deliveries when you come by," he said regretfully. "And I see that you ain't eatin' enough to feed a birdie. I'll get you a nice chunk of Adelina's pecan pie, shall I? Along with that whiskey soda. Glad you're back where you belong. And you brought that nice dog with you, too. I'll see about some scraps for him." He twinkled gently at Sasha and disappeared back into the house.

Bree found herself smiling. Her mother reached over and nudged her. "What?"

"It's good to be home, Mamma."

"It's good to have you home, darlin'." She clapped her hands briskly. "Now, Royal. My little round of phone calls to make discreet inquires about the Chandlers turned up bukiss."

Bree and Royal looked at each other. Finally, Bree said, "You mean bubkes, Mamma?"

"Whatever. I didn't get much of a handle on Probert at all. He kept himself to himself, as the Irish say. A proper Methodist, he seemed to be, and that isn't much of a compliment when you consider John Knox."

"Knox was a Presbyterian, Francesca," Royal said. "But don't be blaming him, either. What your mother is saying, Bree, is that the man stuck to business and family, and ran the both of them in what might be called a parsimonious way."

"You're being gentlemanly, Daddy. Marlowe's known worldwide for predatory pricing practices. They're notorious for driving competitors out of business with cutthroat tactics. And they're perfectly horrible to their suppliers. I know that much from skimming the business pages every day."

"The liberal press version of the business pages," Royal murmured. "Now, don't get your feathers ruffled. Any laissez-faire economy's bound to have a version of Marlowe's. It's the price of doing business."

"It doesn't have to be," Bree said hotly.

General came back onto the porch with a whiskey soda, a fine slice of pecan pie, and a small, steaming teapot. He handed the drink to Royal and the pie to Bree (who set it aside on the table) and poured a cup of tea for Francesca. He dropped a large hambone at Sasha's feet, and then went gently away.

Royal put his right leg over his left knee and sipped his drink. "I made a few calls myself, on your young client's behalf. Did you know Probert had a partner?"

Bree thought a moment. "Yes. I think I did. Lindquist, his name is."

"John Allen Lindquist. He and Probert were frat brothers at the University of Oregon in the pharmacy program. Lindquist's kept pretty much in the background all these years, but he carried a lot more weight than you'd guess, just looking at the company from the outside. He's a registered pharmacist as well as an MD, and has in fact done a whole lot of research into developing generic drugs."

"That's where Marlowe's makes most of its profits, isn't it?" Bree said. "They have a huge plant down in Ames, I think it is, and they manufacture a lot of the generics themselves."

"Actually, the largest plants are in China." Probert held his glass up to the sunlight and gazed appreciatively at the amber color. "Labor's cheap. No one inquires too much into their employee practices, and so far, no one has imposed a whole lot of tariffs on the imports."

Francesca cleared her throat loudly. "Isn't this *interesting*?" she said fervently.

Royal grinned at her. "Francesca. Light of my life. If you wish to duck out on this conversation, I can't blame you one iota."

"Thank mercy." Francesca got up in a flurry of skirts. "If I told you talk about some old plant in China was going to be the conversational highlight of my day, I'd be lying like a rug."

"You'd perk up right enough if you saw what those plants in China are like," Bree said. "They stick those poor workers in warehouses you wouldn't want a cat to live in, and they make them pay for the privilege."

"Now, Bree," Royal said.

"Sixteen tons," Francesca said.

Bree, about to spout off like the fountain in their rose garden out back, was abruptly silenced.

"Of course," Royal said. And then, in a chancy baritone he sang, *"Sixteen tons, what d'ya get? Another day older and deeper in debt."*

Francesca chimed in: *"St. Peter, don't you call me, 'cause I can't go, I owe my soul to the company store."*

"You're both crazy," Bree said, laughing.

Royal set his glass down with a flourish and rose to his feet. "Crazy like a fox. Guess who's coming to the party this afternoon?"

"Oh, I don't know. Tennessee Ernie Ford's been dead a while. So, who?"

"John Allen Lindquist was pleased to accept an invitation to Plessey's annual Guy Fawkes Day Dinner and Dance," Royal said. "What do you think of that?"

Bree shook her head at them both. Parents. "I think that's just fine."

"Then that's all settled," Francesca said with satisfaction. "Bree, honey, I have to go check on the caterers and make sure that Adelina isn't cooking herself dumb and exhausted in the kitchen. And I talked to Antonia this morning. She said you didn't get a lick of sleep last night. So I want you to trot right on up to your old room and take a nice long nap. I'll come and wake you up in time to get ready for the party."

This was the best idea Bree had heard in a week. Her father made his leisurely way down the steps to the front lawn, and Bree followed her mother into the house.

Plessey had been rebuilt as a center-entrance Georgian in the late 1820s, replacing the low-ceilinged cedar wood frame building that had preceded it. The house was three stories, surrounded by verandahs on all three levels. All of the large rooms—the parlor, library, sewing room, and dining room on the main floor, and the bedrooms and sitting rooms on the upper stories—had mullioned double doors that led out onto the porches. When Bree read *Pride and Prejudice* for high school English, she read about the inside of Mr. Bingley's home, Nether-field, with a little jolt of recognition.

The ceilings were high and the walls were trimmed top and bottom with crown molding. Francesca had become very interested in the late Georgian period, so she'd gotten rid of the wallpaper and commissioned hand-painted murals in the public rooms. The private rooms for the family and the staff were painted in a variety of bright, cheerful colors like *eau de nil*, warm persimmon, and cadet blue.

And the house had a smell—one that Bree would have recognized anywhere in the world. It was compounded of lemon floor wax, lavender from Francesca's potpourri bowls, and a comfortable moldy sort of odor that came from the wood frame itself.

She walked wearily up the main staircase to her old bedroom, Sasha bounding ahead of her. Her mother's elderly retriever, Beau, lay in front of her parents' set of rooms, which were directly at the top of the stairs. Beau got stiffly to his feet, wagging his tail slowly. He thrust his head close to Sasha, as if trying to figure out whether he was actually a dog or a fur-coated, four-legged Something Else. Bree had noticed this oddity about Sasha before; other dogs treated him as a noncanine. There weren't any of the jousting, sniffing, tail-flagging behaviors that happened when two new dogs met one another. Beau greeted Sasha and backed off. Then he did what Bree'd seen other dogs do: he extended his forepaws, bent his graying head, and wagged his tail in the upright position, a classic offer to play.

Bree's room hadn't changed since she was six years old and moved out of the nursery and into her own room. A small fireplace occupied the back wall, flanked by a pair of shabby built-in bookshelves. Copies of her best-beloved childhood books were still there: *Lad: A Dog*;

The Lion, the Witch and the Wardrobe; Philip Pullman's Dark Materials trilogy; and a whole slew of Anne of Green Gables. Her bed was spindled four-poster, with an ancient patchwork quilt her grandmother Annette had made as a christening present. General had put her briefcase and her overnight bag under her little vanity table.

Bree was too tired to unpack her dress and hang it up in the pine wardrobe. She kicked off her shoes, fell onto the bed, pulled her pillow over her head to shut out the sunlight, and fell into a deep sleep.

She woke to a place she had been to once before. A field of grass so deep and green it felt like velvet beneath her feet. A scent of flowers and nearby water was in the air and the sound of silvery chimes. Bree opened her arms to a bronze flood of sunlight.

A slight hissing in the grass. A cold hand crept around her ankle. A smell of dead, decaying flesh hit her, as if Something had actually gathered the odor up and flung it in her face. Bree shouted, drowning . . .

And woke with a shriek in her throat and the feel of clawed hands around her feet. Sasha's furious growls assaulted the air. Bree struggled to open her eyes, to get up, to get *out*, and fell off the bed onto the floor with a thump.

Sasha nudged his head into her side and pushed. Bree sat up slowly, leaned against the bed, and put one arm around his neck. After her breathing slowed, she said, a little hoarsely, "That was some nightmare, Sash."

She bent forward to rub her ankles, and snatched her hands away. A smear of filth, grave-ridden and corrupt, covered them from palm to wrist. She looked at the smear in horror. She closed her eyes and took a deep, calming breath. Sasha nudged her again. "The professor said he was going to send some help, Sasha. I sure as heck hope it's soon."

Bree set her teeth. She struggled to her feet, and clutching Sasha by the collar as if he were a lifeline tossed to a sinking ship, she went to take a shower.

After a long, hot shower that scrubbed away every trace of the filthy hands on her skin, she dressed for the party and sat down in the little rocker next to her fireplace. She was still there when her mother knocked and walked into her room.

"*Not* that little black dress again!" Francesca said in dismay. She clapped her hands over her mouth. "What I meant to say is that you look beautiful, honey. But what about that nice red dress you wore at the open house party a few weeks ago? You looked like a queen in that dress."

Bree smiled. Her face felt stiff. "It's still at the cleaner's. If I'd stopped to think this week, I would have picked it up. But I only decided to come at the last minute, Mamma. There wasn't time to go fetch it."

"Well." Her mother fussed around her. "I do have to say I like the way you're doin' your hair. Those braids are brilliant." She looked at Bree with a soft smile. "Once in a while I miss the old look, though. I know it wasn't professional to wear it fallin' down your back. But it was so pretty! So. You ready to come down? You want me to send somebody up with a plate of sandwiches or you want to go down and grab some of that barbecue? People are starting to show up already."

Bree tucked her arm under her mother's. "You let me at the barbecue. I can smell it from here."

She'd slept for several hours. The sun was low, and streaks of pink, orange, and a misty mauve spilled over the lip of the west horizon. White lights twinkled among the branches of the sycamore trees, and the smell of pulled pork and cracklings was mouthwatering. The canvas tents glowed with candlelight from the dining tables. On the opposite side of the low brick wall that separated

the house and grounds from the cotton fields, a giant pyre
of wood stood stacked and ready for the midnight firing.
Once, when Bree was eight or nine, a relative had brought
a Guy to throw onto the fire, the way they did in England.
One of the brattier Carmichael cousins told Antonia it
was a real body. Bree had plunged her hands into the fire
to get the Guy out, to stop Tonia's frantic screams, and
Francesca had banned the Guy ever since. She'd dressed
Bree's burns with olive oil and gauze.

The evening was cool. Bree accepted a silvery wrap
from her mother to wind around her shoulders. She
paused at the top of the steps to the lawn and watched
the milling flow of people. Most were old friends. Some
were clients of her father's firm. And more than a few
were relatives from both the Winston-Beaufort and Carmichael sides of the family.

Bree spotted Aunt Cissy, waved, and plunged into the
crowd.

———◦◦◦———

"John Lindquist? I'd like you to meet my daughter Brianna. Up until a few weeks ago, she was a junior associate at the firm. She's opened her own practice in Savannah
now." Royal clasped Bree's wrist and gently drew her into
the circle of his acquaintances as he spoke. Bree had
wandered out to the wall where the pile of dry wood
stood waiting for the torch, away from the noise of people
chattering and the pianist. She watched her father ex-
pertly shepherd a small group of men toward her.

"So I hear." Lindquist looked like a pharmacist, if
pharmacists could be said to have a look. He was very
clean and neat, of medium height, with a trim, flat body
that spoke of dutiful work at a gym. He looked accurate,
that was the word, as if he rarely made mistakes. He had
pale blue eyes and a rather remote manner. Bree thought

about it, later, and decided that he was a party watcher, as opposed to a party participator. Here was a man who saw little difference between strolling through a museum and talking to actual people.

"How do you do?" Bree extended her hand, and he shook it with an air of mild surprise. Maybe he thought she was an interactive exhibit.

"And you remember Francis and Arnie, Bree." Bree smiled at two of her father's golfing buddies, and waited until they had moved away before she turned to talk to Lindquist. He was looking at the pyre. "Pine, mostly? And a bit of cedar."

Bree blinked. She didn't know much about wood. "Yes. That is, probably. We collect deadfalls all year long and save them up." She considered the height of the pile. "My guess is there's some of the old chicken house in there, too."

"Mm." He shook the ice in his glass, and then drained it. "Carolyn tells me you've taken on Lindsey's defense."

"Carolyn? Carrie-Alice, you mean?"

"She was Carolyn when we were all at school together, and she remains Carolyn to me," he said, rather pedantically. "She adopted this Carrie-Alice stuff when we decided to move some of our operations to Georgia."

"So Marlowe's has a manufacturing plant here, too? I thought most of your divisions were either in Iowa or China."

"Just a small research facility," he said. "And the store itself, of course. Both are under my control. Bert liked the area. Cost of living's good, no state income tax, and what taxes there are, are low. Labor's cheap, too."

Mostly the poor, the broke, and the uneducated. A news story from several years before suddenly popped into her head. "And we don't have as much oversight as some states," she said. "For our aid to dependent children programs and our food stamp bureau. Weren't y'all depending on the state welfare programs to make up for the low wages y'all pay your part-timers?" There'd been a memo, she recalled, that urged the local Marlowe's managers to keep a list of state and federal aid programs on hand. Employees who asked for full-time employment—which would mean minimum medical benefits or more wages—were urged to turn to the state for help rather than to work longer hours and have state labor laws regarding full-time workers kick in.

She couldn't read Lindquist's eyes in the low light cast by the lights in the trees, but he said, without heat, "That's right." There was so much indifference in his voice, Bree had to make an effort to keep her temper. She shifted her glass of white wine from one hand to the other. "I was hoping you could give me a little guidance, as far as representing Lindsey."

"Guidance?" he said blankly.

"I'm going to try and mount the best defense I can. And to do that, I need to get some idea of how Lindsey got to this point."

"And what point would that be?"

The words were more insolent than the tone itself, so Bree said, patiently, "This is a seventeen-year-old girl who seems to have the world by the tail. Her mom and dad are still married after some thirty-odd years. The family's worth the weight of the Sears Building in gold bullion, but they make a point of avoiding the extravagant lifestyle that brings so many kids of wealthy families into trouble. Her older brother and sister seem to have sane, adult lives, too. Her brother's on the way up in the company, but it looks as if he has to earn his way. Nothing's being handed to him because he's the son of one of the five richest men in the world." She let a little annoyance creep into her voice; it wouldn't be a bad thing to rattle this doofus's cage. "And her sister teaches middle school. Now. Does this sound like the kind of family that would send a teenager off the rails?"

"You seem to know a lot about the family." He sounded disapproving.

"I have a terrific staff. Especially when it comes to research."

Lindquist rattled the ice in his glass. "Well, I can tell you this much. Lindsey was a problem from the day she was born."

"Oh?"

He nodded firmly. "Very different from the other two. It was a tough pregnancy, and things got even tougher after the child was actually born. Lindsey was a fussy baby. Didn't sleep much. Had a lot of colicky stuff wrong with her. As a toddler, she was prone to temper tantrums. She even bit her brother once. On the arm. I remember the teeth marks distinctly."

"Fancy," Bree said dryly. "I don't know much about babies and toddlers, Mr. Lindquist, at least not yet, but this doesn't sound like a disturbed child to me. Just a fussy one. There are lots of those."

He nodded eagerly. "Too many, wouldn't you say?"

Bree shrugged. "Maybe. Anything else?"

"Well, she was a poor student. Pulling down Bs and Cs. Almost impossible to motivate her. Bert and Carolyn don't—didn't—believe in excessive reliance on doctors, but they did make an effort to get her treated."

"I don't understand. Treated for what, exactly?"

"She didn't fit in. She was a disruptive influence on the family. Do I need to make myself any clearer?"

Bree made a face into the depths of her wineglass. "Let's take a look at this from Lindsey's point of view. I know that Mr. Chandler and you were close . . ."

"Close enough," he said. "We met at school. We were

all chem majors with minors in business admin. Funny, when you think about it. Not that usual, the combination of business and science, you see. So it was natural for us to gravitate to one another."

"Mrs. Chandler is a chemist, too?" Bree said in some surprise.

"Carolyn?" he snorted. "Not on your life. Where in the name of God did you get that idea?"

Bree knew she shouldn't let this guy get under her skin. "You said you were all chem majors," she pointed out rather tartly. "'All,' not 'both.' So of course I assumed you were talking about three people and not just you and Probert. And why shouldn't Carrie-Alice be a chemist?"

"Steve Hansen was with us for a time," Lindquist said with a "gotcha" air. "And Carolyn's never had much interest in anything outside the home and the kids. The kids, mainly."

Bree bit down on her lower lip, to keep herself from continuing this inane verbal competition. "What I really would like to discuss with you, Mr. Lindquist—"

"It's Doctor Lindquist," he snapped, suddenly testy. "I added an MD to my PhD in pharmacology."

Bree nodded agreeably. "Dr. Lindquist, I'm going to give Lindsey the best defense I possibly can. And to do that, it'd help to know as much as I can about her background. Do you have an opinion about Mr. Chandler's parenting skills?"

"He was a good and devoted father. He loved his children."

Right out of the press kit prepared for you by your New York PR firm, Bree thought. Aloud, she said, "And Carolyn—Mrs. Chandler—you're closer to her? Or am I making another assumption?"

"I don't think I care for the tone of your voice, Miss Beaufort."

Bree shook her head in mock sympathy. "It's a problem that's plagued me all of my life, Mr. Lindquist. My tone of voice. So. You and Mrs. Chandler were how close? Too close?"

He looked at her in contempt and paused for a long, long moment. "She's my sister."

"Your sister." Bree's cheeks got hot. She remembered, too late, the hoary advice to defense attorneys: never ask a question to which you don't already know the answer. His sister! Something she should have known, for sure. Well, she deserved the embarrassment; never, never, never get cocky without being willing to pay the price.

"My younger sister. I only have the one. No brothers."

Bree drew a circle in the grass with the point of her shoe. "Hm. So. As the concerned uncle of this child, what can you tell me that might help me explain to a jury why she mugged an eight-year-old Girl Scout and stole her cookie money?"

"Genes," he said, in an unconscious echo of Hartley Williams's addled diagnosis. "It begins and ends with what you inherit."

"Bullshit," Bree said.

Lindquist made a small adjustment to his tie and gazed at her, his face utterly expressionless. "I don't think I can help you, Miss Beaufort."

"I don't think you can, at that, Mr. Lindquist."

He turned on his heel and marched off across the grass.

"Well," said her father, from behind her shoulder, "that went well." He looked sympathetic. Bree supposed he'd heard the entire conversation.

"It did, didn't it?" Bree swallowed the remains of her wine and set the glass on the top of the brick wall. "Serves me right, I guess. That sanctimonious so-and-so."

Royal chuckled.

"Honestly, Daddy. I suppose I should have handled that better."

"No 'suppose' about it. You surely should have. You let your convictions get in the way of building a good case for your client. It's a charming failing, Bree, but it's definitely a failing. I've told you before, a good lawyer—the best lawyer—suspends her personal beliefs in defense of her client. You're an advocate, my dear. It's an important role."

"It's a lot more honest to be an advocate for the innocent."

At that, her father looked seriously displeased. "I don't need to remind you our whole legal system's built on the presumption of innocence. And the question of guilt is *not* your job. You are not a judge." He tugged at her ear affectionately. "Not yet, at any rate." He glanced at his watch. "Nearly midnight. Time for the fire. I'll get your mother." He turned to walk away, and then turned back. "You're going to be all right, you know. You'll handle this case as well as you've handled all the others. I've got a lot of faith in you, Bree."

She went forward and hugged him.

Royal smiled, patted her back, and then strolled over to the pianist, who struck a series of loud, trilling chords on the piano. He waited until the crowd of partygoers settled into expectant silence. She let her father's speech to the guests wash over her, thinking of all the celebrations like this one, in the past. She wondered if she'd be around for the ones in the future. Sasha's familiar warmth was at her knee, and she bent to stroke his head.

Help, Professor Cianquino had said. He was going to send help. Well, she hoped it got here soon.

She tilted her head back and looked up at the stars. The moon carried herself across the sky like a little ship. A feathering of clouds washed across the very top of the heavens, veiling the Pleiades and the Dipper. When her mother tossed the flaming brand on the fire, the flames shot up with a whoosh! The bright glow pitched the moon and stars into dark relief.

And from the heart of the pyre, two huge black dogs leaped over the wall and landed at Bree's feet.

Ten

Cry "havoc!" and let slip the dogs of war.
--*Julius Caesar*, William Shakespeare

"You've got to be kidding. They're giants! The town house people don't mind looking the other way when it comes to Sasha—I mean, he's such a peach. But these guys? We're going to get fined. Maybe even kicked out." Antonia rubbed her arms nervously. It was early Sunday evening. Bree had left Plessey just after breakfast, her two new guardians jammed into the backseat of her little car like two sumo wrestlers in a rickshaw. "What breed are they, anyway?"

Bree looked at her new companions with some doubt. "Newfoundland, partly. I'm not sure about the other part. Maybe more mastiff, like Sash."

Both dogs stood fifty inches at the shoulder. Their chests were massive and their paws tipped with sharp white claws. Belli opened her mouth and grinned at them. She had a mouthful of sharp white teeth. She seemed to have more of them than the usual canine allotment. Bree was opposed to the flaunting of aggressive, macho behavior on principle, but she was glad to suspend her principles in this instance. These guys made her feel safe.

"Bella. And that's Mee-lace, you said?" Antonia patted the other guardian nervously on the head.

"It's spelled Miles. M-I-L-E-S. And her name's Belli, with an *i*."

"Belli. Kind of a nice name, I guess. Italian?"

"In a way." For the first and only time in her life, Bree was glad that Tonia had flunked Latin.

"But Bree, they can't stay here."

"I'll take them to the office. They'll be there most of the time." She eyed her sister. "You usually like dogs. Do they really make you that nervous?"

"They're just so . . . *still*. You know. They don't move around a lot. They just sit and stare at you."

The dogs had taken positions on either side of the fireplace. There they sat, upright, their watchful eyes following back and forth as Antonia paced around the living room. Sasha pranced around with her, his tail wagging cheerfully. He'd greeted the arrival of his two compatriots with the air of a general reprimanding the late arrival of the troops. Occasionally, he directed their movements with a snap of his jaws and a preemptory bark. Mostly he looked at them with a proprietary air and left them alone. They didn't eat, or if they did, they hadn't, yet. Maybe they ate once a month, like pythons. They didn't like to be petted or brushed, although they accepted both from Bree with an air of indifference.

And they didn't leave her side.

"You found them wandering along the side of the road at some rest stop?" Antonia said again, as if Bree hadn't already lied to her twice about the appearance of the dogs. Although it was only partly a lie. They'd been waiting for her in the parking lot of the Saturn Diner that morning after their brief, reassuring appearance at the bonfire and they had slept beside her bed at night. "I can't believe you just picked them up and brought them back with you. How do you know they don't belong to somebody?"

"They'd been abandoned," Bree said, shortly. "Don't keep going on about it, Tonia. I figured it'd be a good idea for them to keep an eye on things at the office."

"Sash keeps an eye on things just fine."

"He's not tough," Bree said, ignoring Sasha's reproachful look. "These guys are warriors. Ignore them. Pretend they're a pair of porcelain Fu dogs. You know, those Chinese temple dogs. Come on, Tonia. Sit down and tell me all about last night's show. Everything go well?"

Her sister perched on the arm of the couch, and then got up, unable to stop staring at the dogs staring at her. "Let's go into the kitchen. They can stay in here, can't they?"

Bree looked at Sasha.

They stand guard at the mirror.

"I think as long as they know I'm within shouting distance, they'll be fine in here. And I brought you back some barbecue and some of Adelina's pecan pie. I'll heat some dinner up for you. You should eat before you go back to the theater."

Antonia trailed her into the kitchen and pulled a stool up to the kitchen counter. Bree bustled about, putting the barbecue into the microwave and serving the pie up on a small plate. Her sister watched her with the same grave attention as the dogs. "You're, like, totally cheerful."

"Am I?"

"I mean, totally. I can't believe the difference in you."

"I wasn't that much of a gloomy Gus, was I?"

Antonia poked at the pie with her fork. "Not gloomy, no. But really anxious." She swallowed a bite with an air of pleased surprise. "Yum. Nobody makes pecan pie like Adelina."

"I keep telling her she should quit housekeeping at Plessey and go into the pie business. She and General would make a fortune."

"Hm. And she said, 'G'wan with you' and kept on baking, I bet. So, anything particular happen at home? Other than you picking up a pair of elephants to bring back with you?"

The elephants. Thank God for the elephants. "Not really," Bree said evasively. "Mamma looks well. So does Daddy. And I got a chance to interview John Allen Lindquist."

"Who's he when he's at home?"

"Lindsey's uncle. I'd hoped he'd give me some help for her defense, but no soap."

"You're still thinking about taking on that case?"

"I have taken on that case. Hers and her father's, both."

"Her father's?" Antonia's eyebrows went up. "I thought he was dead."

"He *is* dead. But there's some question about how he died." Bree folded a dish towel into neat quarters and leaned against the kitchen counter. "I can't help thinking the two things are linked somehow—Lindsey's behavior and her father's death."

Antonia shrugged. "Whatever. You seem to be attracting a lot of corpses, sister."

Bree shivered. "Yes. Well. I'm going to put Ron and Petru on an intense search for some background on the guy, that's for sure. It's going to be a busy week."

"Anything else?"

"Anything else what?"

"Anything else happen at home I ought to know about."

Bree flushed.

"Mamma called after you left this morning."

Bree bit her lip.

"Said you ran into Abel Trask."

"So I did."

"Said he was moving here to Savannah?"

"Just for a bit. He's taking over the Seaton Stud until his sister-in-law decides what to do with the business."

"Hm."

"Hm, what?" Bree demanded testily.

"Just putting that together with you being so cheerful, sister. That's all."

Bree bit her thumbnail. "Look, I can take care of myself."

Antonia got up and put her plate in the sink. "You've said that from the day I was born. And you know what? You mostly can. But I'm not so sure about this time. Mamma isn't either."

There were times when as much as Bree loved her little sister, she wanted to smack her silly. This was one of those times. Antonia took a quick look at her expression, rolled her eyes, and grabbed her tote bag from its place by the back door. "I'm off to the job. I'll be late. Don't wait up."

Bree thought of Miles and Belli, guarding the mirror. "I won't have to, will I? Thank goodness."

But she said it to the air; Antonia was gone.

The evening passed quietly; the night was still and the nightmares held at bay by the stern bodies of the dogs at her bedroom door. Her cheery mood held well into the next morning, when she arrived at the office so early, even Lavinia wasn't downstairs yet. Sasha went directly into the little kitchen, while Miles and Belli stationed themselves beneath the painting that had heralded so much grief: the *Rise of the Cormorant*. Bree stared at the sinking ship, the hands grasping at air from the depths of the roiling sea, and dared to hope, a little. The scene revealed in that picture had haunted her childhood and brought her gasping awake from dreams of drowning too many nights to count. "And if that bird flies out of there to get me, you two'll bite him, won't you?"

Miles blinked his solemn yellow eyes.

Bree stared at the painting, unafraid, or pretty nearly. There was one face on that ship, one figure, she actually longed to see. The pale-eyed, dark-haired woman who had given birth to her, only to die a few days later, leaving her to Francesca and Royal.

The dogs growled. A slow, subterranean rumble like an aural earthquake. Bree whirled. Her secretary and her paralegal stood at the foyer.

"Oh, my God," Ron said.

"Do not move, dear Bree," Petru said. He raised his cane as if it were a weapon. "I will fend them off. And where is Sasha?"

"He's in the break room," Bree said cheerfully. "I thought you'd know these two. Miles and Belli."

" 'War' and her 'Soldier' brother." Trust Petru to know his Latin. "And where have they come from?"

Ron edged into the room. "Oh, dear," he said fretfully. "I don't know, but I can guess. Armand sent for them, didn't he?"

"You don't know them?" Bree said in surprise. "You haven't met them before?"

"Something has happened," Petru said glumly. "Something not so good, I trust."

"It's all right," Bree said to the dogs. "Hush now, hush." The rumbling died away, as if an avalanche had rolled out of hearing. "Come into my office, then, you two." She didn't wait to accompany them, but forged ahead, and sat down behind her desk. Petru thumped in and took the sole chair. Ron perched on the edge of her desk. "Friday night, I went out to Melrose. Lavinia called on Striker to tell him that . . ." Bree paused and bit her lower lip.

"Somebody's gotten over the Bridge," Ron guessed. "But who?"

"Josiah, I guess," Bree said lightly. "Anyhow, somebody, Archie, I think, suggested these guys as protection, and here they are." She rubbed the back of her neck. "I'm a little puzzled that you two don't know about it."

"Well, we had no idea," Ron snapped. "Honestly. You should know, Bree, that this entire organization is run on a need-to-know basis. It's something I've complained about for centuries."

"This is a distressing turn of events," Petru said glumly. "There is a hierarchy, to be sure. We are all aware of that. But I would have been glad to have been in the noose."

"The loop, Petru, the loop," Ron said crossly. "I'm not surprised nobody told you, but I'm somewhat flabbergasted that no one thought fit to tell *me*."

"Now you both know. And let's not borrow trouble until it shows up at the door," Bree said briskly. "We've got a case to investigate. Two of them. And I, for one, feel much safer going on now that those two are in the picture." She tapped her pen on her desktop. "We've got a lot to do, and not a lot of time to do it in. Cordelia Eastburn is pushing Lindsey's case as fast as she can. I haven't seen you since Friday afternoon, but you should know that Lindsey's absolutely refused to allocute to the robbery and Cordy's headed for trial like a flipping locomotive. So you, Petru, need to dig up as much as you can on Probert, particularly anyone who had a grudge against him. Use the Internet and make me a list. And Ron? We need a complete reinvestigation of the accident out on Skidaway Road. And I want both of you to read over the pleadings for Chandler's request for a retrial. I need a summary of all the cases cited in the original indictment."

"This summary is a paralegal's job, perhaps," Petru said. "Ronald is not equipped to render an opinion on the pleadings."

"I want *all* of us to read them," Bree said firmly. "One of us may pick up something the others have missed. I'm including myself in this, too. Okay? Are we all set with the assignments? We'll have a progress report tomorrow morning about this time."

"I do *not* see the connection between this young girl's case and our client," Petru said. "But I will search diligently for such, dear Bree."

"Thank you. I'll be searching, too. I'm going to talk to Miss Madison Bellamy." She smiled at the looks of incomprehension on the faces of her colleagues. "Nobody knows a girl like her very best friend. And if Lindsey doesn't want to dig herself out of the hole she's in, let's hope Madison does."

Petru and Ron went off on their separate tasks. Bree recalled enough about juvenile law to know that everyone's interests would be better served if she went through Madison's parents first, so she called Madison's mother to set up an appointment.

"She's at school, of course, until just after three this afternoon," Andrea Bellamy said over the phone. "Why don't I ask her to leave school and come home right now?" She sounded anxious, and her tone held the sort of exasperation most parents reserve for their teenagers.

"I'll be happy to come by later this afternoon," Bree offered. "There's no need to interrupt classes."

"Classes," Andrea Bellamy snorted. "It's her senior year and she's already been accepted at Pepperdine. Maddy's body may be in class but the rest of her is in la-la land. The school's done a pretty good job of keeping the TV people off school grounds, but they're waiting like a pack of vultures the minute the bell rings to let the kids out. All this attention isn't doing anybody any good."

Bree, realizing that Andrea Bellamy wasn't going to come up for air anytime soon, interrupted firmly. "Then I'll see you and Madison at three thirty this afternoon?"

"Sure! I'll make you some latte. And maybe you can give me a clue about when all of this is going to die down."

"Soon, I hope." *If I can keep the miserable Lindsey from more grandstanding.*

Bree rang off with relief. Madison had looked like a smart, sensible kid in the surveillance videotape. Maybe, just maybe, she was going to get somewhere with Lindsey's defense. In the meantime, she wanted a clear idea of Probert Chandler's movements on the last night of his life. There was just time enough to get a handle on that, before she was due out at the Bellamys'.

She'd begin with where Probert Chandler spent his final hours as a temporal: the Miner's Club.

The Miner's Club, a bastion of the Savannah Old Guard, was on Abercorn facing the Colonial Park Cemetery Square. James W. Oglethorpe had left a variety of legacies behind him, but the best was the layout of Historic Savannah herself. He'd divided the village into twenty-four town squares. Originally, each square was created as a center for some good civic purpose, like a church, a school, a park, or a government house. Each of the squares was surrounded by homes.

In the three hundred–some years of her history, Savannah had been burned to the ground, ravaged by hurricanes, and bombed by pirates. A hodgepodge of architectural styles was intrinsic to the city's heritage. Queen Anne, Georgian, Victorian, Greek Revival, Spanish, and Art Deco homes existed peaceably cheek by jowl. The Miner's Club occupied a large, New Orleans–type building that had housed, successively, an expatriate French duke, a whorehouse, an orphanage, and a flour tycoon. Bree drove the half mile down Liberty and parked on Abercorn, not far from the old mansion itself. The exterior was blue-green stucco. Scarlet bougainvillea wound its way across the wrought-iron porches and balconies and the last of the hydrangea bloomed like puff-balls against the wrought-iron fence.

Bree pushed open the heavy mahogany door and walked into a small foyer, covered in a thick blue wall-to-wall carpet. A second mahogany door led directly off the foyer. It was partly open. Bree heard the clink of glasses and the low hum of conversation. She pushed the door open all the way and walked into a wood-paneled bar and dining room.

The ceilings were low. A clutch of small round tables sat scattered next to the row of windows that overlooked the street. There were perhaps half a dozen people seated there, mostly men, mostly dressed in suits. Bree waited by the long polished bar until the man behind it finished polishing the doubles glass he held in his hand and put it on the shelf. "Montel," she said, "how have you been?"

He turned and cocked his head a little. "Miss Beaufort," he said, as if satisfied he'd identified the right species of bird. He came toward her, folding his bar towel into a neat square. "I'd like to take this opportunity to tell you how much we miss the judge."

"The judge" was Bree's great-uncle Franklin. His death, and the subsequent inheritance of his caseload, was the reason Bree had the practice on Angelus Street. She'd loved him, but been unnerved by what she'd learned about him after his death. She still wasn't wildly happy about his legacy.

"He did enjoy coming here after sitting on the bench all day," she said.

"May I get you something to drink?" Montel was a grave, slender black man who could have been anywhere from fifty to seventy, a well-known, well-liked fixture at the club.

Bree perched on the nearest bar stool. "Just a club soda, if you would."

Montel took a slim Tom Collins glass from the shelf and filled it with ice, lemon, and club soda. Bree accepted it with thanks and sipped it gravely. She let the silence run on a bit. Then she said, "Uncle Franklin never talked much about Mr. Chandler. I understand he was a member here, too?"

Montel nodded thoughtfully.

"You recall he had that tragic accident just after he left here, the last night of his life."

"Some four months ago, that would be." Montel nodded. "Mm-hm. I do remember that."

"Do you remember who he was with?"

"Now, the po-lice asked me that," Montel said cautiously. "And he met with a number of folks, as I recall. Didn't really sit down with nobody, though. Sat right where you are right now."

Bree looked down at the bar stool. She hoped Probert wouldn't choose this moment to make an appearance.

"Had him more than a few, he did."

"Drinks?" Bree said.

"Drinks. Manhattans, as a matter of fact."

"Hm," Bree said. "His usual?"

"Not like the man at all. No, sir. Strictly a draft beer, if he was here during the week, and on one or another great occasion, a champagne cocktail. But that was about the extent of it. Until that night."

"Did he seem upset at all?"

"That he did," Montel said. "That he did."

"Did he say anything to you? Perhaps mention why he was upset?"

A peculiar look chased itself across Montel's face. "Well, Mr. Chandler was from up North," he said. "He wouldn't be of a mind to talk to me about that, now, would he? Or the members, either." Bree remembered what her mother had said about Probert not being "local."

"You didn't, um . . ." Bree searched for a diplomatic way to ask if Montel had eavesdropped. There wasn't one. "You didn't happen to overhear anything you think I might need to know?" She lowered her voice. "I think we're looking at a case of murder, here, Montel. I wouldn't want you to betray a confidence, but it's important."

"Murder, you say." Montel folded his bar towel into neat thirds. "Blood."

"Blood?"

"He say something about blood. Into his cell phone. Mad-like."

"Mad-crazy? Or mad-angry?"

"Angry. I would say very angry. He was so mad, he was like to spit."

"Was this before he started drinking more heavily than usual?"

"Oh, yeah." Montel nodded in a dignified way. "To my way of thinking, that phone call set him off."

"And he finished how many Manhattans . . . ?"

"Four."

"Yikes," Bree said. "Four. And then staggered out of here and went on home?"

"Well, now, I suppose he did." Montel smiled gently. "His permanent home, you might say."

"You wouldn't happen to recall who was here that night, offhand? People that knew Mr. Chandler?"

"Well, now, he come in with Mr. Lindquist, the one that he started his stores with. And his son, George, was here for a bit. But Mr. Lindquist went off to the opera with his wife. George, he drifted off somewheres. Mr. Stubblefield was here. The judge was here, as a matter of fact, and some others I could name. Mr. Chandler did stop and have a word with Mr. Peter Martinelli."

Bree wrote the names in her notebook. "But Mr. Chandler wasn't here with anyone in particular?"

"No, I can't say that he was. Spent some time on his cell phone, though, after that one call that made him mad." Montel frowned disapprovingly. You didn't do business at the Miner's Club, and cell phones were a particular anathema. But it was a lead, anyway. She could ask Hunter for Chandler's cell phone records. And she could check on Peter Martinelli. The name rang a faint bell.

Bree fished the lemon slice out of her club soda and bit into it. "I may be back to ask more about this, Montel. Thank you kindly for your hospitality."

"You're entirely welcome. You take care, then."

Bree went back into the crisp, sunny day not much wiser than she'd been going in. Except that Montel was a shrewd judge of character and hard to fool. Probert Chandler's drinking the night of his death had been atypical. And a man not used to drinking, on a wet, curving road . . . easy pickings for anyone wanting to cause an accident.

Except that Skidaway Road wasn't the quickest route back to the Chandler home. It was the quickest route out to the Marlowe's on Highway 80.

Bree didn't read a lot of detective stories—sometimes she thought she'd be better off in this new career of hers if she did—but she did recall a useful aphorism from a book she'd found abandoned in an airport on a trip out to Hawaii with her sister. The detective was a huge fat guy who never left his brownstone apartment. He had an athletic young assistant, whom he frequently admonished: never theorize in advance of the facts. Which was pretty good advice. So Bree put a clamp on her imagination—John Allen

Lindquist murdering his former partner for acing him out of Marlowe's billions? Son George killing off Dad to get more shares?—and drove out to the fatal bend in Skidaway Road.

Bree had reviewed the police diagrams of the accident thoroughly. The car had gone off the road opposite a little white house surrounded by a white picket fence. Bree parked her car a fair way beyond the bend of the road, to avoid getting clobbered by traffic headed the other way, and walked back to the spot where it'd happened.

The guardrail was bent, whether from Chandler's accident or another, Bree couldn't tell. She hiked her skirt above her knees and stepped over it. The bank dropped abruptly to a deep swale choked with kudzu. Bree made a face. Four months since the car had gone over the side, and the greenery had grown so rapidly, so ferociously, that there wasn't a sign of where the car had actually landed.

"Chiggers," Bree said aloud. The little bitey creatures would make her legs a mass of blood in seconds. Not to mention snakes, spiders, and who-knew-what lurking in the coils of the greenery. She straightened up with a sigh. If she were smart, she'd come back later, with jeans, rubber boots, and a long-sleeved shirt.

She narrowed her eyes and squinted, hoping to see something, anything, that would keep her from wallowing about in a mess of stuff that had to contain poison ivy, poison oak—anything.

And she found it. There was a huge scar in the trunk of a weeping willow not forty yards from the embankment. The kind of scar made by a car crashing into the tree. Bree hesitated a long moment, cursed herself for a coward, and started down.

Something moved in the grass. She paused, then took a step forward . . .

Into cold. Into cold that bit at her bones with croco-dile teeth. Into a wind that carried death and decay like a trophy. And a sound like a jackhammer tearing up the earth.

Bree stepped back, cautiously, and the vision ebbed. She stepped back again and stumbled over a smooth round object that she knew hadn't been in the grass before.

It was a paperweight. It was made of Lucite, and it contained the distinctive Marlowe's logo, an elaborate 'M.'

Bree picked it up. Waited. Heard nothing, felt nothing. Whatever it was, whoever it was, was gone.

She checked her watch. It was past time to keep her appointment with Madison Bellamy. But first, she'd go back to the office and pick up Belli and Miles. She wasn't going anywhere without the dogs.

Not anymore.

Eleven

A faithful friend is the medicine of life.
—Ecclesiasticus 6:16

"I don't really know how long the media's going to keep an interest in the case," Bree said in response to Andrea Bellamy's repeated question. Madison's parents lived in a large, expensive new home just off the Sweetlands golf course. The floors were composition bamboo. The walls were painted in deep fashionable colors like iron ore gray and grasslands green. The kitchen, where they sat, had an overwhelming array of Smallbone cabinetry, black granite countertops, and stainless steel Viking appliances. The coffee arrived hot and properly milk-infused from a built-in cappuccino maker.

"Decaf, unless you prefer something else." Andrea placed the cups on a place mat that coordinated with the deep green walls, then sat across from Bree at the kitchen table.

"This is fine."

Andrea regarded her with frank, interested eyes. She was a little too thin, with well-cut brunette hair and a dermabrasion-smooth complexion. "So you're Bree Beaufort," she said chattily. "We've read about your family, of course. Your aunt Cissy's quite the thing at the Miner's Club."

"You know her, then?" Bree asked politely.

"Me? No! We haven't applied for membership. I'm not sure we could afford it—and I don't think they'd let us in anyway. Mason," she added, "my husband, is in plumbing. You meet any plumbers at the Miner's Club?"

Bree ignored the edge to her voice. "I don't spend a lot of time at the club." She smiled, opened her briefcase, and took out her pen and yellow pad for taking notes.

Andrea cocked her head. "Huh! I hear Madison. Too bad. I was looking forward to some good gossip about the inner circle." She rolled her eyes dramatically.

"I'd have to disappoint you, there."

Andrea smiled tightly. And she looked snubbed. Bree, remembering her father's caveats about attitude, added cravenly, "But if I had any, I'd be happy to pass it on."

"There's my girl," Andrea said in an artificially upbeat voice as the back door to the kitchen opened. "You made good time, honey. I hope you didn't speed! We've got an officer of the court sitting right here waiting to talk to you!"

Bree got to her feet as Madison came in. She was a slim, well-exercised kid with long red hair that had been well cut and artfully highlighted. A high-rise T-shirt exposed her flat stomach. She wore three small earrings in each ear, and had a small butterfly tattoo on one ankle. She looked just like the hundreds of teenaged girls that swarmed over the Oglethorpe Mall on Saturday afternoons. A nice kid. A well-grounded kid. Not a kid who'd participate in the robbery of an eight-year-old Girl Scout.

"Say hello to Bree Beaufort, Madison."

"How do you do, Ms. Beaufort?" Madison flipped her hair back with one hand, took a bottle of water from the Sub-Zero, and sat at the table, at some distance from her mother. "You're here about Lin and the business at the mall?"

"In a way," Bree said. "I read the statement that you gave the police about the incident. You were pretty clear that Lindsey stopped the car on an impulse, and that neither you nor Hartley Williams had time to stop her."

Madison folded her lips together and nodded. "That's about the size of it. Lin's, like, prone to this kind of pushing the edge. Nothing huge. But it's happened before."

"Robbing a Girl Scout?"

Madison shook her head, taking Bree's flip comment at face value. "Oh, no. But if we're, like, shopping, she'll go: 'Watch this!' and stick a lipstick into her bra, then go out of the store without paying for it. Or if we're at school and there's this tough test she'll write stuff on her wrists so she can cheat. Like that."

"Acting out," Andrea Bellamy said rather piously. "Madison's tried to help her. She's going to be majoring in psychology at Pepperdine, Madison is, and wants to go into social work. She feels, as I do, that she has an obligation to be friends with poor Lindsey. I think her mother and father really appreciate Madison's influence."

Bree bit her lip and scribbled *Yikes!* on her yellow pad, in very small letters. Then she said, "Have you known Lindsey a long time?"

"Gosh, yeah. Forever. Since, like, eighth grade, I think it was."

"That's when we decided to send Madison to private school," Andrea said. "The local schools are so scary, don't you think? And the opportunities there are . . ."

"Mom," Madison said.

"What, honey?"

"Maybe you could leave me and Ms. Beaufort to talk alone. Okay?"

"Honey, I don't like to feel that there's anything in

your life that we can't know about. You know how proud I am of the kind of relationship the two of us—"

"Mom. It'll be fine. It's not secret stuff about me that I want to talk about. It's secret stuff about Lin."

Andrea Bellamy looked very much as if she wanted to hear secret stuff about Lindsey Chandler. "Well, if you're sure . . ."

"I'm sure. Besides, if Ms. Beaufort finds out something, like, detrimental to me, she has to tell you, right? I mean, you're the parent. I'm the kid. Who's in charge here?"

Bree, concentrating hard on the scribbles on her yellow pad, was pretty sure who was actually in charge here.

"If you're sure."

Madison reached forward and patted her hand. "I'm sure. I'll come and tell you all about what's going on in a bit. Have you done your Pilates yet? You go on and start. I'll be in to, like, work out with you as soon as we're through here." She watched until her mother went through the swinging doors that led to the dining room. As they closed behind Andrea, she got up, crossed the kitchen floor on silent feet, and put her ear to the door. She sighed noisily. "Mom!" She cocked her head, waiting until she heard her mother move away from the door, and then trailed back to Bree.

"My goodness," Bree said. "There's more to you than meets the eye, isn't there?"

"Yeah, well." Madison twirled a piece of her hair into a ringlet, and then let it spring free. "She's not bad, as mothers go. I get along better with my dad, though. He's a lot more on the ball. And he doesn't give a hoot about Savannah society or private schools, or being best friends with the Chandlers."

"You don't, either?"

Madison shrugged. It was the Lindsey shrug. The "I'm seventeen years old and what do *you* know?" shrug. Then she grinned. "Well, yeah. I guess I do. I mean, it's better to be rich than poor, right?"

Not right. At least Bree didn't think it was right. But she was honest enough to admit she might think a lot differently if she'd been brought up in a trailer park. So she just said, "It depends, I think, on how you handle it."

Madison's eyebrows went up in a look of mild surprise. "Ha. I suppose. Anyway. About Lin. How much trouble is she in, really?"

"A lot," Bree said.

"No kidding? I mean, she can afford the best lawyers, and that. You don't think you can get her off?"

Bree gritted her teeth. "If the courts decide she's broken the law, I'm going to have one heck of a time keeping her out of jail. I don't care how many *Law & Order*s you've watched, Madison, but in the real world, there isn't one kind of justice for the rich and another for the poor. And if, once in a great while, it may seem that way, well . . . it's not that often, that's all."

"You like being a lawyer," Madison said shrewdly.

"Yes, I guess I do. And I hate it when people think what I do is for sale."

Madison nodded thoughtfully. "Right, I'm cool with that. So, if Lin's looking at jail time, what can we do to, like, make it community service or whatever?"

"Show mitigating factors," Bree said. "You know what those incidents might be?"

"Stuff that shows she was, like, fated to rob the little kid because she didn't know any better."

Bree rubbed her knuckles along her bottom lip to conceal her smile. "Yep. Things like that."

"Hm." Madison leaned back in her chair and took a

long drink from her water bottle. "Okay. Her parents were, like, very distant and strict. But it wasn't because they were all that strict themselves. It was because they didn't like her."

Bree sat up, pleased at the insight—Madison was going to be a very good social worker if she decided that should be her career—and it confirmed her own feelings about Carrie-Alice as a parent. John Lindquist had told her more than he realized. But there was a big gap between parental coolness and parental abuse. And Bree had read enough about bad kids to know that the most devoted parent could be pushed to the edge. Royal had been most insistent about the need to be impartial when you evaluated witness statements. So Bree did her best. "Any real reasons for that dislike?"

"I don't know. She can get on your nerves, no question. But her folks were older when they had her. My mom's, like, thirty-five, you know. She had me when she was eighteen. Lin's mom was forty when she was born and her dad was, like, even older."

Bree, facing thirty, suddenly felt ancient.

"So maybe you should talk to the brother and sister. See what their take is."

"I intend to." She set her pencil down and took a deep breath. "Madison—did you know her father very well?"

"Mr. Chandler? You've got this 'serious issue' look on your face, you know. You think he was, like, having sex with her? No way."

Bree felt older than ancient. She felt positively Methuselahian. When did seventeen-year-old kids get this knowledgeable? "Well, that's one good thing," she said feebly. "There's something about him, though. I keep feeling if I can get a handle on him, I can get a handle on why Lindsey's such a problem kid."

Madison shrugged. "Her folks don't like her. A lot of kids at school don't like her. Sometimes I don't like her much myself."

Bree didn't respond for a minute. Then she said quietly, "That's pretty callous, isn't it?"

Madison flushed bright red. "I guess."

"So. Now that your mom's not in the room, do you want to tell me anything about drugs?"

"Not me," Madison said. "No way. A little weed now and then, you know, marijuana, but nothing else. I swear."

"I'm not concerned with your defense, Madison, I'm concerned with Lindsey's. If you tell me she's not on something, I'll tell you to your face you're a liar."

Madison bit her lip.

"Well?" Bree said impatiently. "I'm checking hospital records, with the school, and if she'd got a juvenile record, I'll find that, too. So you might was well tell me what you know. It'll show up in the blood tests."

"She goes around with this guy," Madison said reluctantly. "And he's sort of known for it, drugs and that, I mean. So once in a while she takes maybe an upper or two. No big deal." She gazed at Bree, her eyes candid. "If she's on something stronger, I don't know a thing about it. Honest. Lindsey, Hartley, and I, we spend, like, practically all of our waking moments together. At school, after school, on weekends. We're in this band together, you know?"

"The Savannah Sweethearts, sure."

"And we go on trips out of state together. If she were taking serious drugs, I'd know about it. And I haven't seen a thing."

Bree rubbed the back of her neck. Madison's hot denial had a truthful ring. And amphetamines might account for Lindsey's behavior the first time they'd met at the Chandler place. "Okay. That's it, then. I may have some more questions for you later . . . and I'm certainly going to have to depose you before we go to trial, but I can't think of anything else right now."

"What are you going to do now? Is Lindsey, like, condemned to the joint, or what? Is she ever going to get back to school? And that Mrs. Chavez decided not to press charges. So that has to count for something, doesn't it?"

"It doesn't matter if Mrs. Chavez presses charges or not—what matters is what the district attorney's office wants to do."

"Golly. So she's in the soup."

"Maybe. I've got a couple more things up my sleeve," Bree said with more confidence than she felt. "I'll have to talk to Hartley again. Maybe she's noticed something you haven't."

"Good luck on that," Madison said with a sudden grin. "I just finished reading *The Three Musketeers* for my French lit class . . ."

Bree blinked.

"Stay with me here. Well, we're kind of like the Three Musketeers. You remember Porthos? Big, sweet, and dumb? Well, I love Hartley like a sister, but she's our Porthos."

Bree rubbed her forehead. Kids. Although there was something endearing about the showing off. "Be that as it may. I'm going to talk to Lindsey's brother and sister. And I'm curious about why Shirley Chavez decided to drop the charges, too. It'll do Lindsey some good if she's willing to stand up in court and forgive her the way she did at the arraignment. Maybe I can get Mrs. Chavez to agree to that. So we're not dead in the water yet." She got up. "Thank your mom for the coffee. Or do you think I should find her to say good-bye myself?"

"Wouldn't she like that, you being a Winston-Beaufort and all? Nah. She's slogging away at her little home gym.

If we interrupt her once she's into her routine, she'll freak. I'll walk you out."

She led the way out the back door. Bree caught up with her and said, "There is one more thing, Madison. This guy you mentioned. The one that supplies her with the uppers."

Madison made a face. "We hang out with some guys, yeah. But the guys in high school are, like, well, so high school. I prefer older guys myself, and my parents won't let me date older guys, so I don't really date at all."

That was the other thing about teenaged girls that Bree'd forgotten: as sensible and grounded as Madison was, it always came back to Me. Bree gave the conversation a gentle shove in a more productive direction. "We're talking about Lindsey, though. She doesn't date, either? This guy you mentioned . . . what's his name?"

Madison, who seemed to be a fastidious soul, wrinkled her nose. "She broke up with him a few months ago. Or rather, she said he did. His name's Chad Martinelli."

Bree went on alert. "Martinelli. He's from around here?"

"Yeah. Chad's, like, a total loser."

"He's in high school with you?"

"Not anymore. He was a year ahead. He was supposed to go on to college, but not good old Chad. Total stoner." She waved her hand dismissively. "Got a job out at Marlowe's, for God's sake. I mean, I ask you. And his dad's some big-wheel lawyer in town."

"You wouldn't happen to remember the name of the firm his father works for?"

"Sure. It's that creepy old geek that runs the late night commercials on TV."

"John Stubblefield?" Bree couldn't suppress a grin.

"I think so."

Suddenly, the Martinelli name kicked in. "And his dad is Peter Martinelli?"

Who was in the Miner's Club the night Probert Chandler died.

"So Chad's what—eighteen? Nineteen?"

"Something like that," Madison said vaguely.

An adult, legally, then.

Madison sighed as she followed Bree out of the garage. "Now there's a guy I wouldn't trust an inch. I mean, talk about drugs. Whoa!" She stopped short. "Are those your dogs?"

Miles and Belli stared silently from the backseat of Bree's car.

"Sort of. They're kind of on loan."

"Awesome." Madison backed away.

"Those two are, that's for sure. But you see that good old boy in the front? That's Sasha. Everybody likes him. Would you like to meet him?"

"Me? No. No, thanks." Madison retreated to the inside of the garage. Her face was pale. "I'm not a real dog fan, if you know what I mean. I got bitten when I was a kid. Never really got over it." She waved at Bree from the coolness of the interior. "Nice to meet you." She turned and slipped inside the house.

Bree got into the front seat and turned to look at her two protectors. "It's not that I don't appreciate you. I do. But if you're going to scare the living daylights out of everybody, I can see that we're going to have a problem."

Belli rumbled at her, like a mountain speaking.

Bree shook her head, and put the car into gear. She'd grab some lunch, and then she'd stop by the Marlowe's where Shirley worked for the father whose kid knocked her daughter flat on the pavement at the Oglethorpe Mall.

And she wanted to speak to Chad Martinelli. She absolutely wanted to speak to Chad Martinelli. Before Peter Martinelli knew about it and stepped in to bring the full weight of Stubblefield, Marwick onto her shoulders.

Twelve

You're breakin' my heart.
You're shakin' my confidence daily.
—"Cecilia," Paul Simon

She drove to the Marlowe's out near the Oglethorpe Mall, and decided to ask for Chad Martinelli before she asked for Shirley Chavez.

Chad was a skinny, sullen kid with a postnasal drip and a long shock of black hair that hung over his eyes. He was also, to Bree's mild astonishment, in charge of inventory. The very polite Marlowe's greeter who met her as she walked in got a shade less polite when she asked to see Chad.

"In the office. He works with the computers."

The administrative offices were behind the returns and exchanges area, immediately to the left of the front entrance. Bree walked down the wide, linoleum-covered hall and tapped at the metal door. There wasn't any answer for a minute, then the door opened to a largish room packed with metal desks, a long rank of computers, and neatly arrayed filing cabinets.

"So what d'ya want?"

Bree glanced at the kid's name tag, which indeed identified him as Charles "Chad" Martinelli. "You," she said bluntly. "I want to talk to you."

Chad looked over his shoulder. There were two other people in the room, both middle-aged women. He stepped into the hall and closed the door behind him. "So you're talking to me," he said. "Who are you and what do you want?" He ran his eyes insolently up and down her figure. "You look like a lawyer. You from my dad's firm?"

Bree's response was immediate and involuntary. "No way."

A brief smile lifted the sneer, and for a minute, Bree caught sight of a shy good-looking kid behind the sullen façade.

"But I am a lawyer. Mrs. Chandler hired me to handle Lindsey's case."

The smile grew into a genuine grin. "You mean the cookie heist?" He punched the air with one hand. "Way to go, Lin!"

"Yeah. Well, it's the way to go if you want to spend a fair amount of time making license plates."

This appealed to Chad's sense of humor. "Heh," he said. "Heh-heh." He bit his lip a little nervously. "She can buy her way out of it, right? People like the Chandlers can always buy their way out of it."

"Maybe. Maybe not. I'll be frank. It doesn't look good. Not good at all."

Chad rubbed the back of his hand against his nose. "No shit."

"No shit." Bree cocked her head to one side. There wasn't any way that this kid was going to admit anything about drugs. But the look on his face when she'd mentioned Lindsey's possible prison term gave her an idea about how to get into Chad's head. "So. Are you and Lindsey seeing each other?"

Chad leaned against the wall and moved his shoulders up and down, scratching himself. "Maybe."

"Madison Bellamy said you two broke up a couple of months ago."

"Yeah?"

"Yeah. And what I want to know is, did Lindsey break off with you, or did you break off with her?"

"Why don't you ask Lin?"

"I will," Bree said with deceptive cordiality. "But I'm asking you now, aren't I?"

"Her folks did it," he said abruptly. He screwed his eyes shut in a brief, spasmodic gesture.

"You mean her father? Probert?"

"Whatever."

"That must have been a while ago." She watched his eyes. "Because he's dead, isn't he?"

"You bet he is."

Bree didn't like the look on his face at all. "Chad?" she said sharply. "When was the last time you saw Mr. Chandler?"

"What's it to you?" That strange tic again; Chad's eyes closed and opened again.

Bree resisted the impulse to grab the kid by his Marlowe's ID tag and pull it tight around his neck. "I'm trying to help her avoid jail time. I'm trying to come up with something, anything, that can help me understand her better."

"You know what would help Lin? To get away from that freakin' family. To get away from those freakin' friends. You accomplish that, you might get somewhere." He shoved himself away from the wall and came toward her, his hands clenched tight. "You want to know when I last talked to that old fart? About forty freakin' minutes before he spun out on that road and splattered his brains all over the place. I told him what he could do with his freakin' 'parental responsibilities.'"

Bree refused to back up. The kid was taller than she was, so she had to crane her neck to look him in the eye. "You told him this face-to-face?"

Chad let his breath out in an agonized sigh. "He ran into my dad." Bree felt a chill run over her at the venom in his voice when he referred to his father. "And jumped all over him about it. Then my dad freaked out at me, and Chandler called me, and the whole freakin' thing with Lin just blew up."

Bree took a minute to sort out the pronouns. "So your father called you—on your cell phone? Yes. And then Mr. Chandler called you. So then what did you do?"

"I was here, wasn't I?" He jerked his thumb toward the office door. "I called Lin, and she freaked, and then I freaked, and I went home."

"By way of Skidaway Road?" she asked softly.

His look was totally blank.

"Chad," she said firmly, "there's something else that can help Lindsey's case enormously. She's got more than a flying chance to get into rehab instead of jail, if we can prove she needs it. We need to talk about drugs."

Chad scowled, suggested she perform an unnatural act, and then slammed himself back in the office.

Bree took a moment to collect herself. She'd put the Company on a search for Chad's record. Ron was good. Petru was even better. Chad's father—and Stubblefield's firm—might have a lot of the wrong kind of influence in Chatham County, but they wouldn't be able to hide it all. If Peter Martinelli's son had been involved with drugs, her angels would find out. And if Chad had been supplying drugs to Lindsey, it could be the best way out for her. The juvenile system had more than a few ways to help drug abusers; there was a lot less support for a kid who was unapologetically mean and nasty.

She took a deep breath, went back to the cheery

greeter, and asked to see the store manager. She found him in the small appliances aisle, checking inventory with a handheld gizmo that scanned the product codes.

"Shirley?" The Marlowe's manager said after Bree identified herself and asked after the worker. "She's not on today." He frowned worriedly. "She in more trouble?" His name tag was clipped to the breast pocket of his bright green Marlowe's shirt: MEL JENSEN. He was middle-aged and middle-sized, with soft brown hair that was losing out to acres of scalp. He held her business card between his thumb and forefinger.

"She's not in any trouble at all, as far as I know."

Bree had regretted her decision to tackle Shirley Chavez at work as soon as she'd walked into the main body of the store. It was massively busy, and unless she could draw Shirley to a quieter spot, conversation was going to be difficult. The place was crowded with cheap, brightly colored clothes, boxed microwaves, stacks of coolers, and boxes of toys from China. Customers of all kinds pushed overloaded carts along aisles littered with candy wrappers, crumpled tissue, and an empty pop bottle or two. Jensen, apologetically, refused to leave the floor so they could talk in private. The manager leaned over, picked up a discarded cotton glove, and looked around in a distracted way. A chemical smell hung in the air; from the solution used to size the clothes, Bree thought. She'd had a roommate in college who washed the jeans she picked up at Marlowe's three times before she wore them. The pharmacy at the far end of the store dominated the space. Long lines of customers waited for service there; most of them seemed to be from among the retirees who'd flooded south Georgia in recent years.

"We're open twenty-four/seven," he said apologetically, in response to a question Bree hadn't asked. "Hard to keep the place picked up."

"It looks just fine," Bree said reassuringly, although it didn't. "And I just dropped by to have a word with Ms. Chavez. No problem at all. Is there somebody here who might know where I can find her this time of day? One of her friends?"

Nervously, he looked her up and down, as if confronting an unfriendly dog. Bree dressed in a professional way when she was working: a skirt, a suit jacket, and a plain silk tee. She carried her briefcase in one hand. "They didn't tell me they were sending you down today, Miss—Beaufort, is it? I would have made sure she was here. She's a good worker, by the way. Very steady." Then he added hastily, "Loves her job. Loves it. She'll make an excellent witness."

For a second, this statement made no sense at all. "Oh! No, Mr. Jensen. I'm not from your company. I'm a lawyer. I represent the girl who's been accused of stealing the Girl Scout money. See? It says so right on my card. Brianna Winston-Beaufort, Esquire."

Mel Jensen didn't seem to be a man who actively disliked anybody. He had a soft, anxious face and the manner of a puppy who wanted to please. But he looked at her with some distaste. "That wasn't a good thing," he said. "Not at all. Shirley's a good worker, and that kid of hers is a good kid. And it's just like that Lindsey to take advantage . . ." He stopped and bit his lip.

"Lindsey comes into this store? Does she come here very often?"

"I'd prefer not to comment."

"Absolutely," Bree said. "But you know what? I could have guessed that. You know that Mrs. Chavez stood right up in court and said she didn't want to press charges against my client. The Chandlers are a pretty powerful family, Mr. Jensen."

Jensen's jaw set stubbornly.

"As for Shirley, we're very grateful to her. Only a really nice person would have withdrawn the charges, don't you think?" Or somebody who's gotten a hefty bribe. But she didn't say that aloud.

"But she's still a witness in a criminal case," Jensen said, unexpectedly shrewd. "Maybe you shouldn't be talking to her."

"She's taken Sophie right out of the case altogether, Mr. Jensen. She's refused to let her testify at the trial. The DA's office has her deposition and Sophie's, the tape from the security camera, and the testimony of the girls who were with my client. That's what they're going to trial with."

A very large woman in sweatpants, flip-flops, and a baggy sweatshirt stopped in front of them with a pointed "Excuse me."

Jensen flashed a smile. "Can I help you?"

The woman had a small toaster tucked under her arm. She thrust it at them. "These were supposed to be on sale. This is the last one. And it's the one without the box that's been sitting on the shelf having everybody and his brother poking at it. I want a fresh one."

Jensen unclipped his scanner from his belt, read the bar code, and told the ruffled customer a new one was on its way from the warehouse. "Two days," he said, "maybe less. Come on by and pick it up anytime after Thursday." A second, equally determined customer caught sight of his scanner and marched determinedly toward them.

"I'm sorry," Bree apologized. "I shouldn't be taking up your time like this." Jensen stepped out of the mainstream of traffic and directed the second customer to a clerk a little further down the aisle. Bree stepped aside with him.

"Well," he said with a somewhat strained smile, "if that's all I can help you with . . ."

"Chad Martinelli," Bree said promptly. "He may be connected with another case I'm working on."

"Chad?" Jensen looked bemused. "Well, smart as a whip, of course. What about him?"

"Any problems with him, as an employee?" Bree longed to ask about drugs, but didn't dare.

"Not really. He's not the most reliable worker we've got, but like I said, he's a smart kid. And of course, he and Miss Chandler . . ." He shifted on his feet. "I think maybe we've talked enough now. I can't see that Martinelli has anything to do with this. And I sure can't see why you need to harass Shirley."

Bree placed her hand on his arm. "Honestly. We're not out to hurt anybody, Mr. Jensen. I'd just like to talk with her. Please. The family's in a position to do her some good, you know. If things work out the way they should."

He fiddled nervously with his tie—a small, tired guy who was just trying to do his job. Bree didn't think she had the heart to put any more pressure on him than she had already.

"I guess it wouldn't hurt. She has a second job, you know."

"Then perhaps I should call on her at home."

"No, no. That's not such a good idea. Her husband's all worked up over this thing. It's an insult to his kid, this whole thing. He'd like to sue the pants off this Lindsey character, and I can't say as I blame him."

"Oh, dear." Bree dithered, fighting the temptation to call on the Chavez home and suggest just that. And take her lumps from the Review Board when she was brought up on charges of unethical behavior. Phooey. "Then perhaps I should drop by and see her at her other job." She smiled. "Is that employer as kind as you?"

He smiled, a little sheepishly. "Nice folks out there. Nice folks."

Bree waited.

"She's a stable hand at the Seaton Stud." His eyes widened at the look on Bree's face, and he checked himself. "Anything wrong about that? She loves the job, even though she has to work her tail off. It seems like a pretty good place to work."

"No," Bree said. There seemed to be a frog in her throat. She cleared it. "There's nothing wrong."

"You know how to get there? It's not far. You get onto 80, on the way to Tybee Island."

"I know the way, Mr. Jensen. Thank you. I appreciate your help."

She retreated to the parking lot and her car. Bree dumped her briefcase in the backseat, then poured Sasha, Belli, and Miles each a bowl of water from her water bottle. Sasha lapped it up. Belli took a tentative sniff, then emptied the entire bowl with great scoops of her huge pink tongue. Miles put one outsized paw on the water bottle after he'd emptied his bowl. Bree refilled the bowl for him and wondered if she should stock up on a couple of hundred pounds of dog food. Like the rest of the Company, Belli and Miles had temporal requirements when in temporal bodies, and they'd have to eat pretty soon. She'd offered each of them a fast-food hamburger on the way back from Plessey the day before, but they'd turned up their massive noses at it. Maybe they just hated Burger King.

Sasha put his paw on her knee and barked.

"Right," Bree said. "I'm dithering. This is me, putting the key in the ignition and me driving straight to the Seaton Stud." She stroked Sasha's ears. "He's probably not even there. Off on a buying trip."

It was a lowering day, with a threat of rain to come. Bree rolled the windows down, and all three dogs stuck their heads out and faced into the breeze, ears flying. The sight of two huge, fierce faces sticking out of either side of her car caused more than a few double takes from the other drivers on the road. Sasha, as usual, merely looked beautiful.

Abel's brother, Charles Trask, had married into the Seaton Stud, which was an old, long-established racing farm for Thoroughbred horses. His widow, Missy Seaton Trask, had a side interest in three-day eventing. She'd branched out into the light draft breeds, with an emphasis on Trakehners and Swedish Warmbloods. As a result, the Seaton racing reputation had ebbed, and winners at the track were scarcer now than they had been in the past. According to Aunt Cissy, at least, who had been full of information at Saturday's party, Missy was facing some pretty significant cash flow problems.

Bree pulled into the long flat road that led up to the main house and the barns. The place looked a lot shabbier than when she had been here last. Which was what? Eight years ago, at least. Maybe ten. Three-railed fences ran for a mile or more on either side of the asphalted drive. The fences were in poor repair, and the edges of the verge needed mowing. The slightly rolling pastures were filled with mares grazing under sycamores and oaks. By this time of year, the year's crop of foals had long been weaned, and the mares bred back. They grazed peacefully under the gray skies, their bellies rounded with the foals to be delivered in spring. They, at least, looked in great condition. Whatever her cash situation, Missy wasn't skimping on the feed.

Bree pulled to a stop at the head of the drive. The sign announcing the farm was still there, considerably weathered. Letters picked out in dark green said: SETON HORSE FARMS, INC., CHARLES AND MELISSA SEATON TRASK, PROP., EST. 1883.

The barns lay to the left, the house to the right. The

office was directly in front of her. The barns were long and low, with green metal roofs and gray metal siding. The house and the office building dated from the mid-nineteenth century. Both were brick, with Carpenter Gothic white trim and small mullioned windows. Bree parked and got out and addressed the dogs. "The three of you are going to stay here, right? No roaming around and scaring folks."

She grabbed her briefcase, with a rather confused idea that if she did run into Abel, he'd see at once that she was here on business. The blinds on one of the office windows moved, as if someone had looked out at her. Then a short, muscular woman came out the front door and trudged down the steps. She wore jeans, green rubber boots, and a flannel shirt. She had short, bristly hair and a pugnacious jaw. Missy Trask. And she hadn't changed a bit. Bree hadn't known her well, but her looks were memorable. "No salesmen, no salesmen!" She stumped up to Bree, her eyes slitted against the daylight, and stopped dead in her tracks. "My God. It's Bree Beaufort. I haven't seen you in years."

"Ten at least," Bree said. "I was here for the Hunt Ball."

Missy's gaze shifted past Bree to the dogs, who were looking around with interest. "And what the hell are those?"

"My dogs," Bree said. "Totally quiet. Totally obedient. They'll stay right there."

Missy squinted so hard her eyes almost disappeared between folds of flesh. "What kind of breed are those big black ones?"

"Newfies," Bree hazarded. "Nicest dogs on the planet."

"Newfies, my ass," Missy said. She swung her turretlike gaze to Bree. "And what are you up to these days?"

Bree mentioned her need to see Shirley Chavez, and offered her card.

"Attorney-at-law," the woman mused. Then, accusingly, "You're kin to Cissy Carmichael."

"My mother's sister." Then, in case this wasn't enough, she added, "My aunt."

"*Those* Winston-Beauforts. Abel ran your cotton farm a few years back. It's all coming back to me now." She gave Bree a knowing, very unpleasant look.

"That's right."

"Good to see you again, I guess." She stuck out her hand, and Bree took it. It was hard and calloused, the rather grubby nails clipped short. Her eyes were small, bright brown, and very sharp. "So," she said, as if she'd come across an unusual and not particularly useful artifact, "you've come out to see Abel?"

"No!" Bree said, rather more violently than she'd intended. "I thought I mentioned that up front. I'm working on a case. I'm representing Lindsey Chandler, and one of the witnesses to the incident works here for you. Shirley Chavez."

"Shirley? Yes. She's a stable hand. Part-time. And a good worker, too." Her face was weathered, in the way of those who work outdoors, and the dry wrinkles around her eyes deepened as she looked Bree up and down. "So poor little Sophie found herself mixed up with a bunch of snotty girls all in the name of the cookie charity. Huh. What's your business with Shirley?"

"If you don't mind my taking a few minutes of her time, I'm afraid I'll have to discuss that with her."

"Oh, I don't mind." She looked at Bree's leather pumps. "You might not like what's going to happen to your good shoes, but that's all in a day's work for you lawyers, eh?" Without another word, she turned and stamped off toward the barn.

Missy Trask's legs were short, but she moved like a runaway train, and Bree found herself almost jogging to keep up.

The barns formed a square around a paved courtyard. The buildings were all one story high, with the exception of a gambrel-roofed structure filled with hay. Each of the one-storied buildings held twenty horse stalls, with Dutch doors that opened to the center yard. The top halves of the doors were fastened open. About half of the stalls were occupied, and a row of brown, gray, black, chestnut, and bay heads bobbed up and down as Bree followed Missy to the farthest building. A couple of workers were mucking out, dumping the manure and straw into wheelbarrows. "Yo! Shirl!" Missy shouted. "Someone here to see you!"

A small, skinny figure propped her pitchfork against the barn wall. Wiping her hands down her jeans, she trotted toward them.

"This is Brianna Winston-Beaufort, Shirl."

"We've met. Or rather, I know who she is. I saw her when I was in court."

"Right. Well, you know then that she's been hired by Probert Chandler's widow to represent Lindsey Chandler's criminal case. You don't have to talk to her, but she won't lie to you, from what I know of her. You have any questions, you can come and talk to me anytime. Would you like me to stick around?"

"No," Shirley said quietly. "But thank you just the same, Mrs. Trask."

"Then I'll leave you to it. If you wouldn't mind, Bree, would you stop on and see me before you go?"

"Surely."

Missy whirled and stamped in the direction of the office.

A soft, misty rain started to fall. Shirley drew the cowl

of her hooded sweatshirt over her head and gestured toward the stall she'd been cleaning out. "We can stand partway in there. But you'll get your shoes all messed up."

"I should have thrown a pair of boots into the car. I would have, if I'd known I'd be stopping here."

"It's a nice place to work." Shirley stepped all the way inside the stall, which was empty of horse but full of straw, and turned to regard Bree with candid gray eyes. "I like it. They treat the animals real good, and the people, too."

Shirley had handled herself with a certain amount of dignity in court, although Bree had seen that the judge, the phalanx of officials, and the high, imposing ceilings of the courtroom itself were intimidating to her.

"Is that Lindsey in jail still? I saw that the cops came and got her again, after I stood up and told the judge I didn't want to press charges."

Bree set her briefcase onto the straw. "No. She's out on bail. In the custody of her mother, and supervised by the juvenile court. She has an ankle bracelet."

Shirley smiled faintly. "Bet she finds a way to ditch it."

Bree looked at her closely. "You don't like her much, do you?"

She shrugged. "Kid that's got all she got—why'd she have to go after my Sophie?"

"Beats me," Bree said frankly. "Your Sophie's adorable, Mrs. Chavez." And wasn't that the truth. Sophie had big dark eyes, long curly black hair, dimples, and an amazing sangfroid in the face of the TV cameras. Although Bree had noticed that most kids under twenty seemed totally at ease in front of cameras. Maybe it had something to do with a life lived on YouTube. "And I can't see her going the way of the Lindsey Chandlers of this world. You take awfully good care of her."

"We try, Luis and me. We've got five, you know. Both

of us work the two jobs to keep the right kind of money coming in. My oldest, Luisa, does a lot more babysitting than I'd like. 'Course, now . . ." She stopped and sucked her lower lip.

"Now what?" Bree asked patiently, although she was pretty sure what was coming.

"Nothing."

"Mrs. Chavez, you know that I'm Lindsey's lawyer. That I'm on her side. Not the side of the courts. Necessarily," she added, since a lawyer was, in fact, an officer of the court. "I'll get to the point, shall I? I'd like to know if anyone from the Chandler family gave you money to drop the charges against Lindsey and the family itself."

Shirley looked at her feet.

"I'm not here to take it back or anything." She held her hand up. "And I'm not here to give you any more. If you sued the family in civil court, you'd probably collect damages. So if someone did give you a check, it was a private settlement, anticipating a court-ordered one. At least, I could defend it that way if I had to. I just need to know if . . ." Bree stopped and tried to think of a phrase less provocative than "paid off." "If you've received some consideration."

"Yes."

"You did receive money."

"For Sophie."

"Of course, for Sophie."

"And for Luis and me, too. Since we had all that hassle."

"May I ask how much?"

Shirley smiled. "Half a million dollars."

Bree had long ago learned to keep a poker face when dealing with her cases. But she almost lost it now. "Half a million dollars?"

"We're investing it, Luis and me. Some people, see,

when they win the lottery, they, like, quit their jobs, buy a lot of fancy cars, like that. Not us. We're putting the money in the bank so all the kids can go to a good school, and we're going to look at maybe a house with four or five bedrooms instead of the one we got now."

Bree put both hands on the back of her neck and pressed her palms into her head. "Whoa," she said. "Well."

"But alongside of that, we aren't supposed to say anything to anybody. And we got to keep our jobs, so it don't look like we all of a sudden got rich." Her smile widened. "But we sure enough did."

"Yes. Thank you, Mrs. Chavez, for letting me know."

"You being the family lawyer and all, it's okay to tell you, right? I figure it's okay to tell you."

"Right. I should advise you not to mention to anyone else, though."

"Heck, no." She shifted uncomfortably. "Just a few people, who won't say a word, honest to God."

"Sure." Bree took a deep sigh. "I just have a couple more questions for you. You knew Lindsey by sight, before she grabbed that money from Sophie."

"Oh, yeah. She used to come into the store. We all knew who she was. The boss's boss's daughter. The big cheese."

"Did she come in for any particular reason?"

Shirley looked away and rubbed her lips with one hand.

"I was wondering if it was to see her boyfriend. Chad Martinelli."

"Him," Shirley said. She leaned forward, in a confiding way. "They said his folks and her folks didn't get along. Thought he was some kind of bad influence, that Chad."

"And is he? A bad influence?"

Shirley snorted. "You're kidding, right? You know how often our warehouse's been robbed?"

"Your warehouse?"

"Yeah. It's huge, you know. And it's part of the research center, which is way in the back of the Marlowe's lot. We carry all kinds of drugs, and tons of them. Ever since our store started offering those cheap generics, we got the whole state of Georgia coming in to fill prescriptions in this one store here alone. Just imagine what the rest of the U. S. of A. uses. So, in the past six months, the warehouse gets robbed, like, once a week."

"Once a week!" Bree was stunned. "But there hasn't been a word about this with the police. Or in the papers. Has there?"

Shirley shook her head wisely. "The old man. Probert. He didn't want a word of it to get out. So it didn't." She rubbed her thumb and forefinger together in a provocative way. "Money talks, Miz Beaufort. And Mr. Probert, I guess he figured we could crack down on those crooks ourselves. So. No cops. No police report. Just a pile of extra security and a lot of the bosses poking around into all the employees' business."

"And Chad Martinelli is one of the people they're taking a look at?"

Shirley rolled her eyes. "Who knows? But me, I got my suspicions." She leaned forward and dropped her voice to a whisper. "I'm his backup."

"Pardon me?"

"His backup. You know, for inventory. We're all trained for two or three different jobs at the store, so we can back each other up. That Chad calls in sick one, two, maybe three times a month. So I take over tracking shipments for him. You know what I found out? Last three times that warehouse was robbed it was the day after we got the containers in from China. It was like the robbers *knew* ahead of time. And the only person that knows that from our end is the inventory dispatcher. Which is Chad.

And me. Like I told . . ." She stopped and looked confused. "Never mind," she muttered.

"What do the robbers take?" Bree asked. "Anything in particular? I mean, they can't just waltz in with a truck and roar off with the whole warehouse."

"Nah," Shirley said, with the pleasantly officious air of someone who knows something you don't. "It's the PSE. Comes in pallets about yea big." She held her hands about two feet apart, and four feet off the ground. Easy enough to load on a pickup."

"And PSE is what when it's at home?"

"I can't pronounce it, but I can spell it," Shirley said promptly. "P-S-E-U-D-O-E-P-H-E-D-R-I-N-E. I looked it up on the Internet. It's some drug they use to make meth."

"Pseudoephedrine," Bree said. "Good grief. But how . . . ?" She realized she was gaping at Shirley and closed her mouth. She had no idea how the Marlowe's powers had managed to keep this from the police. They couldn't. They wouldn't. For one thing, legitimate sale of the drug was tracked through at least one federal agency, not to mention the attorney general's office of the State of Georgia.

"No police?" she said to Shirley.

"Not a one," Shirley said. She smiled cheerfully. "No skin off my nose, is it? Mind your own business and nobody will mind yours. That's what Luis says." Her smile faded. "I can tell what you think of that, Miz Beaufort. About mindin' my own business. I can tell you this. The one time I didn't mind my own business, it came back to bite me in the ass."

Bree wasn't about to pass judgment. She stood in the straw and turned this new information around in her head. It'd have to be verified, of course. But the Chandlers were a secretive bunch. And what connection could this have to Lindsey and the Girl Scout heist? With Probert Chandler's murder? *Lindsey. Marlowe's. Blood. Blood. Blood.* Her client knew the connections. And her client had had his one phone call, so to speak. So it was up to her.

Time to talk to Sam Hunter about the robberies.

Bree picked up her briefcase and stuck out her hand.

"Thank you, Mrs. Chavez. I really appreciate your help, here. I've just got one more question, if you don't mind."

Shirley nodded agreeably and shook her hand vigorously. Bree held it for a moment.

"Who actually gave you the check? For Sophie?"

"One of you lawyers," she said. "A real good-looking guy. Built. Gorgeous sort of violet blue eyes. You know who I mean."

"Oh, yes, I know who you mean." Bree released Shirley's hand and smiled at her. "When he gave you this check, this lawyer, did he tell you that you had to keep quiet about it?" That would compound Payton's misdemeanor. Bribery. Hah! "Did you sign anything that said you had to keep quiet?" It was okay to keep quiet about the amount. It was absolutely not okay to deny the fact of the payoff.

"No, not him. Some other guy came along later and told us to keep our mouths shut. Not the cute one." Her sigh was regretful.

So the rodent had known exactly what he was doing and sent someone else to do the dirty work. Couldn't pin coercion on him, worse luck. Bree snorted. "Those gorgeous blue eyes, Mrs. Chavez? Contact lenses."

"No kidding!"

"Fact," Bree said. Then, for the sake of thoroughness,

she asked, "This other guy. The one who told you to keep quiet about the pay—that is, the money. What did he look like?"

"Now, he was pretty cute, too. Older, though. And he had a scar under one eye. Kind of romantic looking, actually. And the business about keeping quiet about the money—he just sort of added that on."

"Added it on to what?"

"Those warehouse robberies," Shirley said patiently. "He didn't want us to talk about them, either. I'd been working late shift the night of the last one, and he was all over me about what I saw, and whether I could point out any employees that maybe had something to do with it. I didn't say a word about Chad, of course. Poor kid."

Bree mentally ran through the roster of the attorneys at Stubblefield, Marwick. The description didn't fit anyone she knew, but it was bound to be one of the many lawyers assigned to handle George Chandler's affairs. He sounded pretty distinctive. She could track him down if she needed to. And if she decided it would be pretty satisfying to nail Payton's cute little behind to the wall, she might just do that.

"What color are they for real?"

"Sorry?" Bree said.

"The cute guy that gave us the check. What color are his eyes for real?"

Bree gritted her teeth. "Rat gray, Mrs. Chavez. Rat gray." A rat for sure, and slimy enough to assign the threat to keep quiet to somebody else altogether.

She stamped back across the courtyard, at first barely noticing the rain, which had increased from a mist to a shower. By the time she reached the office, her hair was soaked. Rain dripped down the back of her neck, and her white silk tee clung to her chest in an annoyingly revealing way. She knocked briefly at the front door and pushed it open, unwilling to stand in more wet.

"Well, look what the cat dragged in," Missy Trask said. She turned to the man sitting behind the office desk. "She looked pretty good before the rain got to her."

"Hello, Bree."

Bree sighed and set her briefcase down. "Hello, Abel."

Thirteen

What is character but the determination of incident?
—Partial Portraits, Henry James

"Oh, dear, oh, dear," Ron said. "Are you sure you don't want to go home and change? You're soaked."

"I'm fine," Bree said glumly. She draped her jacket over the back of her chair. Her tee had dried quickly, once she'd put the heater on in the car, but it'd dried all wrinkly. Her shoes squelched, and she kicked them off. She was very thankful that her generation had put a stop to wearing panty hose. Wet panty hose would have been the limit.

"Anything of interest to report?" Ron said brightly. "Because I've got a carload, a truckload, a *train*load of new info. I'm brilliant!" Petru, who had appeared in the doorway from the kitchen, gave him a look.

"In a minute," Bree snapped. "I've got some leads of my own."

Ron raised his eyebrows. "And that's what put you in a snit? Solid leads on each case? We're making progress by leaps and bounds."

"I am not in a snit," Bree snapped. She hadn't been, at least, until the hotly uncomfortable meeting with Abel and Missy. Both were in overprotective mode, demanding to know that Shirley Chavez and her daughter were

safe from the machinations of wicked city lawyers. Bree
wanted to spit. She had, she hoped, handled herself with
aplomb. Both knew about the payoff. Both were suspicious, and rightly so. The spot of light in the gloom
wasn't too bad, though; Payton was bound to land in a
peck of trouble with the bar association if Shirley continued to keep her news of her found money to "just a few
people, honest to God." Of course, the downside was that
she, too, could be caught in the mess, just by virtue of
association. And Abel thought she was party to that kind
of crap! How could he!

"Grrr!" Bree said. She covered her face with her hands.
She wanted to cry.

She looked out her small office window. It overlooked
the cemetery, which the rain made even more dank and
drab. The Spanish moss dripped sullenly over the gravestones. The magnolia tree drooped like a petulant wraith.
She tossed her car keys on the desk and stretched back in
the chair. "Let me bring you up to speed on Lindsey's
case, since that one's time-sensitive. I saw two witnesses
today. First, Madison Bellamy, who gave me a lead to a
possible defense. It looks like Lindsey's involved in
drugs, in a very low-key way, admittedly, but at least I'll
have a little bargaining power with the juvenile courts.
My talk with Shirley Chavez was even more interesting,
although less productive as far as our client is concerned.
The Chandlers paid the Chavez family off. Or rather,
Payton McAllister the Third, Rat Fink of the Universe,
did. I don't know who's going to make it to the finals of
Sleazy Lawyer of the Year. Payton, or that skunk boss of
his. My money's on Payton. Anyhow, I need you, Ron, to
dig up what you can from Lindsey's pediatrician. If she's
been taking uppers or downers or whatever, my guess is
that her doctor would have some kind of record. And you
checked her juvenile records?"

"Nothing," Ron said. "Not a whisper."

"I'm not surprised. Her family's insanely committed to keeping things out of the public eye." She looked at him. "You used The Smile, didn't you? With the police, I mean. It's even more important with the doctor's office. It can be a little dicey, getting medical records, and even worse when it's a juvenile."

"I would hope," Ron said a little stiffly, "that I am always polite and professional when I deal with Company business."

"Of course you are!" Bree said.

"I have no idea what you're talking about regarding my smile," Ron continued. "But I can assure you that what information needs to be gathered will be gathered." He looked at her with an expression close to seraphic.

"Terrific." Bree sighed. "Now for the rest of what I've found out. Shirley had some truly valuable information, although I'm not sure yet how it fits into solving Probert's murder. There have been a string of robberies at the warehouse in back of the Marlowe's store on Route 80. The thieves are stealing pseudoephedrine, which, as you all probably know, is a primary ingredient in making crystal methamphetamine."

"Oh, dear," Petru said.

"Oh, dear is right. Chandler seems to have ordered a cover-up. As far as I know, he succeeded."

"Why?" Petru said. "Why the cover-up?"

Bree lifted her shoulders and let them drop. "Who knows? Worst case, he was involved in the meth labs himself."

"Surely not," Ron murmured. "He would hardly have asked for an appeal if that were true."

Bree put both hands over her eyes and rubbed hard.

"Coffee," Ron said sympathetically. "Good for what

ails you. And Lavinia had a cooking frenzy and made us all some shortcake. You want some?"

"Sure."

Ron trotted out to the break room behind Petru, who retreated from the doorway. Bree stared at the cemetery, which depressed her even further. She could see Josiah Pendergast's headstone from where she sat. The grave beneath it yawned empty, like a horrible grin in the face of the dirt. She drummed her fingers on her desk. The Beastie Boys were on patrol in the front room, thank goodness, posed beneath the *Rise of the Cormorant* like sphinxes before a tomb. Dog food. She was going to need a lot of dog food.

"Phone messages!" Ron caroled from the break room. "You might want to call Miz Eastburn back. She's called twice."

Bree picked up the stack of While You Were Out message slips: her mother—no surprise; her sister—no surprise; Cordelia—hmm; Sam Hunter—excellent. She needed to talk to him about Chad Martinelli's drug record, if any, and shake loose any information he had about the robberies. And there was a call from Payton— Sssst!

Her duty to her living client came first. She dialed the DA's office, gave her name, and waited while the strains of "A Horse with No Name" pulsed too loudly in her ear. "Why," she demanded, when Cordelia came on the phone, "does America have to sing through its collective noses? And why do I have to listen to it, anyway? What's wrong with having a small series of reassuring little beeps when you're on hold? Like a nicely ticking EKG."

"I do feel your pain," Cordelia said. "Listen, girl. You want to meet me for a drink after work?"

"You don't drink," Bree reminded her. "You have high

blood pressure. But sure, I'll meet you for a drink. Should I be prepared for anything in particular? It's the Chandler case, I take it."

"Mm. Shall I pick you up at your office?"

The only people who could find 66 Angelus were dead, or living in a body borrowed for the purpose. Neither case fit Cordelia. "Umm, no, that's not going to work for me today. Why don't I meet you down at the court-house?"

"No, sir." Cordy's reply was immediate and firm. "What do you say to Huey's around six? We'll run into each other there."

Bree caught the undercurrent. A casual meeting, at a popular after-work spot. And there were quiet booths in the back. "Okay. Got it."

Cordy dropped the phone into the cradle, which cut Bree off with a thud. Cordy didn't believe in unnecessary or prolonged farewells.

"Here we go." Ron swept in with a tray in his hands. Petru thumped along behind, a thick file under one arm. Ron set the coffee tray with a plate of cookies on her desk.

"It's my shortbread," Lavinia said, peeping in the office door. "Figured you'd need a little sugar boost right about now." She carried a duster, to maintain the fiction that she wasn't attending meetings but was the landlady, tidying up. She walked in and set to work on Bree's sole bookshelf, which was a spindly thing, set under the office's only window.

Bree bit into the cookie, which was delicious, and then took a cautious sip of coffee. "You figured right, Lavinia." She closed her eyes briefly. "I can feel the energy just pouring into me. And our client is innocent. Both our clients. I'm practically positive." She looked her staff over. "So. What about you guys? Who wants to go first?"

"I do," Ron said promptly.

"Okay. But you'll wish you'd heard what I've got to say first. What have you got?"

"We've got a method of murder," Ron said with enormous satisfaction. "Are you people ready to applaud like mad? Because I deserve it." With an air of enormous triumph, he laid a sheet of paper in front of Bree.

"Tush," said Petru in disgust. "You have already fallen prey to several of the seven deadly sins in this life, Ronald. You are about to add vanity to the list?"

"Guys," Bree said absently, "cool it for a second, okay?" She looked up at Ron, unable to suppress her own grin of triumph. "Hotcha!" she said. "And three cheers for you, Ronald Parchese!"

"What's he got there?" Lavinia demanded.

"A witness statement!" Bree said. She waved it excitedly in the air. "Listen to this:

"'My name is Helen Ford Nussbaum. I am seventy-two years old. I've lived on the corner of Skidaway Road and Parsons for over forty years. It is the white house located at the bend of the elbow, as Skidaway turns south. I was sitting at home watching *Frazier* on TV at eight thirty on the evening of July the third. It was the episode where . . .'" Bree broke off, read a few sentences on, and then said, "Blah, blah, blah. Okay, here's where it gets real, people. 'There was someone in my rose garden. A man, with a hat pulled low over his head. Maybe a woman? I don't know, would a woman do such a thing? He crouched just inside my white picket fence. A car came around the bend, where Skidaway turns south. It was not going too fast. The man behind the fence jumped up and shone a light right at this car's windshield. It was a bright light, the kind my late husband used to use to jack deer.'" Bree shuddered. "Ugh. Anyway. 'The car spun off the side of the road and into the ravine on the other side.

There was a terrible crash. The man jumped over the fence and ran down to the ravine.'" She looked up, her face grim. "Oh, my. The ghost of Probert Chandler said he didn't die in the car. Do you suppose he was whacked over the head? I'll bet you a basket of beignets he was. Ugh. Ugh. And Mrs. Nussbaum didn't go outside to check on him, I suppose. Anyway. To continue: 'My neighbors called the police, I think, because about ten minutes later an ambulance and a police car came. The man in the car was killed, I think.'"

Bree dropped the statement onto her desk. "Why in the name of heaven didn't the police interview this witness?"

"This lady hasn't been outside her house in years," Ron said. "She's agoraphobic. The cops did come to the door to get a witness statement, but she locked all her locks—she's got at least a dozen on her front door and more than that on the back—and yelled at them to go away."

Bree frowned. "Is she mentally competent?"

"Oh, yes. Just scared of the big bad world out there. And who's to blame her?" Ron's face grew grave. "You're not going to like the rest of this. The day after the crash, she started to get threatening phone calls. She took the phone off the hook and ordered locks for the windows."

"Would she be able to identity the voice?"

Ron thought about this. "Probably. But it's not going to be admissible evidence, Bree. We're going to have to get this statement verified by someone from the police department if we're going to use it in the temporal courts, and I don't know if I can coax her into going into it all over again."

Bree didn't need to ask how he'd gained Helen Nussbaum's confidence. It was the smile. Everything and everyone melted before that angelic smile. "Wow," she said.

Then again, "Wow. This is brilliant. We've got confirmation, guys! Probert Chandler was murdered!"

"I, too, have had some success with my Internet searches already," Petru said. He placed his cane crosswise on his knees and placed the file he'd brought carefully on top of it. "The plaintiff told you Marlowe's had a role in his demise, did he not?"

"We're making an assumption," Bree said carefully. "But I think it's a safe one. Especially because of the robberies."

She sat back in her chair and grinned at them. "Ron? How would you like to go undercover?"

Ron beamed and said, "Can I wear my fedora?"

"You can wear a bag over your head for all I care," Bree said recklessly. "Just get a job at the Marlowe's, and find out all you can. I want to know what was stolen, when it was stolen, and why there's been a terrific effort at a cover-up."

"No fedora," Ron said. "But I've got a great bowling jacket I can wear with my J.Crew jeans."

Petru cleared his throat.

"And yes, Petru. Now your summary."

"If we are to make a list of those connected with Marlowe's who wished to see Mr. Probert Chandler consigned as quickly as possible to the afterlife, it will be extensive. So I focused particularly on recent lawsuits, of the bitterer kind, on persons who lived here in Savannah on or about June third, and on men, of course, after I demanded that Ron share the results of his interview with Mrs. Nussbaum with me." He looked disapproving.

"How did you decide the depth of the bitterness?" Bree asked.

"The amount of fear expressed by persons in news articles and media interviews." Petru shook his head.

"La, la. It is quite remarkable, the hatred this man inspired, and equally remarkable that it has been most discreetly handled. Only the larger journals described these things. The *New York Times*. The *Wall Street Journal*."

"If it doesn't concern a rocker or a movie star, there's not a lot of interest from the public," Ron observed. "So you can forget about a lot of TV or Internet media time. But we can depend on the biggies."

"Perhaps. It is better for us. These unnoticed items will allow us to be clever." Petru took the top sheet from his file and handed it across the desk to Bree.

"Oh, my," she said in dismay. "You've listed what, eleven names here, Petru. All these people live here in Savannah and have an active motive for murder, so to speak?"

"I have divided the motives according to the most statistically probable reasons for same," Petru said. "We will set aside domestic and gang reasons. You would agree that this is not a domestic?"

Bree thought about it. "We can't rule it out. But I don't think Carrie-Alice cares enough about life to murder anyone, even a husband. And even if she did, well, she doesn't have the sneakiness, if you see what I mean. As for poor Lindsey, she doesn't seem to have the discipline. This murder was planned, and it was clever. And I'll bet you anything it was over money."

"I agree," Petru said. "And this light, that is used to terrify the deer, and indeed that terrified Mr. Probert Chandler, it is used by deer hunters, is it not? So I thought it would be an excellent thing if we began by eliminating those who love animals and begin with those that hunt them down. Thus, my preliminary list."

Bree wasn't too sure about the deer hunter angle, but it was as good a place to start as any. Petru could factor in the robbery motives after she had a good talk with Sam Hunter.

She looked at the names on Petru's sheet. Most of them small businessmen, it appeared. In four cases, Petru had appended a brief description of the lawsuits. Two of the men had criminal records, one for felony DUI, the other for fraud. "It's as good a place to start as any. We'll divide it up. Four for you, Petru, four for you, Ron, and three for me. Since we have an eyewitness that places the murderer at the scene, we'll begin with alibis. If any of these people were in Topeka on the night in question, for example, we can put him at the bottom of the list."

"Now you just give me them three," Lavinia said firmly. "We want to establish alibis for the night in question, ain't that so? I got me a great line in telephone interviewing. As a matter of fact, if you two come a-cropper with your interviews, you just leave those folks to me."

"Wow," Bree said, reviewing the list one more time. "Suspects. We've actually got a list of suspects." She sat back in her chair, the humiliating meeting with Abel finally at bay. "It's a long shot. But that's exactly how the police would go about solving this case, isn't it? And you know what? Sam Hunter's been willing to work off-line in the past. He might give us a hand with a background check on these guys. And once I turn Mrs. Nussbaum's witness statement over to him, he's got to reopen this case as a homicide."

Ron hesitated. "Mrs. Nussbaum's really nervous, Bree. And she's got a wonky heart. It wouldn't take much to send her home a little sooner than she should go."

Bree looked at the stacks of reports on her desk. The autopsy, the forensics exam of the automobile. There was a lot to absorb before she sat down with Cordelia at six.

"I'll keep Mrs. Nussbaum out of it, totally. I won't give Hunter her name—just the gist of what she saw. The murderer plunging down the hillside to nail poor Probert with that flashlight." She clapped her hands. "Suspects!

Can I keep this copy of the list, Ron? Sam Hunter might have some information about them. And Cordelia, we can't forget Cordelia. She'll want to get this case if we nail the murderer. It's high profile enough to give her a head start on the governor's race."

―――― ⚬⚬⚬ ――――

"You can forget the jury trial, Bree. I'm here to tell you we'll accept a plea."

Bree stared at her. Cordelia sat opposite her in a quiet booth at Huey's and stared coolly back. Bree hadn't been in the restaurant since she'd lost her temper and tossed Payton McAllister over the bar and started a small riot. She'd marched in the front door with an air of owning the place, figuring the best offense was her Brazen Hussy act. It worked. Other than a sharp, suspicious glare from Maureen the bartender, who was pretty good at the Brazen Hussy act herself, nobody said a word. But she didn't have to wait for service. She got her glass of white wine in record time.

"So make me an offer," Cordy said.

"You're kidding, right? You're dropping the case against Lindsey?"

"I don't want a lot of hoo-rah from you, Bree. Just talk to your client's mother and make me an offer."

"Wow. I didn't think God Himself could lean on you, Cordy, much less the Chandlers. Somebody *really* wants this to go away." Bree thumped her forehead. "Sorry. That was incredibly stupid. We, of course, would like credit for what my client's been through. Restitution's been made. The victim's withdrawn her complaint. She's already spent time in custody . . ."

"A couple of hours," Cordy said, expressionlessly. "And . . . ?"

"And had the humiliation of wearing the ankle brace-let. So. That's enough punishment, right? She's done."

"Okay. We'll send over the paperwork in the morning." Cordy ignored the remains of her diet cola and made a move to gather her purse and briefcase.

"Wait just a cotton-picking minute."

That made Cordy laugh, although not very hard. "I haven't heard that expression since I was a kid. As for the case—let it lie, Bree."

"I'll say it again, then. Somebody really wants this case to go away. I can't believe that somebody got to *you*, Cordelia. You were so sure about the justice of prosecuting this case. Officially, of course, I'm delighted to see that my client is being treated with the consideration she deserves. And unofficially, I'd really like to know who got to you."

Cordy stood up. She was a small woman with a big presence, and she loomed over Bree like a linebacker. "You're dramatizing this out of all proportion, Bree. This is a small-time crime with no real victims. As for me?" Her eyes narrowed and her face grew fierce. "Don't you ever think I can be bought. But I do know when to pick my battles. And this case of petty theft isn't worth it."

"It's not just a case of petty theft. It's a case of murder."

"What!" Cordelia sat down with a thud. She looked really angry. "Nobody's dead. What in the name of sweet Jesus are you talking about?"

"Probert Chandler's death. I have proof it was murder."

Cordy closed her eyes, as if she'd reached her limit. "First off, what does Probert Chandler have to do with the Girl Scout mess?"

"I don't know yet."

Cordy sniffed contemptuously. "So when you do, let me know."

"I don't know yet," Bree continued doggedly, "but there's a connection. As for Probert Chandler, I've got an eyewitness that says somebody jumped out at Chandler's Buick as it was coming around that bend and jacked the car with a deer light."

Cordy stared at her. Bree held her hand up in an "as God is my witness" gesture. "That's solid?"

"Yes."

"And the witness is who?"

"Can't tell you that yet." Cordy swelled, a bit like an angry bullfrog. Bree grabbed her hand and clung to it. "But I'll let you know just as soon as I can. Trust me, Cordy. Please."

Cordy rubbed her chin and muttered under her breath. "If that's true, there is a case. I'll give you that. But I don't know that it's murder, though. Reckless endangerment, maybe. But murder?" Cordy's interest was caught. That was clear from the set of her jaw. She grabbed her diet cola and sipped it. "What else have you got?"

"He didn't die in the car," Bree said.

"Come again?"

"Chandler didn't die in the car. Somebody knocked him off the road, hopped down into the ravine, and killed him. I looked at the autopsy report just after we spoke today." She dug into her briefcase and pulled out the sheet listing the body's injuries. "He died from a crack to the skull, *probably* after striking his head on the windshield, but you can see for yourself." She waved the autopsy report in the air. "It's a definite maybe. There's a strong suggestion that there was a second blow, a harder blow that conclusively caused the brain damage."

"A car going down that ravine would bounce around a lot."

"And he smacked his head in the same place twice?"

"He was strapped in, wasn't he? Fixed in place."

"He didn't have his seat belt on, according to the police report. But!—and this is an important but—there are marks on the chest consistent with abrasions from the belt. So he was strapped *in* when he went off the road. And then somebody unstrapped him and slammed him over the head with a roundish, heavy object."

"Like the dashboard."

"Like a huge flashlight for jacking deer."

"Could the belt have loosened in the crash?"

"You know the likelihood of that happening. Practically zero, unless the buckle was defective. And it wasn't. It was a new car. And there's nothing in the reports about any damage that could have sprung the seat belt mechanism. Not only that, there were grass stains on his trousers."

"He could have gotten those anywhere. He'd been golfing that afternoon, for God's sake."

"We can check that, of course."

"Huh." Cordy's responses indicated she was on autopilot. She mused for a long moment. "You really think there's something in this." It wasn't a question.

"I really do."

"And this eyewitness. Is he willing to come forward? Is there any backup to this stuff?"

"No and no. Not at the moment. But I think if I keep digging I'll be able to come up with sufficient evidence to make a real case." She hesitated. "There's something else, too. Something big, although not as big as murder. I was planning on running it by you this evening, but under the circumstances, maybe not. Not yet."

"What circumstances would those be?"

"Somebody's putting pressure on you, Cordy. So until I've got a whole truckload of cold hard facts, I'll keep it to myself."

"Fine by me. Go ahead and stay cryptic." Cordy

cocked her head and looked at Bree assessingly. "So who's your client? The widow?"

"I'm not at liberty to disclose that just now."

"But you're telling me somebody's hired you to bring a case of murder to the attention of my office. Somebody with a stake in the outcome, say. The widow?"

"I'm not at lib—"

"Yeah, yeah. Well, you watch your step, Miss Bree. You find evidence that a crime of this magnitude's been committed on my patch, there's not enough governors in the United States of America to keep me off it. Oops, forget I said that."

The governor's office. Well, well, well. Bree smiled. Cordy's verbal slip was dropped with just the right air of "golly gee."

"I've got a church meeting." Cordy slipped her purse strap over her arm and slid out of the booth. "You know Sam Hunter, at the PD? 'Course you do. The man's smitten. Smitten." She chuckled at the chagrined expression on Bree's face. "No one should know better than you that this is a small town, Miss Bree. But he's a good man in a pinch, or so I hear. And pretty discreet. You might want to run that stack of 'maybe so's' and 'what if's' right by him."

"Thanks. I just might do that."

"You get anything I can use in a court of law, I want to hear about it. Sooner than quick."

"It's a deal."

Cordelia took her time leaving Huey's. She stopped at the bar and shook a few hands, lingered by a few tables, then left the restaurant trailing goodwill and determination. She'd make one heck of a governor when the time came. But she was too wily a politician to stick her neck out on so tenuous a case, and Bree, for one, couldn't blame her.

She looked at the remainder of white wine in her glass, and left it. It was close on seven, she still hadn't had any dinner, and she had to drop in on the Chandlers to discuss the plea with Lindsey and her mother.

And perhaps get herself an official client, one that could support her investigation into Probert's untimely demise.

Fourteen

What is incident but the illustration of character?
—*Partial Portraits*, Henry James

"You think my husband was murdered?" Carrie-Alice looked faintly disgusted, as if she'd discovered ants in her sock drawer. "No one's said a word about that before."

"An eyewitness has come forward."

"Now? After all this time? Why?"

"A matter of conscience, I suppose." Bree hesitated, then smiled briefly. "Put it down to the offices of a good angel."

Carrie-Alice got up and walked agitatedly around the room. She'd been at home, sitting in front of the TV in the near dark, when the maid let Bree into the house. "I can't believe it. I just can't believe it." She'd turned on one lamp and turned off the TV and the room was dark with shadows. The freesias sitting in the vase on the mantel were dying and a scent of rotting flowers filled the air. She picked up a framed family portrait that sat on the coffee table in their living room. Carrie-Alice and her husband stood side by side, their three children grouped around them. "I suppose this will be smeared all over the news, just like this thing with Lindsey." She laid the photo facedown. "Why can't people just leave us alone?"

Bree didn't bother to point out that their staggering

wealth was one reason why, and Lindsey's provocative behavior was the other.

"Well, I can't imagine what you want me to do about it," Carrie-Alice said with an exhausted sigh. "Murdered. It doesn't make any sense."

"The DA's office is willing to take a look at this, as long as we can provide them enough evidence to make a case. Right now, we don't have it. I mean, we do, but it isn't admissible. I'd like your permission to take things a little further."

Carrie-Alice worried at her lower lip with her teeth. "I don't see that it's going to do anybody any good, digging up the past." Her lips quirked in a grim smile. "Or Probert himself, for that matter." She hesitated. "My kids are home. George and Kath, I mean. I asked them to come home for a while. This thing with their sister's just worn me out. I suppose you should talk to them about it. But I can't see that it would make any difference." She looked around the large living room, as if she'd misplaced all three of them. "They took her to the movies."

"Lindsey? George and Katharine took Lindsey to the movies?" Bree was exasperated and finding it harder than she should to keep her tone courteous. She wanted to take Carrie-Alice by the shoulders and shake her. She hoped she wasn't becoming callous. The woman was recently widowed. She was dealing with a lot of unwanted notoriety. Maybe she was just too overwhelmed. Maybe that explained her lack of real concern. And maybe it didn't. Maybe she thought her son and her older daughter had something to do with the murder. It wouldn't be the first time. Look at the Menendez brothers. The only thing Bree knew for sure was that Carrie-Alice Chandler was a hard woman to figure out.

"Yes. Lindsey was whining about being cooped up. The only one of her friends who's been to see her is

Madison." Her glance at Bree was unexpectedly shrewd. "And I think Madison dropped by more because Andrea insisted than anything else."

Some of Bree's coolness must have shown in her face. Carrie-Alice looked away. She put her hand to her forehead. "I'm sorry. I'm forgetting what few manners my folks taught me. Can I get you some coffee? Tea? A cola?"

What Bree wanted was dinner and a glass of white wine and a good night's sleep. And maybe a workout at the gym. Her back muscles ached with the inactivity of the past few days. "Perhaps both of us could do with a glass of tea," she said brusquely.

There was an intercom on the wall next to the foyer. Carrie-Alice pressed it. "Norah? Could you bring tea for us, please? And some crackers and cheese? Thank you." She clasped her hands together, sank back into her chair, and took a deep breath. For the first time since Bree had met her, she let her guard down. Her eyes lost that distant, detached look. She said, as if admitting to murder herself, "I just can't get used to not doing things myself. You know? And to having somebody who isn't family in the house, touching my things. Bert was the same way. There's so much stuff that comes with having the kind of money we've got. I hate it. I just hate it. Having maids, and cooks, and people to do the gardening. I resisted it for a long time. Then I'd be up at three in the morning trying to get the ironing done, and scrubbing out the bathrooms, and Bert finally put his foot down. So we hired staff." She looked sidelong at Bree, a little timidly.

"There's a lot of satisfaction in doing your own work, surely," Bree said. "And it's got to be hard, adjusting to the sort of wealth Mr. Chandler amassed." On impulse, she reached over and put her hand on Carrie-Alice's. It was icy cold. "You aren't all that comfortable with your husband's success, I take it."

"You don't know the half of it."

The maid, a quiet, neatly put together woman of about Carrie-Alice's age, came in and set a tea tray on the table. She began to pour out.

"But there's a lot of very satisfying things that you can do with piles of money. Why, look at the Gates family. You can take care of things yourself—maybe just not the old, familiar things like housework."

Carrie-Alice made a face. "Bert didn't hold with most kinds of charity. It begins at home, he said. And I'll tell you this. He came up from nothing. Absolutely nothing. And look where it got him. This is America, Miss Beaufort. Bert always felt people with enough drive can get anywhere, and I think that, too. People who are poor want to be poor."

Bree shot a glance at Norah, who winked and said, "Anything else, Mrs. Chandler?"

"No, thank you. Now look at Norah," Carrie-Alice continued, as the maid left the room. "We pay her the going rate for a woman with a high school education. And she chooses to be—what's the expression Cissy uses?—in service. Nobody forced her to come to work for us. Just as nobody forces people to work at Probert's stores. I mean, slavery went out in 1863. Everybody's got a choice."

"That's not true," Bree said, keeping her voice as even as she could. "There's not much of a choice when the higher paying jobs have been driven out of an economy because of stores like Marlowe's." She held her hand up. "I'm not here to get into a wrangle over the cost of free markets with you, Mrs. Chandler. But I will say this. I do believe that the more you've got, the more you're obligated to share. And I apologize for upsetting you when I'm a guest in your home. I do have an obligation to talk this offer from the DA's office over with you, however. So perhaps we should discuss that."

Carrie-Alice's face was pink. Bree was pretty sure her face was pink, too. Any brief rapport the two women had was gone. "Well!" she said. She looked at her watch. "George and Kath took Lindsey to the six o'clock show at the multiplex. It's over by now and they'll be back any minute. I waited dinner for them. As far as Lindsey goes, I suppose we'll do whatever it is that she wants to do." She raised her head at the sound of activity at the front door. "There they are," she said with obvious relief. "We can get this over with."

Probert Chandler's two older children walked into the room. George looked exactly like a twenty-something Harry Truman, down to the wire-rimmed glasses and the genial smile. Katherine was a tubby, untidy woman with soft brown hair and sensible shoes. She was dressed in an extremely well cut pantsuit.

Both of them looked worried.

"Where's Lindsey?" Carrie-Alice demanded.

"We'd hoped she was here." George looked around the living room. "She's not?"

Katherine sat down in a chintz chair with a grunt of annoyance. "We walked all over the darn multiplex looking for her, Mother. And then when we decided to give up and come home, we discovered that she'd swiped the car. And she's not answering her cell phone."

"She got up to go to the john and didn't come back," George said. "Kath went in to look for her and she wasn't anywhere to be found." He bent over the tea tray and took a cookie. "We had to take a cab back here. Cost me eighty bucks."

"She can't have gotten far," Bree said. "She's wearing the ankle bracelet, isn't she?"

"I didn't think of that!" George said. He scowled. "What do we do now? Call the police?"

"More police," Katherine wailed. "I can't stand it!"

"If she's gone out of the permissible range of the signal, the police will be tracking her," Bree said. "She's not a high-priority risk. If she were, the police would have contacted you by now. But yes, it'd be a good idea to call. You want her brought back here, I take it?"

"Would they keep her downtown?" Katherine asked. The three Chandlers looked meaningfully at each other. Katherine spoke first. "Just kidding. Of course she's got to come back here. This is her home."

Bree nodded. She took out her cell and dialed the station number from memory. "They've got her on radar, so to speak," Bree said, after she concluded the call. "It shouldn't be long."

"This is Miss Winston-Beaufort," Carrie-Alice said belatedly. "She's here because the DA's office is willing to bargain, or negotiate, or something. We may not have to go to trial after all."

"So we got that Eastburn woman to see some sense," George said. "Good."

Bree took a closer look at him. There was a lot she needed to know from Mr. George Tyburn Chandler. "Did you have something to do with this, Mr. Chandler? This sudden"—she searched for a politic word—"accommodation on the part of the State?"

"Me?" His glance slid sideways. "There've been some discussions on how to handle this at the home office, sure. I wasn't about to see my little sister spend time in the joint."

The slang sat awkwardly on him, like an ill-fitting suit.

"The discussions seem to have borne fruit," Bree said dryly. "I think if we petition the DA's office to dismiss the charges based on time served, we'll be successful."

"What about this upset tonight?" Katherine asked. She joined her brother at the plate of cookies. "She's breaking parole, or something."

"We'll see," Bree said. "But I don't think the DA's any more anxious to pursue this than you are."

"She's here on another matter, too," Carrie-Alice said. "It's about your father."

"Dad?" George brushed crumbs from his chin. "Something about Dad?"

Bree got up and strolled toward him, so she could see his face clearly. She was going to hold her questions about the warehouse robberies in reserve, until Ron came back with more information and until she'd talked to Sam Hunter. "Yes, there's some pretty compelling evidence that the car crash that killed him was no accident. That it was murder."

The word hung in the air like dirty laundry.

"What!" Katherine clapped her hands over her mouth. Then she said, "You've got to be kidding. This is some kind of horrible joke."

George shook his head. "I don't think it's a joke. And I think Miss Beaufort's right." He nodded at her. "I've had a lot of questions about Dad's death. It's about time someone else had questions, too."

"She wants to look into it more," Carrie-Alice said. "More reporters hanging around the house. More news stories. I can't stand it."

"We've got to do what's right." George sat down on the couch next to his mother and took out his checkbook. "So we'll hire her to get right on with it."

∽∽∽

"So that kind of squashes any hope I had of patricide," Bree said.

Antonia choked on her yogurt. "Will you *listen* to yourself?"

Bree grinned. "I'm a tough cookie, aren't I?"

Antonia waved her spoon in the air. "The toughest!

I'm so proud. That's my sister, folks." She sang (and paraphrased) Professor Higgins's song about being an ordinary man: " *'She has the milk of human kindness by the quart in every vein. A simple girl she is, down to her fingertips, the sort who never could, never would, let a rude opinion pass her lips.'* I did tell you we're doing *My Fair Lady* after the Holmes run is over, didn't I? What do you want to bet on me doing Eliza?"

"I won't bet on a certainty."

Antonia looked enormously pleased.

The two of them lay relaxed in the living room. Antonia was on her third cup of yogurt. Bree was too tired to eat anything. She'd driven home from the Chandlers' with a check for five thousand dollars in her briefcase and a hollow taste of victory in her mouth. "I totally get it about your cynicism, though."

Bree was startled. "Was that cynical? Am I getting cynical?"

"And why not? You've told me over and over again that justice works just as well for the rich as it does for the poor . . ."

"Most times," Bree said. "I said most times."

"And here's a prime example of a little brat princess getting off of a particularly heinous crime . . ."

"I wouldn't call snatching a shoebox of money from a Girl Scout heinous," Bree said doubtfully. "Crummy. Impulsive. Ill judged. But not heinous. Heinous is whacking poor old Probert Chandler over the head with a giant flashlight and leaving him for dead in the rain."

"True," Antonia said soberly, "very true."

"But I am glad that I can proceed with the investigation into Chandler's death with some legitimacy now." She chuckled. "Although George may not like the commotion over the warehouse robberies, if robberies they were, and if we're able to get the police department on to them. This is all connected somehow, Tonia. I'm sure of it."

"It is?"

"Absolutely. The Girl Scout incident, the warehouse robberies, Chandler's murder—all three."

"If you say so," Antonia said dubiously. "You're pretty sure of yourself, don't you think? Isn't Daddy always telling us not to jump to conclusions? Feels to me like you're doing the broad jump."

Daddy didn't have a ghostly client telling him the case rested on those connections, either. But Bree didn't say that aloud. *Lindsey. Marlowe's. Blood. Blood. Blood.*

"Don't you think it's truly weird that the corporation's making this big effort to keep the warehouse robberies out of the news? And isn't it even weirder that they're managing to do it? Can you imagine covering up that scale of crime?"

Antonia shrugged.

"So the question is Why? I know why," she answered herself. "Bad publicity is a big part of it. Like a clutch of Caesar's wives, they are. Needing to be above suspicion or reproach. But there's something else. And I'm going to get to the bottom of it."

Antonia yawned. "So you've got another fat-cat paying client, Bree. Good on you. But what convinced you that this Chandler was murdered? I mean, you figured that out way before all this stuff about the autopsy and the eyewitness statement from poor old Mrs. Nussbaum came out." A looked of pleased awe came over her face. "Hey! Maybe you're psychic! Are you, Bree? Would that be totally cool, or what?"

Bree shook her head and glanced nervously at her twin sentinels. Belli and Miles sat on either side of the fireplace, staring at them both with yellow eyes. Antonia had anticipated the need for a hundred-pound bag of dog

food and picked up a huge bag of Iams on her way back
from her afternoon duties at the theater. She'd fed the two
huge dogs herself, and Miles, at least, had unbent enough
to lick her face. That was enough for Tonia, who loved
animals as much as Bree did, as long as, she said, they
didn't remind her of a Godzilla movie.

"Which, you know, they still do. Remind me of a
Godzilla movie, that is. But it's a nice kindly Godzilla,
not the pissed-off one."

"Hm?" Bree had been gazing up at the mirror over the
fireplace. The frame was made of some old bronzy metal.
She remembered the day Great-Uncle Franklin had
dragged it into the town house. She'd been about ten, she
thought, and the family was taking a long weekend in Savannah, as they occasionally did. Her mother had pitched
a fit. A Francesca-style fit wasn't all that dramatic, unless
you were a family member and used to her generally sunny
disposition. "Remember Mamma demanding that Uncle
Franklin take that mirror to the dump?"

"No. Should I?"

"You were about four at the time. So never mind."

They were both sprawled on the couch in front of the
fireplace. Antonia poked Bree with her toe. "How come
you didn't call me back earlier today? The theater's dark
on Mondays. I thought maybe we'd go down to Huey's for
a big shrimp salad. But it's too late now."

"Phone calls," Bree said. "Darn. I meant to call Sam
Hunter back. But you're right. It's too late now."

"Oh, yeah?" Antonia wriggled her eyebrows. "Maybe
he wanted to take you out to Huey's."

"It's more likely he called to tell me to butt out of the
Chandler case. Ron was over at the PD today, scarfing up
autopsy and forensic reports. That's bound to set him
off."

"But he's going to change his mind now, right?" Antonia yawned suddenly. "Gosh. It's only ten thirty, and I'm beat. I think I'm going to go to bed early for a change."

Bree grabbed her sister's ankle and shook it affectionately. "Good idea. I'm going to take a long hot bath, and go to bed myself."

"Well, I'm taking a long hot bath first."

"Make it a shower and use the little bathroom, will you? I don't want to hang around waiting for you to finish piddling around."

Antonia flounced off the couch and made a rude noise. But a few minutes later, Bree heard her banging around in the small bathroom, so she got up and unpinned her hair. Sasha, who'd been dozing in the middle of the living room floor, woke suddenly and stared intently at the phone on the stand by the front door.

The phone rang. Bree froze. The sound was insistent and invasive, and she was very sure she didn't want to answer it. Sasha looked at her.

Bad news.

"How bad, Sasha? It's not Mamma, is it? Or my father?"

Sasha squeezed his eyes shut and opened them again, and the worst fear ebbed from Bree's heart. But she still didn't want to answer the phone.

The bathroom door banged open. "Are you going to get that?!" Antonia shrieked excitedly from the hall. "It might be L.A. calling! It's only seven thirty there!"

Belli and Miles growled like a pair of ore trams rattling through the depths of a mine.

"Bree!" Antonia danced angrily into the room, wearing a large towel, sarong-style, and a furious expression. "For God's sake!"

"Why would L.A. be calling?"

"Because I've signed up with an agent there, that's why. You knew that." She grabbed the handset and said, with an abrupt change of tone, "Hel-lo. Antonia Winston-Beaufort here. Oh. It's you. Yes. She's here." *Sam Hunter,* she mouthed at Bree. "And she was going to call you back today, Lieutenant, but as you know she's busy busy bus—"

Bree snatched the phone out of her hand. "Hello, Lieutenant. Why am I sure I don't want to hear what you have to tell me? It's not Lindsey, is it?"

"Lindsey Chandler? No. Patrol picked her up about forty-five minutes ago and took her home. I called because of something else."

"What is it? Where are you?"

"I'm at the Seaton Stud. The owner here, Missy Trask, asked me to call you."

"Missy couldn't call me herself?" Bree said stupidly. "Is she all right? What's wrong?" An urgent, utter panic hit her. "Abel? Is Abel okay?"

"She's in a bit of a state." Hunter was tired, and when he was tired, he got brusque. "Might be a good idea if you can get on over here."

"Lieutenant!" Bree's voice was tight. "What's going on? Why are you there?"

"Why?" he asked grimly. "Because I'm at a crime scene, Miz Beaufort, looking at the body of Shirley Chavez, lately of this parish."

Fifteen

"This is *all* your fault!" Missy Trask's face was blotched with tears and cold with rage. "Stirring things up! You come out here with those damn black dogs like some damn vulture and look. Just *look*!" Her sturdy body quivered with fury. She wore the clothes she'd worn that afternoon. The flannel shirt was the worse for wear; she'd pulled the tail free from her jeans to wipe her face and tucked half of it into her waistband. The other half flapped free.

Bree looked, although she didn't want to. The Chatham County scene of crime team had erected huge floodlights in a fifty-foot-wide area around Shirley's body. Her hands and feet were bagged in plastic. A photographer snapped pictures of the gory mess of her skull. She'd been shot down in an alleyway between two of the barns. Worried horses poked their heads out of their stalls. Their stamps and snorts added a surreal undercurrent to the mutters of the swarm of technicians and police officials. A small family group huddled against the walls of the barn to the left of the corpse. Mr. Chavez, most probably, and two olive-skinned, dark-haired teenagers. All three were weeping.

"I'm afraid you might be right," Bree said quietly. She closed her eyes and swallowed. This *was* her fault.

"She was so excited over that whacking damn check you people gave her. Well, you bought her and then you buried her. I hope you people are proud of what you've done."

"Missy." Abel stood by quietly. He came forward and took her gently by the shoulders. "I want you to go into the house and wash your face." He glanced over her head at Sam Hunter, who was standing with his hands shoved into the pockets of his chinos. "Are you through with her?"

"We'll need a signed statement from her about the discovery of the body, but yeah, go on ahead. I'll send someone on up to the house as soon as we've finished here."

Abel smiled at Bree, a rueful twist to his lips. "I'll be back in a few minutes. I've got to get Virginia settled. Will you be here a while?"

Bree nodded. Her face felt frozen. Sasha stood at her knee, subdued, his attention drawn to the busy figures at the site of the body. Hunter glanced swiftly from Bree to Abel and back again. He waited until Abel's tall figure led Missy off into the darkness that lay beyond the circle of artificial lights.

"I'm sorry about this," he said. "Mrs. Trask said you'd visited Shirley Chavez this afternoon. She seemed to think you'd have some idea of the motive behind the killing. I didn't realize she was so upset with you."

"She liked Shirley." Sasha thrust his warm nose into her hand, and she cupped his head. There was something very calming about the shape of a dog's head beneath your hand. Bree stroked the dog and stared at the ground. Anything rather than look at that poor huddled form beneath the lights and hear the weeping family in the shadows. "Missy has a right to be angry. She lost her husband just three weeks ago, so she's a bit fragile to begin with. This is another horrible injustice. You knew Charles Trask had died?"

Hunter nodded. "Fell and broke his neck jumping a horse over a fence." He sounded faintly surprised that something like that could happen. "I've been a good city kid all my life. Can't see the attraction in it."

"Hunting can be a dangerous sport."

"Especially for the fox."

Was that disapproval in his voice? Bree looked up. "They haven't had a live hunt here in years. They use a drag."

Hunter quirked his eyebrow up.

"A drag is a pouch saturated with a chemical scent. The hounds follow that instead of . . . you're trying to distract me up, aren't you?"

"I'd like to get that look off your face."

Bree looked at her feet again. "I do feel responsible for this, Hunter."

"You want to tell me why?"

She hesitated, trying to order her thoughts. "There's some connection here. It's just not clear to me yet."

"Connection between what?" Hunter demanded.

Marlowe's. The warehouse. My daughter. Help me. Help me.

"This murder. Probert Chandler's murder. And a couple of robberies at the Marlowe's warehouse on Route 80."

Hunter's lips tightened to a thin line. But all he said was, "What robberies?"

"I was hoping you could tell me." She leaned forward, the better to see his expression.

Hunter's face darkened in the glare of the harsh lights. "I don't have time for this," he said tightly.

"You haven't had any reports of any break-ins out at the Marlowe's warehouse?"

"No." He stared back at her, his gaze as assessing as hers. "You know something. What?"

He wasn't hiding anything from her. She was sure of it. "Shirley told me someone's been stealing pallets of PSE from Marlowe's. And that the corporate types have been all over the local guys, trying to keep it quiet."

Hunter didn't say anything for a long moment. His face was totally expressionless. Finally, he said, "Let me get back to you on that."

"You promise?"

"If you promise to tell me about anything, *anything* that you turn up as soon as you get it."

"Sure. As long as you give me a little time to set up my own case."

Hunter rubbed the back of his neck and stared up at the night sky. She could hear him taking several deep breaths. "You aren't seriously suggesting I compromise an investigation on behalf of a civilian? Or that I forget that I'm working for the Chatham County Police Department?"

"Of course not!" Bree straightened up belligerently. She looked around the busy area. "Is there a place where we can sit down?"

"I'm finished here, for the moment. Forensics is in the middle of doing their thing, and I've got two detectives taking statements from the workers. Let's go into the farm office." He flipped open his cell phone, told whoever was on the other end of the transmission where he'd be, and followed her back across the paved courtyard to the old brick building. Somebody had made a fresh pot of coffee in the automatic pot that sat on the worn pine credenza. Bree poured both of them a cup. The heat warmed her hands. The shock of the incident was wearing off.

She sat down in the chair across from the desk and tried to kick her brain into first gear. "Let me start with what I know for sure: a representative of the Chandler family authorized Stubblefield, Marwick to give the Chavez family five hundred thousand dollars to drop any civil charges against Lindsey."

Hunter crossed his arms and rested his head against the office wall. "Okay. Quite a sum. But I suppose they can afford it. This led to someone blowing a hole through Shirley Chavez's skull?"

Bree ignored Hunter's bluntness. "The Chandlers can afford to buy the state of Rhode Island. I don't know which Chandler it was. And it's important. Because I think Shirley was killed because of what she knows about a series of robberies at the warehouse."

"I haven't heard—"

Bree cut him off with an upraised hand. "This is all conjecture, Sam. Can you just let me think aloud for a second?"

Something in her voice—which was almost shrill with her tension—made him back off. Or maybe it was his given name, which she rarely used. "It was George who authorized the payoff, possibly. He seems to have a little more influence with the corporation than I'd been led to believe. And he's Stubblefield, Marwick's client."

Hunter focused on her statement. "Wealthy heir to the family fortune starts in the mailroom and works his way up?"

Bree's smile was wider this time, and genuine. "Well, that's just it. I called my paralegal as I was driving over here, to see if we had any information on who inherited what when Probert Chandler died. He'd already settled a relatively modest amount of money on each of his children as soon as they hit twenty-five. The remainder of the family fortune is left in trust to his wife, who in turn will leave it to the three kids, although Lindsey's will be in trust until she's twenty-five, too. The mind boggles at the thought of that kid with a third of twenty billion. Anyhow. This is a traditional family—can you imagine leaving twenty billion dollars to your widow? That just isn't done with these huge fortunes, Hunter. Trust me. There are all kinds of tax issues. Anyway, so none of the three kids benefited by his death. At least, not on the surface. If Carrie-Alice had been in the car with Probert, that would have been another issue altogether." She broke off, thinking about this. Hunter cleared his throat impatiently. "These trust funds include huge amounts of voting stock. So, of course George will get whatever George wants in that company, despite the fact that his job title is junior mailroom clerk, or whatever it happens to be. A lot of the wealth is in stock." Bree took a deep breath. "I'll tell you what's impressed me so far about this case. The spin. The fact that the public perception of Probert and his clan is poor boy makes good. That George is the humble scion of a thrifty hardworking billionaire. The complete silence around the warehouse robberies. Squashing Cordelia, which is almost impossible to do. And this is all *after* Probert himself has died."

"So George calls the shots?"

"That's my guess. But it's a guess, at this point. Now for more puzzles. You know as well as I do that buying off a victim is illegal, the way that Payton McAllister did it. Which is stupid. Because if they'd gone the private-settlement route to settle a civil suit, nobody would think twice about it. Just another rotten-rich family buying justice. You see what I mean? So that's an anomaly. The only possible reason to buy off the Chavezes this way is speed. The Chavezes withdraw the complaint and boom! the case drops off the radar. Shirley said Payton McAllister was out at her house by four o'clock the afternoon of the assault on Sophie. George—if it is George behind this—hadn't counted on his sister loving the limelight. Instead of the case being decently buried, next thing he knows, she's on Savannah's most notorious talk show, being as bad a kid as she can possibly be. And they can't snatch her off to a nice little clinic somewhere, because the police and DA's office are already involved, and she's under arrest." Bree suppressed a laugh. "George must have felt as if he was playing Whac-a-Mole."

"And the murder?"

"Which one?" Bree got up and began to pace around the room.

"Cordy gave me a call," Hunter said after the silence had stretched on.

"She did," Bree said. She darted a glance at him. His face was forbidding. But he wasn't yelling at her to turn over the name of the witness. At least not yet.

"Unofficially," he said wryly. "And I had to agree to sit on it until you delivered on your promise. She said something about forty-eight hours?"

Bree made a face. "If that's what she said, that's what I get."

"So you think this guy, the one that jacked Chandler's car in Skidaway Road and then went down into the ravine after, is the same guy who showed up later to keep Shirley quiet?"

"It leaps out at you, doesn't it? I mean it tracks."

Hunter yawned. "Sorry. I had a late night yesterday, and tonight's not going to end early. No, it doesn't necessarily track. It's a theory. And you're making way too many assumptions."

"Which is why you should let me go forward with investigating this case. So I can clear up these assumptions."

"Here's something to investigate." There was more

than a trace of sarcasm in the tone of his voice. "Why kill Shirley Chavez? So word leaks out there's been a payoff. So what?"

"Well, that should leap out at you, too, Lieutenant," she snapped. "Because I've been poking around into Probert Chandler's murder, that's why. If I find the guy that killed Shirley, I find the guy that smashed Probert over the head with the high-beam flashlight." She bit her lip to keep her tears back. The image of Shirley Chavez's shattered skull was as real to her as the look on Hunter's face. "Missy was right. I stirred this whole thing up." She cleared her throat loudly. "This should make it easier to catch him, anyhow. He must have left some forensic evidence this time. And you guys are good and thorough, right?"

"Maybe." Hunter flipped his cell phone open and spoke into it. "Markham? I want you to include something else in the background check on everyone who set foot on the farm today. I'm looking for a connection to Marlowe's or the Marlowe's lawyer. Stubblefield, that's right." He grinned sourly into the phone. "Yeah, wouldn't that be nice? But he's got a gofer on point for this one. Lawyer by the name of Payton McAllister." He slipped the cell phone back in his pocket. "Interesting leads. There'd be more than a few of us on the force that'd be happy to nail Stubblefield."

Bree's own opinion was that it'd be a true community service, but she said, "What can you tell me about the case here? Missy Trask found the body? Is that right? Did anyone see anything? Do you have any leads?"

Hunter stood away from the wall and stretched. "I'm going to get Mrs. Trask's written statement right now. I can't stop you if you want to go with me."

This, from Hunter, was a major concession. But Bree hesitated. Abel was with Missy. And Virginia, too. Bree was tired. It'd been a long day with a truly hideous end. If she had to confront Missy's accusing face one more time, and in front of Abel, too, she'd die on the spot. Virginia would be there, too, who'd loathed Bree from the moment she'd set eyes on her all those years ago at Plessey. But God hates a coward, and most policemen do, too.

"Fine," she said aloud. "I'll just tag right along, if you don't mind."

She trailed Hunter out into the dark. The rain had cleared, and the sky was swept with mist. The moon showed palely through the wisps, and the night was still, except for the clatter from the barns where the forensics team tramped up and down. There were no media yet, but it was only a matter of time.

When Ashbury Seaton invested in racehorses in 1883, he'd had a lot of cheap labor to run his stable and a lot of land to build on. Seaton House was a two-story, rambling structure that had started out as a small, six-room plantation house in the late eighteenth century. Succeeding generations of Seatons grew cotton, then tobacco, and finally, with a prescience not usual to Southern businessmen at the time, moved into railroad stock and freed their slaves just at the start of the Civil War. The brick office building had been sort of a dower house, where a succession of strong-minded Seaton matriarchs found themselves banished as their sons and daughters married and took over the business. It was located less than two hundred yards from the big house. The shortest route between the buildings was this brick-paved path that led to the kitchens in the back.

The light from the office windows spread a faint glow over the ground outside. Bree looked for the little wooden gate that fenced off the brick path to the house, and unlatched it, letting Sasha go through first. She motioned Hunter to follow. "We'll go this way," Bree said. "It's shorter, and maybe we can coax Missy into the kitchen, away from the crowd." She stepped onto the path. Late rambling roses reached out for her ankles, and she tripped a little over a particularly obtrusive root. Hunter caught her arm and eased her upright. "You've been here before?"

"This afternoon, obviously," she said tartly.

Hunter glanced at her, the same sharp, penetrating look he'd given Abel. "You know the family well?"

"No. Not well. When I was younger . . ." She ignored his derisive snort. "Okay, a few years back, when I was still riding, I was here drag hunting a couple of times. It's a good hunt. And the horses are marvelous. My folks bought more than one hunter from the Trasks, and not a dud in the bunch."

She could almost feel Hunter's withdrawal, as he walked along the path behind her. Well, he'd asked, hadn't he? And she couldn't change her family, or her own past experience, and it was just too flippin' bad if he didn't like it.

The lights were on in the kitchen, as she'd expected them to be. She knocked lightly at the back door, and smiled at the woman who opened it. "It's Delight Rawlings, isn't it?"

"That it is," she said gravely, "and you're Miss Bree Beaufort. I remember you from the hunt breakfasts a few years back."

Bree stepped inside the kitchen, Hunter and Sasha both at her heels. "This is Lieutenant Hunter from the police. Lieutenant, Delight Rawlings is the woman who holds the household here together. We're here to see Mrs. Trask, Delight. We thought we'd come in the back way and avoid creating too much of a fuss. Everything must be at sixes and sevens up front."

"That it is," Delight said with an explosive sigh. "Such goings-on, I never did see. Well, now, I'm a liar. It's just like *Law & Order*. But that's TV, if y'all know what I mean, and this here's real life. You want I should fetch Miz Trask?"

"Please." Bree sank down in a chair at the huge pine kitchen table.

"I'll just do that. You help yourselves to coffee if you want some. And there's some oatmeal cookies, fresh baked." Her eyes slid to Hunter. "I sent some of the cookies out to your folks. I hope that's all right."

"Very kind of you, ma'am. Very."

"I'll be back directly."

Hunter wandered around the kitchen as the housekeeper rolled out the swinging doors that led to the front of the house. The kitchen was large, perhaps twenty by forty, and it was dominated by a large brick fireplace with an old iron spit. An ancient ten-burner gas stove sat under the windows that looked out over the back gardens. The cabinets were a hodgepodge of styles, ranging from battered pine cupboards, painted a peeling white, to a couple of Home Depot specials faced with synthetic thermo glaze.

"Not quite what I expected," Hunter said. He stared up at a ham that dangled from the rafters.

"There's a smokehouse out back. It's still in use. But Missy cares more about the barns than the house. Most of her family did, too. They never did spend much on the inside of their houses, the Seatons." She raised her head and listened. Sasha, sprawled at her feet, raised his head, too.

Four of them coming; one's in a wheelchair.

Wonderful. Virginia was still up.

And still a shrieking pain in the neck. She was first through the doorway, shoving the swinging doors aside with an impatient hand. She barreled through at top speed, or so it seemed to Bree, who jumped out of the way as Virginia rolled to a halt.

"Bree Beaufort, as I live and breathe."

"Hi, Virginia. You're looking well."

Virginia had been a beautiful girl when Abel married her fifteen years before, and she was beautiful still. She had the soft, peachy complexion of a camellia petal, with wide, velvety brown eyes fringed by thick, curling lashes. Her mouth made Bree's hackles rise; it was sweetly curved and full and somehow repulsive. Her lower lip protruded as she considered Bree's remark. "Kind of you to say that. That I'm looking well. When I'm just lookin' a hag, especially after this horrible event today. But you've always been kind, Bree." She smiled slyly. "Makes a sort of a religion of it, don't you think, Abel? But you're not sayin' what you're surely thinking, Bree: 'What's this poor child doing in a wheelchair?'" She smoothed her legs, as if petting a cat. She wore a dark blue silk pant-suit, with a brilliant turquoise tee that set off her complexion and her dark blonde hair. "A turn for the worse, the doctors said. Stress, most likely. That's a real trigger for this disease. Multiple sclerosis," she said, in Hunter's direction. "Intermittent relapsing MS. Came on just after I married my Abel."

Hunter observed her silently, and then said, "Very sorry to hear that, ma'am. It's fortunate that you're here, however. You were here on the farm all day today?"

"I was."

"And you didn't leave at all."

She flirted up at him. "Now, do I look like I could have taken myself off anywhere, Lieutenant? My husband was out all day, and I was here all by myself . . ."

"Except for me, Miz Trask," Delight said. "I was here right along."

"Well, yes. Delight and I were here alone until suppertime. Abel and Missy came in to eat around seven. And then, of course, Missy went out to do evening rounds and this all happened."

"Then we'll need a statement from you," Hunter said smoothly. "Mr. Trask? If you could take your wife to the front—parlor, would it be?"

"That's right, Lieutenant," Virginia said graciously. "These fine old Southern homes do indeed have parlors."

Hunter smiled. He had, Bree realized, quite an attractive smile, when he chose to deploy it. And that's what he was doing now. "I'm a city boy—New York City—and this style of living is all new to me."

"Well, it *would* be, wouldn't it," Virginia said. "And you need a statement from me, you said?"

"From all of the family members," Hunter said smoothly. "If you'll make yourself comfortable . . ."

"Comfortable!" Virginia indicated her wheelchair with a sweep of one red-nailed hand.

"As is possible, with your situation. I'll send Sergeant Markham to you right away."

Virginia shot Bree a malevolent glance. "Abel. I'll need you there with me."

Abel turned to Missy, who had washed her face, combed her hair, and exchanged her flannel shirt for long-sleeved cotton. "You going to be okay with all this?"

She jerked her chin in a gesture of acceptance. Abel opened the swinging doors and Virginia rolled through. Hunter waited until the doors banged closed, then pulled out his cell and called Markham.

Missy stuffed her hands in her jeans and rocked back and forth on her heels. She addressed Bree without looking at her. "Sorry," she said shortly.

"It's all right. You just voiced what I'd been thinking." Bree shook her head helplessly. "I can't believe it."

"Neither of us, Abel or I, think you had a hand in poor Shirley's death. I didn't mean what I said. About you having murdered her. I did mean what I said about dealing with that dreadful kid Lindsey and her family, Bree. How could you?"

"Everyone's entitled to the best representation the courts can offer," Bree said stiffly. "I won't apologize for that."

Missy tried to smile. "Now you sound like your daddy."

"And you sound like you've had more experience with Lindsey than seeing her strutting her stuff on TV." Bree looked encouraging. "Well?"

Missy sat across from her with a sigh, and accepted a cup of coffee from the silently sympathetic Delight. "You've noticed things look a little run-down around here."

Bree demurred, then said, sympathetically, "Hard times?"

Missy grimaced. "You could say that. I made a mistake going into hunters, Bree. Charles was great about it. He was always good about letting me make the big decisions. But it diverted attention from the track, and the track paid the bills. You know what happens when you let things slide. First you start placing second and then you show third, and then you don't come into the money at all. By the time I woke up and smelled the coffee, we were thinking about selling off some of the land."

Bree made a sympathetic noise. With the sudden jump in the number of retirees looking for second homes, land around Savannah had doubled, tripled, and quadrupled in value in the past few years. Missy was sitting on a fortune.

Behind them both, Hunter stowed his cell phone, leaned against the stove, and listened.

"I thought maybe the quickest way to pay the bills was a riding school. You know what has to happen with those horses that don't make it at the track."

Bree did. It was a hard fact of life that a stud like Seaton sent horses off to the knackers several times a year.

"So we reschooled a couple of the old boys who had the temperament to make it as hacks, and took on students." An impish twinkle lit her eye. "Girls with mammas with more money than sense, most of them. And they knew squat-all about horses, but that's another story. So, to cut to the chase. Lindsey and her two friends signed up for the basic English hunter classes. Madison and what's her name, Hartley. They were okay. Madison in particular has the makings of a pretty good rider. And she's a good kid. But Lindsey." Her lips tightened in disgust. "Pulled her off the horse, called Carrie-Alice, and banned her from the property. For life."

Bree winced. She remembered Lindsey poking at Sasha with the stick. "Really bad? Actionable?"

Missy flapped her hand dismissively. "Just creepy. Picking sores in the horses' hides, that kind of stuff. Couldn't trust her with a crop. But I'll tell you, Bree, that kid is on something. I don't know much about kids and drugs. Lydia and David never seemed to get caught up in any of that stuff when they were at home. Or if they did, they sure as hell kept it from me. But that girl was on something. Sure as you're born."

"I think so, too," Bree said. "I'm going to ask Mrs. Chandler's permission to take a look at any hospital records. And perhaps talk her into arranging for a total medical exam."

"I don't get it," Missy said. "I thought you were through with all this. You bribed Shirley . . ."

"I did *not* bribe Shirley!"

"Well, paid her off, then. And that case is over, right? So what's up with the poking around into Lindsey's life?"

Bree gestured vaguely. "Just tying up a few loose ends."

Missy frowned. "Do you think *Lindsey* could have had something to do with Shirley's death?"

"Until the family asks me to back off, I'm still representing her interests," Bree said. "So, thanks for the heads-up. If you can remember anything more about her time here, would you let me know?"

"It was as short as I could make it," Missy grunted.

"Then you'll give me a call, if you think of anything at all, won't you?" Bree scrabbled in her purse and pulled out a card.

"I've already got one. Threw it out, though." Missy took it, read it, and said, "Angelus? I'm Savannah born and bred. Where the heck is Angelus?"

"Little side street off of East Bay. Very easy to miss."

Missy turned and handed the card to Delight, who walked to the kitchen counter and put it in the cookie jar. "It's where we keep the important stuff," Missy said. "Drives poor Abel crazy. I put the bills and the petty cash in there, too." Her eyes narrowed, and she took a breath. "About Abel, Brianna . . ."

"I may have mentioned that we need a written statement from you regarding the discovery of the body," Hunter interrupted. "It's late. We're all tired. But if you could go through it again it'll help us move the investigation forward."

Missy scrubbed at her eyes with both hands. "Sure. Fine. Especially if I don't have to see you all again. No offense, Lieutenant, but all this is playing hell with my barn routine. The sooner you get your people out of here, the better."

He pulled a tape recorder out of the breast pocket of his jacket and set it down.

Bree listened closely to Missy's account, which was straightforward, unembellished, and bare of anything resembling a clue. She and Abel had supper at seven, and

then went out again at eight thirty for evening rounds.
The barn manager, Neely Sandman, went with them.
Missy checked on each of the forty horses under her care.
Feed changes were discussed, any performance or veterinary issues noted. In the case of the horses headed for the
track, racing schedules were debated. The four barns surrounding the brick quadrangle each held twelve stalls; in
the fourth barn, the one assigned to Shirley Chavez,
Missy was perplexed to discover that the mucking out
had been abandoned partway through. "There's ten
horses in that number four barn, and she'd finished eight
stalls. The last two were filthy, with a day's worth of manure in them, and of course, that idiot Patch Brogan had
just slammed Belle and Flyer in there without so much as
a by-your-leave and didn't say a word about it." She shook
her head in disgust. "It's damn hard to keep help. The
wages suck, the work's hard, hot, and dirty, and you don't
get to mess around with horses much. So if you love animals, the way Shirley did, there's precious little reward.

"Anyway, Shirley's on from nine in the morning until
three. She begins mucking out around eleven. It takes
about thirty minutes to do each stall right; you rake out,
put fresh sawdust in, scrub out the water buckets. Neely
said she started right on time. She was one hell of worker,
Shirley was." Missy glanced sidelong at Bree. "She took
about twenty minutes out of her day to talk with you. Oh,
this is being taped, right? She stopped work for about
twenty minutes at one o'clock to discuss a private matter
with Brianna Winston-Beaufort, a local attorney. She
went right back to work. The ninth stall was partways
done, Patch Brogan said. He kicked the sawdust around
to cover the patches Shirley'd raked out. So as near as I
can figure, she must have been killed about two thirty,
two forty-five." Missy stopped, tears in her eyes. She

scrubbed at the tears with the tail of her shirt, and went on. "Sorry. We heard the shot, but the woods are filled with hunters this time of year . . . and who knew?" Anyway, Abel, Neely, and I split up to look for her when she didn't come in for her day's pay. She would have stopped halfway through to get a load of sawdust, so I checked the alleyway between barn four and the storage silo. And there," Missy said bleakly, "she was."

"And then," Hunter prompted.

"I called 911, of course. Then I came up to the office and called her home phone and talked to"—her voice faltered—"talked to Luis. Abel went out to where the part-time help park, and her old Chevy was still there." She held her hands up and let them fall back into her lap. "And we waited for the police."

"Anyone unfamiliar come onto the farm today?" Hunter asked.

"Just her." Missy jerked her thumb at Bree. "Miss Winston-Beaufort."

Hunter gazed over the top of Bree's head. "Did anyone see Shirley after Miss Beaufort left the premises?"

Bree made a noise like "Phuut!"

"I did. I had a short talk with Bree—Miss Beaufort. After she left, I went down to barn four and asked Shirley if she needed any help, any advice. She said no, that Miss Beaufort wanted to know who'd given her the money. She was worried that she'd told us—Abel and me—about it, and I told her not to worry about it. Then I went on with my day. The last I saw her, she was scrubbing out the water bucket in stall four-six."

Hunter turned the tape recorder off.

"Did Shirley seem unusually worried about who knew she and her family had gotten the check?" Bree asked.

"We've got her cell phone," Hunter said. "And yes, she

put in a call to your friend Payton at Stubblefield, Mar-wick. And no, I want you to stay out of that particular briar patch."

"Any calls you can't trace?"

"Apparently she only got as far as the receptionist at the law firm. And yes, there was one call after that."

Bree's heart beat a little faster. "And?"

"We're on it."

"But, Hunter!" Bree took a deep breath. "The timing's so close! An hour, maybe less. That means the murderer . . ."

"Could be twenty miles from here, in any direction. That's a surface area of six hundred miles, give or take."

"Oh," Bree said, deflated.

"And if I had to guess, I'd bet the call was to a phone that's at the bottom of the Savannah River right now."

"You're probably right." Bree looked up at the kitchen clock. Fatigue hit her like a hundred-pound sack of oats. "It's going on one o'clock in the morning. I think I'm done." Missy had purple splotches under her eyes, and Bree looked at her with concern. "And you need sleep. I'm calling it a night."

"Morning rounds at five," Missy said. She shoved herself away from the table. "Lieutenant? Any idea how long your troops are going to be tramping around my property?"

"We ought to be wrapping up now. Sergeant Markham will bring me up to speed."

"Then I'll show you both out."

"I don't think I've met Sergeant Markham," Bree said, as she and Hunter followed Missy down the short hall to the front rooms. "Is he new?"

A scrappy-looking redhead in uniform stood at the front door, scribbling in a notebook. She straightened up as the three of them came forward, and sketched a salute.

"Markham? This is one of the Chandler lawyers, Brianna Beaufort."

Bree looked at Hunter indignantly, but she shook hands with Markham. She was a year or two older than Bree, with a lot of freckles and cold hazel eyes. "Ma'am," she said.

"You got the statement from Mrs. Trask?" Hunter asked.

"Yessir." She gestured toward the ceiling with her pencil. "He got her upstairs to bed, finally. But I'm not sure why—"

"That'll do, Sergeant. This Mrs. Trask is going to bed, too. Bree? I'll see you to your car."

Outside, the mist had thickened, and the night was damp and cold. Bree shivered.

And an eerie howl split the air.

"Jesus Christ," Hunter said. "What the hell is that?"

Her car was entirely wrapped in a white fog. The dogs' yellow eyes gleamed eerily from the rear windows. Sasha growled. A horribly familiar stench wafted through the air.

"Stay there," Hunter ordered.

Belli and Miles roared. There wasn't another word for it. It was a wild, feral scream that stilled the small night sounds into silence. Hunter tensed, shoved Bree behind him, and put his hand on his pistol. The mist around Bree's car whirled in a sudden eddy of freezing wind, then drifted up and thinned to nothing.

"Miles and Belli," Bree said, her voice shaky. "I sort of inherited them."

The dogs subsided.

"Some relative left you those things?" Hunter demanded.

Bree put Sasha into the passenger seat. Then she got into the car and fumbled for her keys. The corpse smell was stronger here. A gobbet of dirt smeared the floor near the accelerator pedal. She bent down, shuddering at the slimy feel, and tossed it out the window. Hunter peered into the backseat. Miles and Belli regarded him unblinkingly.

"Sort of."

Hunter slapped the car door, and then backed away. "Jesus," he said again. Then, with a glimmer of a smile, "Don't speed on the way, okay? I'd hate to have one of the uniforms come across those guys in the dark. It'd scare the pants off him."

Bree smiled back. Markham glowered at them from the front steps of the house. "Or her," she said pointedly. "Stay well, Lieutenant."

Sixteen

Lasciate ogni speranza, voi ch'entrate.
Leave behind hope, you who enter.
—*The Inferno*, Dante

"You look like something the cat dragged in," Goldstein said frankly. "No offense meant, of course."

"None taken." Bree had slept badly, troubled with dreams of the ship in the painting and her mother's face shadowed by a great winged bird. Not Francesca, but Leah. She hadn't braided her hair, the way she normally did, and tendrils curled around her ears from the knot of hair she'd swept up on the top of her head. "This is quite a case, Goldstein. I need some help."

The recording angel pursed his lips. "I'll see what I can do. There are limits, of course."

The Hall of Records on the seventh floor of the six-story Chatham County Courthouse looked exactly as it had four days before, when Bree and Ron stopped by to pick up the pleadings on the Probert Chandler case. The monks were bent over their wooden daises, scribbling away with quill pens. The torches shone brightly, throwing pools of light on the well-scrubbed flagstone floor. Sunshine came through the stained-glass windows that lined the great hall, dimmed to a mere glow by the fantastically colored glass. Bree wondered what she would see if she looked out of one. A celestial city? The Celestial City? Or that most familiar Savannah sight, the Front Street Market and the street musicians who played there?

Goldstein cleared his throat in a marked manner. "Maybe you ought to go home and get some sleep."

Bree came to with a start. "Sorry. This is quite a peaceful place, isn't it? Easy to sleep here."

"Not a good idea," he said firmly. "Trust me on that. We've had a few temporals snooze over their research. Look over there."

Bree turned around. A middle-aged man in judicial robes dozed over a thick stack of parchment. "Judge Crater," Goldstein said in a near whisper. "He's going to be very, very surprised to discover what century he's in when he does wake up."

"Oh, dear." Bree suppressed a giggle. "Hm. Well, if you catch me dozing off, pinch me, will you?"

"Maybe," Goldstein said primly, "and then again, maybe not. Now, what kind of questions do you have?"

"I'm wondering about the celestial penalties in law. My first client, Ben Skinner, was consigned to Purgatory. You may know this already," she added modestly, "but I won that case."

Goldstein looked unimpressed.

"Probert Chandler has been consigned to the ninth circle of Hell."

Goldstein looked very grave. "Yes."

"I reviewed the pleadings early this morning. He was condemned for the sin of treachery."

Goldstein hunched his shoulders in agreement. A small, pearly feather drifted upward on a current of air.

"In the temporal legal system, the worst punishment is execution, in many of our states, at least. The next most severe is life imprisonment with no possibility of parole.

I'm guessing here, but the ninth circle of Hell is the equivalent of that?"

"Yes." Goldstein half closed his eyes and thought a bit. "You want a handout? You could use a handout." He bent down behind the counter, and then came up with a stack of laminated cards, about the size of the refrigerator calendars Bree got from her insurance company every year. He flipped one at her. On one side was printed in screaming red:

CIRCLES OF INCARCERATION

I.   Limbo/Misdemeanors/Venial Crimes

II. Felonies: Crimes of Lust

III. Felonies: Crimes of Gluttony

IV. Felonies: Crimes of Usury and Greed

V.   Felonies: Crimes of Rage and Anger

VI: Felonies: Crimes of Heresy

VII: Felonies: Crimes of Violence

VIII: Felonies: Crimes of Fraud and Deceit

IX: Felonies: Crimes of Treachery

Bree flipped the card over. The opposite side read:

Beazley & Caldecott
Attorneys-at-Law
33 Styx at Charon Square

"They're pretty aggressive about promotional mailings," Goldstein said with an expression of slight distaste. "On government money, too. Nothing illegal about it, you understand. Just tacky."

Bree studied the card with a feeling of unreality.

"But helpful. The card, I mean. It should orient you a bit."

"Yes," Bree said. "Thank you." Thoughtfully, she stuck the card in her purse. "And the specifics of Chandler's crime—sins—crimes—whichever . . ." Bree pulled her yellow pad from her briefcase and referred to her notes. "Treachery and betrayal of family, specifically his daughter, Lindsey. Goldstein, it doesn't say what he did."

"It does."

"It doesn't," Bree said, exasperated. "It doesn't say *how*."

"No," Goldstein admitted, "it doesn't say how. It says what. Why should it say how? We're not concerned with how. We're concerned with what. Do you have any idea how long the pleadings would get if we recorded every single bleeping sin this guy committed in fifty-eight years? That's twenty-one thousand one hundred and seventy days, over five hundred and eight thousand hours, thirty million . . ."

Bree held her hand up. "Stop." She rubbed her temples with both hands. "So how is the gravity of the crime established, if not through facts entered in evidence?"

Goldstein clasped his hands together and opened them. A foot-high balance scale stood on the counter. It was made of gold, or a substance very like it, and it shimmered in the torchlight. "It goes like this," he said, rather testily. "Helping little old ladies across the street, so many ounces on this side." One of the plates dipped, slightly. The little arrow on the base pointed up. "Stealing the little old lady's pension fund, so many ounces on this side." The other plate dipped way down, and the arrow on the base pointed down. "It goes like that. On your own personal Day of Judgment, You Know Who looks at the balance. You're allowed a trial if you ask for it. Chandler asked for it, obviously, or he wouldn't be filing for a retrial now, would he? It's the accumulation of acts and behaviors that leads to salvation or damnation."

"I can't work with that," Bree said. "It's not fair! I need specifics! I can't defend my client against a vaguely established weight of evidence!"

"You've got the physics of this all wrong," Goldstein said in an annoyingly superior way. "We rely on Summaries and Condensations. You aren't foolish enough to think there's a precise analogy between celestial law and the temporal?"

Bree scowled at him. "I might be foolish enough to smack an angel upside the head." Then, as Goldstein looked seriously offended, she said, "Ha-ha. Just kidding," although she hadn't been. "But really, Summaries and Condensations! With no access to the facts stipulated to, either. What a crock!"

Goldstein smiled, rather gleefully, Bree thought. "So you'll just have to get St. Parchese and Father Lucheta nosing around a little harder. Ha! Ha!" He leaned forward and patted her hand in a kindly way. "Look. We'll listen to reason. We always do. Go out and dig into what weighed heavily enough on Probert Chandler's scale to send him to the worst part of Hell and see if you can mitigate it. If I were you, I'd start with the murder of that poor soul Shirley Chavez."

"Yes," Bree said soberly. "Yes. Has she . . . I mean, is she okay?"

Goldstein smiled at her. Bree felt the comfort and the warmth of that smile. And she knew, with utter certainty, that wherever Shirley was, it was a safe and peaceful haven. This was some consolation, although not nearly enough to outweigh the outrage of her death. "Well," she said. She gathered up her yellow pad and picked up her briefcase. "Thank you."

Goldstein bent forward in a courtly bow, sending yet

another small feather ceilingward. "My pleasure." He eyed her in a kindly way. "And how is the investigation progressing?"

Bree heaved a deep sigh. "I'm mired, Goldstein. Mired."

"Yes. Well. The patient accumulation of data. That's the trick."

—∞∞∞—

Bree left the Hall of Records and took the elevator down to the first floor, where a small crowd of the decidedly unangelic citizens of Chatham County milled about. Four portly gentlemen in the brown and cream uniform of the Chatham County Sheriff's Department glowered at the line filing through the arch of the metal detector. Two young guys in the dark blue uniforms of the Savannah PD marched a sulky-looking lady in pink curlers across the broad terrazzo floor. "You there in the suit! You a lawyer?" the lady in the curlers shouted. "I need me a lawyer!" Another pair of uniforms came through the back from the holding pens.

Between them was Payton McAllister.

Bree stopped and stared.

His Italian-made suit was wrinkled. He was tieless. His pink-striped, white-cuffed shirt had a coffee stain down the front. He glared furiously at her. A fourth man, in a conservative seersucker suit, trailed behind them. Beyond the glass doors that led to the parking lot outside, the van for WSAV TV pulled up, and a gorgeous young blonde spilled out, followed by a cameraman and a Steadicam.

Bree bit her lip to stop from grinning. Her first thought was to let the lady in the pink curlers know that *there* was a lawyer, right there. If not Payton himself, then the guy that walked behind him. Her second was to offer a sympathetic shake of the head and slip unobtrusively away.

Just then Payton jerked his arms free of the officers and shook his fist at her. "You bitch!" he shouted. "This is your fault!" So she had a third option; she smiled, waved, and caroled, "*Good* morning!" The younger of the two men in uniform dropped her a wink.

Bree paused in the middle of the foyer and mentally flipped through the possibilities. There was only one, really, and that was to sit down and have a heart-to-heart talk with Lindsey herself.

But she'd have to make sure to catch the news at noon; Payton's gorgeous blue eyes were nicely bloodshot. The cameras should catch it all.

∞

"She's not here." Carrie-Alice wasn't all that pulled-together this morning, either. She wore the cotton twinset that she'd worn the night before. There was a run in her stocking. She'd neglected to put on any makeup. It made her look younger, and more vulnerable. Murder investigations certainly seemed to have a deleterious effect on the way those concerned presented themselves. Bree tucked her tee more neatly into her waistband and tried to look calm, collected, and competent.

"I'm here to help, Mrs. Chandler. I think Lindsey may know more than she realizes."

"About what?"

"I'm not precisely sure," Bree admitted. "But if I could just sit down with her, alone, get her to relax a bit . . ."

"I told you, she's not here." Carrie-Alice twisted her hands together and walked to the front window. The security guards were back. And beyond them, the quiet street wasn't quiet anymore. A small contingent of reporters and cameramen crowded together at the foot of the driveway. Carrie-Alice watched them with something like despair on her face. "Why can't they leave us alone?"

"They arrested one of the lawyers from Stubblefield, Marwick this morning," Bree said. "Or at least, brought him in for questioning. The folks outside are probably after a comment from you."

"About what?"

"Bribes. To pay off the Chavez family, I should think." Bree leaned back against the couch. "If someone from the family in fact authorized it, the police will be here to inquire about it."

"George!" Carrie-Alice shouted. *"George!"*

Bree jumped. This was very unlike Lindsey's detached, remote mother.

Norah came quietly into the living room. "Is something wrong, Mrs. Chandler?"

"George is in his father's office," Carrie-Alice said distractedly. "Ask him to come in here, please."

Norah left as quietly as she'd come and returned with George a few moments later.

"You handle this," Carrie-Alice said abruptly. "I'm going upstairs to lie down. I didn't get a wink of sleep last night. I'm exhausted." She left the room, half running.

George watched her go, a look of mild concern on his face, and then sat down in the chair across from Bree. "You'll have to excuse Mom," he said. "This has been really hard for her. Hard for us all, actually. Have you got some news for us already?"

George, at least, was neatly dressed. His tan chinos were pressed, his blue dress shirt had just come from the dry cleaner's, and his tie was precisely knotted. Bree wondered if this meant anything other than that he kept cool in a crisis. Or was too thick-skinned to care.

"I really need to talk to Lindsey, Mr. Chandler."

"Call me George, would you? I haven't quite adjusted to Dad's death. He was always Mister Chandler."

Bree suppressed a sigh. "I really need to talk to Lindsey, George."

"She's not here, I'm afraid."

"Then I need to go where she is and talk to her." Her lack of sleep was definitely affecting her temper.

"But you're not representing Lindsey anymore. That case is over and done with." He looked over his shoulder uneasily, as if a TV anchor lurked under the davenport. "And she doesn't know anything that could help you in Dad's death."

"She might."

"Like what?" He looked genuinely bewildered. "She's a kid. And she's never been an easy kid, as you know by now. The likelihood that Dad would have confided in her is slim to none. I don't want to shock you, but I don't think he liked her much. I'd prefer to be logical about this."

Too thick-skinned to care, obviously. Poor Lindsey. Bree's sympathy was well and truly stirred. If she could just get to the kid, something could be done to help her, couldn't it? Everyone deserved a shot at redemption. Everyone needed a champion now and then. Bree forced herself to think fast. What sort of plea would a neatly pressed, "life's logical" person like George respond to? "Just dotting my i's and crossing my t's, George. There's no real trick to good solid investigative work, you know. It's a lot of slog, slog, slog."

"That's true. Dad always said that God is in the details."

"Exactly."

"Okay. Mother's not going to be happy about this, but we'll set it up."

"Where is she?" Wild ideas zipped through her brain. Lindsey stuck in a sinister clinic somewhere? Held captive by hired thugs?

"At the Cliff's Edge Academy. We had her taken there last night, after the police brought her home. It's been in the works for a while. To be frank, it may have been the reason behind this latest escapade with the Girl Scout. Mother had talked to her about it a week ago. The Savannah School thought it'd be best if we transferred her out. And the academy has a decent reputation for handling challenged children." He frowned. "Expensive, though." The heir to the world's tenth-largest fortune stood up and shook the creases from his khakis. "I'll call them and set up an appointment. Is there a time that would be convenient for you?"

"It's a two-hour drive from here, up toward Atlanta? Late this afternoon would be just fine."

The doorbell chimed. Norah rustled by. There was a murmur of voices, and the noise of several people moving out in the hallway. "Mr. Chandler!" somebody shouted.

"Excuse me," George said. "That's the head security guard. Would you mind getting the Atlanta phone book while I take care of this, Bree? There's a copy in Dad's office."

"You need the number for the Cliff's Edge Academy?"

"Please." He waved a hand at her as he disappeared toward the front door. A practical man, George Chandler, not one to waste a few bucks on a 411 call to information services.

Bree felt a small twinge of anxiety about returning to the scene of Probert's appearance, offset by a lunatic hope that his ghost would appear with the name of his murderer on his lips. She edged into the room with some trepidation, and spotted the Atlanta area phone book on the credenza. She picked it up and said quietly, "Mr. Chandler? Probert?"

Nothing.

She cleared her throat. "Anything more you can tell me about this case? I'm off to see Lindsey this afternoon."

A small current of air stirred the papers on top of the desk.

"I can't help but feel she's at the heart of the murders, here. You know that, of course, since it's why you're, well, where you are."

A howl shattered the air with the sound of an enormous hammer on a huge block of ice. Bree fought the temptation to run like hell and held her ground. Hot air burst through the room, flinging papers, magazines, books, and folders in the air. The U of Oregon photograph of Probert and his friends flipped off the wall and landed with a crash at her feet. The family portrait fell off the desk and shattered. The City of Savannah phone book flew into the air, struck the wall opposite the window overlooking the pool, and ricocheted into the wastebasket.

The desk began to vibrate. It was a massive piece of furniture, topped by a thick slab of mahogany. It shook as if possessed. The bottom drawer sprang open. Bree clutched the phone book to her chest and wondered what George Chandler was going to say when he saw the complete mess his father's ghost had made of his office. The bottom drawer jumped forward, as if being pulled by invisible hands. It flipped over, spilling the contents on the floor.

A syringe. A Marlowe's paperweight the size of a baby's fist. A lab report. Bree picked the lab report up first. It was a simple blood test, and it identified Carrie-Alice's type as O negative.

The wind died with the suddenness of a power failure in the middle of a storm.

Bree hadn't realized she was holding her breath. The room was so quiet she could hear her blood pounding in her ears.

She addressed the air. "Anything else?"

Nothing. The air was still. No tortured figure appeared before her, hands outstretched in appeal. A distant door slammed; George, she guessed, and the sound of his footsteps meant he was headed this way. Bree retrieved the phone book, stuffed the syringe and the paperweight in her suit coat pocket, and slipped out, closing the office door behind her.

George came down the hall toward her, an abstracted frown on his face. It lightened a little when he saw her. He frowned at her. "What's that you've got there?"

Bree looked down. The lab report was crushed in her right hand. "Just a piece of paper that marked a place in the phone book," she said brightly. She crumpled the paper into a ball and shoved it between the syringe and the paperweight. "It marked places that deliver pizza," she added unnecessarily. "Lindsey must have wanted to order out." She leaned against the office door and tucked the phone book into the crook of one arm. "I'll just look up the academy's number, shall I? We can give them a call on my cell. And it'll be more comfortable in the living room, don't you think?"

"What? The living room? Probably not. We can use the phone in here." He reached past her to the doorknob. Bree didn't budge. His breath smelled like scrambled eggs. "Any trouble up front?" she asked brightly.

"Excuse me," he said firmly. She backed off. He opened the door and walked into the office. She heard him exclaim. Bree briefly considered making a dash for it. "Well?" he said called out impatiently. "Is there something wrong, Miss Beaufort? Are you coming in?"

She peered around the lintel.

The office was as neatly arranged as when she'd first walked in to retrieve the phone book. She considered the properly stacked piles of paper, the neatly arranged magazines, and the orderly row of stapler, penholder, and writing pads on top of the desk. All four drawers were in place and firmly closed. George was crouched down by the bottom drawer. "This is weird," he said. "These keys of Dad's have been missing since he died. And I found them under the desk." He held them in his hand as if weighing them. "Funny how that happens, isn't it? Huh! And here's that old picture of Dad and his disco band. Must have fallen off the wall." The glass was intact. He picked the photo up and positioned it back on the wall. He tossed the keys on the desk.

Keys? Should she have picked up the keys, as well?

"Keys to anything important?" Bree asked casually.

"To the manufacturing plant and the warehouse near the store here. I had the security locks changed both places, just to be sure, when the keys turned up missing. Darn. I could have saved ten grand if I'd just searched for these hard enough. Shoot. I could have sworn I'd looked all over this place." He sat down in the leather executive chair with a sigh.

Bree took a few steps into the office and stared at the photo on the wall. "That's John Lindquist."

George seemed not to hear her. "Anyway. Sorry for the brief delay out there."

"What happened?"

George took a handkerchief from his pants pocket and wiped his forehead. "A couple of big black dogs were loose in the garden. One of the TV people claimed Capshaw set the dogs on him. We don't own any dogs. I have no idea where they came from, or where they went."

"Oh, dear," Bree said. "No one was hurt, I hope?"

"Nah. Just a momentary diversion. If you ask me, one of those reporters brought 'em along just to see if they could get one of us out of the house. The minute I went out there I got a microphone stuck in my face and they started with the questions about the so-called payoff to Miss Chavez."

Bree's hand went to the syringe and the paperweight tucked in her pocket. "I can get an injunction to keep them off the property, George."

He shook his head dismissively. "I've got people to handle that. Let's call Cliff's Edge and get on with this. The sooner I can get back to real work, the better."

Seventeen

It's a white whale, I say.
—*Moby-Dick*, Herman Melville

"Uncle Jay drew blood from me," Lindsey said with a shrug.

"You mean John Lindquist," Bree said.

Lindsey nodded. "And when he wasn't around, Dad did. No one was supposed to know about it." She looked at the syringe Bree had laid on the table in front of her. The headmistress, a Miss Violet Henry, had offered them the use of a well-appointed, quiet conference room on the main floor of the beautiful old mansion that housed Cliff's Edge Academy. "You read Anne Rice?"

"What? No, no, I'm afraid I don't."

"When I was little, I used to think they were vampires, Dad and Uncle Jay. Or that they were using the blood for some weird rite, you know? Like in that video game, Vampire's Bloodlust. And then I'd pee in a cup."

Lab tests, Bree thought. Weird rite, indeed. But for what?

"So?" Lindsey challenged her.

"I think that's the creepiest thing I've ever heard."

"Yeah?" Lindsey said. "You believe me?"

"Of course I believe you," Bree said gently. "What I

have a really hard time understanding is why. I mean, don't you get regular physicals?"

Lindsey picked at her upper lip. "I've got AIDS, I guess. They didn't want anyone to know."

"What!" Bree reached across the table and took Lindsey's hands in her own. "Who told you that?"

"Well, it's got to be something like that, doesn't it? Uncle Jay told me if anybody knew what I had, there wouldn't be a school in the country that'd take me, and I wouldn't have any friends."

Bree turned Lindsey's hands over and looked at the nails. They were bitten down to the quick. But the color was good, her hands were warm, and, as hospital records might have expressed it, hers was the body of a well-nourished white female approximately seventeen years of age. Other than the troubled hunch of her shoulders and her sullen expression, Lindsey looked perfectly healthy. Which, as Bree well knew, was no proof at all that the child wasn't dying of something awful. If she had been on uppers, there was no sign of it now.

"Are you taking any kind of medications for this condition, Lin?"

"Vitamins."

"That's it?"

"Well, yeah!" She slouched further down in the chair and glared at Bree like an angry cat.

"And what about other kinds of drugs?"

"That's the first thing any of you think when you talk to kids," Lindsey said. "Drugs drugs. Blah blah blah. I've said it before and I'll say it again. We don't do drugs." She looked away and drummed her fingers on the table.

Bree caught the use of the word "we" and sent up a brief apology for the deception she was about to practice. She said smoothly, "That's not what I hear, Lindsey."

Was that a flicker of alarm in those angry eyes? It was. Good.

"I've talked to Chad."

"Chad." Her tone was absolutely flat.

"Madison and Hartley, too."

Silence. Lindsey hunched her shoulders and shut down.

Bree let it roll on. It's surprisingly hard to maintain total silence between two people. Bree remained perfectly still, her hands folded in her lap, her eyes steady on Lindsey's bowed head. She knew what she had to do. If anyone needed Bree's services as a lawyer, it was poor Lindsey.

"Just a few uppers once in a while," Lindsey said. She rubbed her nose fiercely. "And a downer or two. And only from Chad. And then when—" She clamped her mouth shut.

"When what?" Bree asked gently.

"My dad found out. He made us break up. He threatened to do something totally gross to Chad's dad, like taking away his law license."

Bree doubted even Probert Chandler could accomplish that. But she had a brief, unwelcome vision of the celestial scales of justice and the little dial that pointed down down down. "When was this?"

Lindsey sighed. "A couple of weeks before he died. I dunno. The accident was in June, right? So it was later. A couple of weeks after Chad was supposed to graduate from high school."

"This didn't happen the day of your father's . . . accident?"

"Nope."

"You're sure?"

"Of course I'm sure." She stared at Bree, and then barked with laughter. "You think Chad had something to do with my dad's death? No way. No way. Chad, he's . . . well, he's comfy. You know. Cosy. Nice. Besides," she added earnestly, "he's a vegetarian."

Bree pinched her knee hard, so she wouldn't laugh, and took a moment to compose herself. Then she put her elbows on the table and leaned forward to stare at Lindsey eye to eye. "Then, I want the whole story about this syringe. From the first you remember up to right now."

There wasn't much more to the story, actually. Lindsey didn't remember a time when her view of the universe failed to coincide with the expectations of the world around her. As nearly as Bree could tell, Lindsey arrived in this world with a permanent inability to do the good thing and, worse yet, a positive drive to do the bad.

When she left, she took Lindsey's supply of vitamins with her.

———⟨∞⟩———

"It's a horrible story," she said to Hunter several hours later. "I don't know what to do. I don't know what to think. She remembers talking to a series of doctors when she was little. And the blood draws started after she turned ten. She has that specific a recall because she screamed when a few blood drops got on a pair of jeans she'd gotten as a tenth birthday present. They had sequins on the cuffs, she said. And she outgrew them way too fast." She wanted to put her head in her hands and weep. Instead, she took a bite of her Cobb salad. "I stopped back at the office before I came here, and Ron had dug up her medical records for me. I'm so bummed I don't even want to take a look. What the hell do you suppose was going on?"

"I think you've gotten way overinvolved in this case." Hunter ate his Brunswick stew with calm efficiency.

They'd met for dinner at Isaac's. It was late, after ten,

and Bree felt as if she hadn't slept for days. Her eyes were sandy. Her head ached.

"It sounds to me like she's just a troubled kid."

"Just!"

He reached out and placed his hand flat against the manila folder that held Lindsey's records. "May I?"

"Those are confidential," Bree said automatically.

"Well, I won't ask you how you got them so quickly if you don't nag me about looking at them." Hunter didn't wait for her reply, but paged through the neat stack of photocopies. Bree separated the bacon bits in her salad neatly from the chopped tomatoes and sprinkled salt over the diced hard-boiled egg. Then she ate all the black olives.

"Almost all of this is behaviorally oriented," Hunter said. "Physically she's fine." He held up a densely printed sheet of cream-colored paper that listed lab results. Bree caught the first line: Blood type AB−, followed by a normal range for the hematocrit, sed rate, blah blah blah.

"And through the years," Hunter said, "the blood draws were to test levels of various antidepressants, mood elevators, and serotonin reuptake inhibitors . . ." He tossed the file flat on the table. "All of this crap was in the vitamins. You know the drill." He tapped the papers into a neat pile. "You haven't seen this yet."

"No. I don't think I want to."

"You might want to take a look at the name of the prescribing physician." He lifted the top paper off the stack and handed it to her.

"Lindquist!" Bree said. "That son of a bitch!" For a. brief, unsettling moment, the world tilted and she saw the restaurant, Hunter's grim and angry visage, the stack of incriminating reports in a sea of red. Her hands clenched. A breeze rose around the table and stirred her hair. Her breath came short. With an effort, she calmed herself, but it was several minutes before she could speak. She knew Lindquist was a rat—but this violation of his oath as a physician was too much.

"The blood draws," she said. Her voice was hoarse with rage. She took a sip of water. "They were just making sure the levels of the drugs they were giving her were safe."

"Looks like it."

"Well, that sucks," Bree said furiously. "She's a minor. Half that crap hasn't been tested on kids. Who knows if it's safe? What sucks the most is that they didn't tell her."

Hunter spread his hands in a gesture of demurral. "The tentative diagnoses are all pretty grim. Suicidal tendencies. Depression. Paranoia. Probable manic-depressive illness . . ."

"Bipolar disorder," Bree said. "It's called bipolar disorder now." She contemplated the pile of grilled chicken that topped her salad and felt suddenly cheery. "I've got a lot of ammunition for a defense, at least."

"If the Chandlers let you use it."

Bree nodded. "And he was *trying* to save her, God help him. At the very least it's mitigating."

"Who was trying to save her?"

"Never mind," Bree said. "Hey! Listen. I'm beginning to get a handle on Lindsey's part of the problem at least. I just need the answers to two questions. First, I assume Payton McAllister spilled his guts with little or no prompting from you guys."

Hunter grinned.

"He did. So who authorized the payoff to the Chavez family?"

"John Allen Lindquist."

"Really!" Bree sat back. This was interesting. She would have made (and lost) a large bet that George was behind the cash payment. Maybe she was wrong about

George. Or perhaps George and Lindquist were working together. She thought about George's reaction when she'd last mentioned Lindquist to him. "And do you know who put the pressure on the DA's office to make Cordy reconsider pressing charges in the cookie robbery?"

"It's just scuttlebutt," Hunter said cautiously.

"Then nod if it's Lindquist."

Hunter jerked his chin at her. She smiled grimly. "I thought so."

"Any reason why you thought it was Lindquist?"

"He could close the Marlowe's store here—that's over five hundred jobs at risk, and it's an election year. And he's turned out to be pretty sneaky, all things considered. He and Probert double-teamed poor old Lindsey. And that rat George must have known, and let them do it." She drummed her fingers on the table. "I wonder if I can sue the two of them, on Lindsey's behalf. Putting her through all that trauma, all those years. All the secrecy. The fear she was dying of something horrible. What is *wrong* with people, Hunter? Maybe I can petition the court to get her away from them. I'm representing her now, did I tell you that? I'm going to tell George and his mother to go fly a kite. First thing in the morning."

"Just to make this perfectly clear: you intend to sue your soon-to-be-former clients based on information received while they *were* your clients?"

Bree stared at him, her mouth slightly open. She sat that way for a long, agonizing moment. "Oh. My. God," she said. "I can't believe . . ." She buried her head in her arms and shouted silently into the tabletop. She raised her head, took a deep breath, and said, "I have to tell them I am going to resign as their counsel. And I have to do it now. And I've got to get some kind of retainer from Lindsey."

"I'm sure they're already well aware that you've been to see her."

"How could they be?"

Hunter smiled. It wasn't a very kind smile. It was a "gotcha" sort of smile. "Did you overhear George's phone call to Cliff's Edge?"

"Did I? No. Do you think I'm the kind of person who'd listen in on somebody's private phone call?"

"You'd better be, if you're going to become any kind of an investigator."

"As a matter of fact," she said with a rather pitiful attempt at dignity, "I went out to check on my dogs. Someone must have let them out of my car and let them run around the Chandler place, creating all kinds of havoc. I can't imagine how they got out otherwise." Well, she could, but she wasn't about to let Hunter in on why.

"I can't imagine anyone coming within half a mile of those animals voluntarily, much less putting a hand on the door of your little car. They'd eat whoever it was alive." His look over his Brunswick stew was suspicious.

"Well, they were safely tucked up when I left them to drop in on the Chandlers and they were just as safely tucked up when I went out to check on them. We could go ahead and ask them what happened. Only I vote you do the talking."

"Let's get back to the point here," he said patiently. "You drove up to Cliff's Edge about just after lunch?"

"And got there about four, yes. Violet Henry arranged one of the conference rooms the school sets aside for family."

"And Henry didn't stay with you throughout the interview?"

"No. Should she have?" Bree slammed the palm of her hand into her forehead. "Damn. Damn, I am so stupid. My conversation with Lindsey was taped, wasn't it? Oh, I should be smeared with molasses and hung in a beehive."

"And the tape turned over to the family by now, don't you think?"

"Double damn, damn, *damn*." Served her right for leaving Sasha with Belli and Miles in the car. Sasha would have alerted her to the tape recorder. She was sure of it. But she hadn't wanted her precious dog anywhere near the tormented Lindsey.

"Here," Hunter said in a kindly way, "beat yourself over the head with this." He pulled a baguette from the breadbasket and offered it to her with a flourish. "I don't need to add that civilians rummaging around in police investigations leads to precisely this kind of thing, do I?"

"If you don't shut up," Bree said fiercely, "I'll stuff that stew right up your nose. And I mean it."

There was a well-dressed couple in the booth next to their table. The woman, a little older than Bree, glanced at them, shifted nervously in her seat, and whispered to her male companion. Bree fought the impulse to stuff stew up her nose, too. "What do we do now?"

"We? Got a mouse in your pocket?" Hunter sighed and shook his head. "Sorry. But you do realize your behavior violates at least three separate tenets in your canon of ethics."

"I'm sorry. I am *so* sorry."

"You're risking your license to practice law. No skin off *my* nose."

"Thanks for the sympathetic ear," she said sarcastically. "I didn't stop to think. I was a fool. Worse yet, I've been unethical. My father," she added gloomily, "is going to spit rocks."

Hunter's face softened, just a little. "Get some sleep. Back off a little. Give yourself time to calm down. You get tired or you let a case get to you, you're going to lose your objectivity and make mistakes."

Bree swallowed another piece of the baguette, along

with the lecture. She waited until the flush had cooled from her cheeks and her blood pressure had returned to a relatively normal state. "So how's the investigation into the murder of Shirley Chavez?"

"The call to the cell phone she made after she talked to Stubblefield's office was to a cell phone with prepaid minutes. And we're sifting through the forensic evidence we gathered at the murder site right now. Not much hope there, I'm afraid." He look tired, and older, all of a sudden. "There's nothing harder to solve than a seemingly random, opportunistic act like this one, Bree. If we don't get a break in the case, it doesn't look good. That eyewitness to Probert's car crash? You wouldn't care to pass that name along?"

Bree remembered her promise to Ron. "That person's not going to come forward," she said. "Not unless we get a miracle."

It was on the tip of her tongue to ask about the robberies. She couldn't. Not until she knew more. Not until the pattern between these two cases started to make some sense.

And not until Sam Hunter's respect for her had come back. Just a little.

"It'll take a miracle to solve this sucker." Bree stared out her office window at the graveyard. She'd resigned from representing Carrie-Alice and George. Although the morning had dawned bright and sunny, the sun never seemed to reach under the boughs of the live oak tree. Josiah Pendergast's grave gaped wide. She imagined she could smell the dank and fetid air that rose from it, and rubbed her arms as if she were cold. At least she'd gotten some sleep the night before. And she'd gone for a run by the river early in the morning; she felt rested, and her head was clear.

But the case looked worse than ever.

"I don't know about miracles. Some good investigative work will help. We've narrowed down the suspect list." Ron placed a sheet of paper on her desk with an air of triumph. "Three of the people on this list have no alibi for the time of Mr. Chandler's death. All three have a grudge against him or the company, and have threatened him in the past. And all three have committed felonies related to crimes against property."

"As opposed to crimes against persons," Petru said with an air of helpfulness. "We thought that the warehouse burglaries were of some significance."

"I wish I knew for sure why the Chandlers are turning cartwheels to keep it quiet." Bree took a look at the list: Stephen Hansen; Marvin Kleinmetz; Tiffany Burkhold. The name Hansen rang a faint bell. Was she thinking of the notorious spy? She hoped they weren't whistling in the wind. What if Probert had been killed in some insane, random act? What if Shirley—no. There was no possible alternate interpretation for what had happened to Shirley. She had been murdered. It was murder, clear as daylight and twice as strong. And it had to connect to these other events. It had to. And it all had to connect to Marlowe's.

"What's the grudge each has against Chandler?"

"Hansen's owner of a small family pharmacy that went totally bankrupt when Marlowe's built that store off of Highway 80. He brought a nonsense lawsuit, lost, and threatened to kill Chandler, right there in open court. The guy's not too tightly wrapped, according to his neighbors. One interesting thing—his pharmacology degree's from the University of Oregon. Same year as Lindquist and Chandler, as a matter of fact."

Bree sat up. *We were all chem majors,* Lindquist had said during the party at Plessey. Steve Hansen, Bert, and me.

"There's more. He's been indicted and convicted for tax fraud in the past. And he apparently has quite a gambling habit."

"Gambling," Bree said.

"Money is always a motive," Ron offered. "One of the best."

Bree bit her lip to keep from yelling hoorah! and behaving like an idiot in front of her staff. "Wow. This is looking better and better."

"Isn't it?"

Petru made a grumbling noise. Ron smirked. "As for these others: Marv Kleinmetz is a union organizer, with a long history of thumping people's heads. He's been trying to organize the Marlowe's workers for years. He was fired for theft last year, and Marlowe's prosecuted. He was released from prison a week before Probert's accident out on Skidaway. And he's a big-time deer hunter." He raised his eyebrows at Bree's puzzled look. "The deerjacking flashlight, remember? Not conclusive, to be sure, but inertia plays a large part in human behavior. You tend to use what's at hand."

"Did you get any details on the theft?"

Ron's smile was beatific. "He was in charge of inventory control. When he was hauled off to the pokey, the store manager replaced him with Chad Martinelli and Shirley Chavez. Ready for the finale?"

"Ready."

"He's the registered owner of a .38."

"Well," Bree said. "Well, well, well. And the third person?"

"Tiffany Burkhold is a former employee. She was

fired from Marlowe's four and a half months ago—a couple of weeks before the car crash."

"So she would have worked with Shirley."

"Oh, she worked with Shirley, all right. Shirley caught her swiping prescription drugs from the pharmacy and turned her in. Tiffany lost both the Marlowe's job and her part-time job as a teller at the Bank of Savannah. She wrote a letter threatening Probert personally. Stubblefield, Marwick got a restraining order on behalf of Chandler. She does have a record as a juvenile. It's sealed, but it's relevant. She was involved in a series of snatch-and-grabs as a kid."

"Shirley turned her in?" *The one time I didn't mind my own business, it came back to bite me in the ass.*

"So Tiffany's still paying for offenses committed how long ago?"

"Twenty-five years, at least."

"Yikes." Bree traced the names on the paper with her finger. "Did you turn these names over to Sam Hunter?"

Ron nodded. "First thing this morning. He said to tell you he's on it."

"Shirley's death changes things," Bree said.

"Lieutenant Hunter said to tell you he's on that, too."

Bree bit her thumb and brooded.

Ron sat on the edge of his desk and swung his legs jauntily. "So what's next, chief?"

"There's something very off, here." Bree frowned. "All three of these people made public threats against Chandler himself. And Chandler responded the way any citizen should: he called the cops. And he used the court system."

"So why the deep silence over the warehouse robberies, perhaps?" Petru said.

"Exactly." Bree bent over the list again. "I like Hansen

for it. I like Kleinmetz for it. Tiffany, not so much." She looked up. "Uncle Jay, a.k.a. John Lindquist," she said. "I really, really want to talk to Uncle Jay. And then Tiffany Burkhold. And then Kleinmetz. In person. Hansen. Do we have an address for him?"

"Not yet. He seems to have disappeared. But I'll find him." Ron shook his head. "You think this is all connected with Marlowe's?"

She thought of the keys. "It has to be."

<hr />

Lindquist agreed to meet her at the manufacturing plant, which was located near the Marlowe's retail operation on Highway 80. On the way to the meeting, Bree had a brain wave of an idea. She stopped at the store, made several purchases, and tucked them away in her briefcase.

Both the research center and warehouse were located a quarter mile from the Marlowe's store, at the very rear of the Marlowe's property. It was pretty clear which was Marlowe's property and which was not: all of the trees and shrubbery had been cleared from the land, to be replaced by lots of concrete and grass mowed within an inch of its life. Parts of the research center were still under construction. A large sculpture of the Marlowe's logo in front of the two-story building was in the final stages. The concrete pad around the base was newly poured and drying in the sun.

Concrete trucks and bulldozers rumbled past Bree as she pulled into the traffic circle at the main entrance.

Lindquist himself met her at the front desk, and insisted on creating a photo ID for her before he led her inside. "Corporate espionage," he said. "Bert agreed with me, by the way. The security in this place rivals that at Fort Knox."

Bree didn't think he was kidding. Guards with guns

swarmed all over the place. Security cameras were tucked into every possible corner. They whirred and rotated as Lindquist led the way to the labs.

Lindquist's office was as utilitarian as the man himself. A steel gray carpet covered the floor. The furniture was chrome, glass, and black leather. One entire wall was made of glass, and overlooked a fully staffed chemical laboratory. The air-conditioning was set so low Bree wished she'd worn a sweater. He seated her at the small glass conference table, and then pushed a switch. A set of blinds whispered down from the ceiling, closing the lab from Bree's view.

"I don't have much time," Lindquist began.

"I don't either." Bree bent down and pulled out the products she'd bought at the store twenty minutes earlier. "Lindsey's vitamins," she said, "and something that wasn't her choice." She set the bottle of vitamins next to the sole ornament in the room, a glass paperweight bearing the Marlowe's logo. She tossed the syringe and vials onto the tabletop. They bounced across the glass toward Lindquist, and then fell to the floor. "Well, Uncle Jay? These are Lindsey's. I sent the contents to a private lab in Atlanta for testing not half an hour ago. What do you think they'll find?"

He looked at the exhibit with absolutely no expression. "The vitamins are a mix of B_{12} and B_6, as well as D, E, and C. I take them myself. Everyone connected to the family does. You'd benefit from them yourself." He set the vials aside. "And we thought that Lindsey's supply might be on its way to the labs in Atlanta. Is that why you're here, Miss Beaufort? Because I can guarantee"— he leaned forward and dropped his voice to a hiss— "*guarantee* that you won't find anything but legal compounds in those samples."

"I don't think I will, either," Bree said quietly. "As a

matter of fact, my guess is that you and your brother-in-law were dosing the child with a variety of antidepressants in an effort to change her behavior. And those are legal. What you did is contemptible. Treacherous. But not illegal. Not when prescribed by Lindsey's physician. Which is you. And aided by her father—her legal guardian and the person responsible for the state of her health. Some of the stuff you gave her undoubtedly has grave medical consequences, especially in patients under eighteen. The reason for the blood draws, I imagine."

Lindquist's face suffused with rage. He stood up, his hands clenched. "You have no idea! You have *no* idea of the trial that miserable 'child,' as you call her, has been to my sister! She's a devil! A spawn of the devil!"

Bree, who could identify spawns of the devil better than most, shook her head. "She's made a practice of living her life on the edge, Dr. Lindquist. There's no denying that. But I can't help but wonder how much easier her life would have been in a family less concerned with discipline and more with affection. Did you ever think once about taking her for outside help? As for buying her silence with threats about a disease . . ." She wanted to spit, but didn't.

"Don't be absurd. You saw how the media leaped on this business with that eight-year-old. And she does have a disease. She's a malignant blot!

"People like us live in a fishbowl, Miss Beaufort. You can put a little pressure here, lean on a few people there, but by and large we're at the mercy of the ghouls with their cameras." His face had paled to an ashen color. "And you know what happens when the great American public turns against you? You start to lose, and you start to lose big. First thing you know, you've got unions organizing the workforce. That drives prices up. You have protest groups urging a change in the tariff. That drives prices up. You start getting huge punitive damages in jury trials, and they're held up on appeal. And prices go up. And you know what happens when prices go up? People buy somewhere else. And the stores close. And nearly three hundred thousand employees are out of work, and you end up with nothing. Nothing."

Bree had absolutely no response to this. She stood up and said quietly, "I'm leaving now."

"To do what?"

"Contact Child Protective Services, for one. And I'm going to get Lindsey a good lawyer, someone well versed in juvenile law.

"Then I'm going to do my best to solve a pair of murders."

She headed to the outer door. She could feel his glare between her shoulder blades.

"This isn't over yet, Miss Beaufort."

The glass paperweight flew past her head and crashed into the wall. Furious, Bree picked it up, whirled, and held it out to him accusingly.

Lindquist backed up, his hands flung wide. "Hey," he said, "hey. All I can tell you is, I didn't go near that thing. The construction vehicles do strange things to the stability of the building."

"Temper, Mr. Lindquist, is going to get you nowhere at all."

She slammed the door on her way out.

Eighteen

Mi ritrovai per una selva oscura.
I found myself again in a dark wood.
—*The Inferno*, Dante

"Tiffany Burkhold works at a bar on Whitaker," Petru said. "The Spur It On."

Bree tucked the cell phone against her ear while she scrabbled in her purse for her notepad. "What's the nearest cross street?"

"West Broughton."

"Near the market, then. It's eleven thirty. Do you think she'll be there?"

"They are open for lunch," Petru said. "It is possible, yes. And your interview with Mr. Lindquist? Successful, perhaps?"

Bree sighed and stared out the car window. Traffic was heavy. It threatened rain. She was suddenly discouraged. "He's a jerk. But he's got zero motive to do Probert Chandler in. And he doesn't know Shirley Chavez from a hole in the ground." Bree tapped the steering wheel thoughtfully.

"By the way, Mr. Payton McAllister made the noon news. I have taped it for you."

Bree grinned. "Things are looking up, Petru. Things

are definitely looking up. Any word on where we can find Stephen Hansen?"

"Not yet. But I anticipate success."

Bree said good-bye and drove up Whitaker to the Spur It On.

The bar was tucked into the first floor of an old extension of the Cotton Exchange. A narrow neon sign ran the length of the storefront. Silver spurs cupped the lettering like spiky hands. At some point in the past, some hopeful owner had installed large windows. An Open sign glowed red in the one nearest the solid steel door. A Dos Equis sign blipped on and off underneath it.

Bree parked on the street. The dogs poked their noses out the passenger windows and looked hopefully outside. "An hour, no more," Bree promised them. "And then we'll go for a walk near the river."

The front door opened outward. The rush of air was filled with familiar scents: beer, the undercurrent of disinfectant, fried foods, and a moldy, woody odor that was characteristic of old bars everywhere. The inside was dimly lit. Bree made out a line of booths against the wall opposite the long wooden bar top. A mass of old pine tables stood jumbled together in the center. The place was almost empty: a few retirees, mostly, older men in golf shirts and shorts despite the coolness of the day and their placid wives in pantsuits and bright costume jewelry. Behind the bar, a woman in a white shirt and black pants slapped at the countertop. She looked up when Bree walked in.

Bree figured she'd stick out like a sore thumb in her city suit. She took a seat in the booth closest to the door. The plastic-sheeted menu was sticky. Bree read down the printed page. Hamburger, quesadillas, French fries, and onion rings. Hunter would love this place, if he hadn't found it already.

"Help you?" The bartender stood with one hip out-thrust, an order pad in one hand. She didn't have a name tag. The bio Ron had provided for Tiffany Burkhold said she was in her early forties, divorced, with one son, who was grown and out working on his own. This woman could fit the profile.

"BLT on wheat, please."

"Coke-cola?"

"Iced tea. Unsweetened." The waitress nodded and sauntered off. A couple at one of the center tables got up and headed toward the cash register at the front corner of the bar. Bree's waitress looked over her shoulder, stuck her head in the open doorway that let to the kitchen, and yelled, "Front!"

A woman in her forties bustled out of the back and up to the register. She was thin, with nervous, birdlike move-ments. Her hair was dyed a stark dark brown. A slash of red lipstick cut across her face like a warning sign. "Is that your bill?" she chattered at the couple. "I see you had the hamburg. Wasn't it good? They make the best ham-burg here. No. Sorry. We don't take American Express. Visa or MasterCard only."

"Pay her in cash, Harold," the female customer said. She addressed the cashier. "I swear, I'm going to ditch that AmEx card. Nobody takes it."

Harold muttered, and plunged his hand into his shorts pocket. He withdrew a money clip and began to count the money out.

"You've got cash today? Good. Good. Makes it easy, doesn't it?" The cashier took the bills Harold offered. "Thirty? On a twenty-five forty bill? You want to leave a little something for Trudy?"

"Just give me two back," Harold said.

"Got it right here." The cashier dug her hand into her skirt pocket and handed the two dollars over. "'Bye, now!" She watched the couple leave. She busied herself at the register. She refilled the bowl of mints, neatened the pile of matchbooks, and, so quickly that Bree almost missed it, put the thirty dollars into her pocket.

Bree's waitress came out of the kitchen balancing a sandwich plate and a glass of iced tea. She set both in front of Bree, and then went to clear the dishes from the table where Harold and his AmEx-hating companion had been sitting.

"Damn," she said. "The cheap bastard didn't leave a dime."

The cashier made a sympathetic sound.

"I swear to God, Tiff, I'm going to get me a job over to the Pancake Hut."

"Too close to the old folks' home," Tiff whispered brightly. She darted into the dining area and began to straighten up the little piles of salt, pepper, and ketchup on each table. "The old buggers tip worse than the folks here." She twinkled at an elderly couple in the far corner.

"Keep your voice down," Bree's waitress said in mild reproof.

"Deaf as a post, the two of them," Tiff said scornfully.

"*She* ain't." Bree's waitress nodded in her direction. Bree smiled, waved, and then beckoned at Tiffany.

Tiffany bit her lip, and then picked her way across the room to Bree's booth. "Help you?" she said.

"I'm sure you can," Bree said pleasantly. "Although I have to tell you in advance all I've got with me is an AmEx card."

"Oh, we take . . ." She stopped and flushed. "Look, I don't know who you are or what you're up to, but we don't take kindly to your sort here."

"I beg your pardon?"

"Art!" she shouted. "Artie!"

Bree heard a clang of pots from the kitchen. Artie's belly preceded him through the doorway to the kitchen. Artie himself was moonfaced, with a beard problem.

"She made a pass at me!" Tiffany said indignantly. "She scared me to death! I want her out of here!"

Bree put her head down and laughed. Then she pulled out her wallet and flipped it open to her Bar Association card and held it up. "I'm an officer of the Chatham County court system, Artie. And I need to talk with her. And I promise I'm not about to give her a big fat kiss. Although," she added, as Artie disappeared back into the kitchen, "I might just give you a slap up the side of the head. Sit down, Tiffany."

Tiffany perched on the edge of the seat opposite her, her hands clenched.

"You're quick," Bree said, with no small degree of admiration. "You must have driven the folks at Marlowe's absolutely crazy."

"Is *that* what this is about! I didn't have a thing to do with those robberies. Not a thing!" Her voice quivered with outrage.

"The warehouse robberies?"

Tiffany looked at her suspiciously. "You know who's behind them, don't you? I told them. It's that geeky kid who sits in front of the computers all day. He's got a record, you know. His daddy's a big-deal lawyer in town. So do they go after him? No. They go after me. Just because of some little trouble I got in years ago. I was barely a kid myself."

"You're talking about Chad Martinelli? Is there any proof that you know of, Tiffany?"

Tiffany leaped to her feet. "Everybody's always on about proof. Proof! I told you! I didn't have a thing to do with it! There's no way you can take me to jail."

"I believe you." She wasn't going to get anywhere with this lunatic if she didn't get her past the fear of arrest. "But you know all about what happened, don't you? I have to say, you seem pretty smart to me. I'll bet not much gets past you."

"Not much does," she said with a trace of smugness.

"Was it Mr. Jensen, the store manager, who first looked into the robberies?"

Tiffany worried her bottom lip with her teeth. "I guess. I don't know."

"You worked the night shift?" Bree guessed. "And at the bank during the day?"

"That's right." Tiffany glanced nervously around the room, then sank back into her side of the booth. "I was cashiering. We were open twenty-four/seven, and Mel, that's Mr. Jensen, was pretty understanding about my not being able to work the late late shift from eleven to three. Because I had to get up for the bank in the morning."

"Right."

"But once in a while, I'd get stuck. We had to rotate, see, and no matter how much coffee I drank, I'd get sleepy." She jiggled her foot rapidly up and down. "See, caffeine has absolutely no effect on me."

Something sure did. Either Tiffany had ADD or a severe adrenaline imbalance.

"So once in a while, I'd just need to take twenty minutes, or I was just going to drop where I stood. And that's when the first robbery happened."

"What was taken, exactly?"

"Drugs. A lot of drugs, from the warehouse. Mr. Jensen figured somebody had a duplicate set of keys." Her eyes shifted away from Bree's. "And the pharmacy. Some bitch worker planted the ones from the pharmacy in my purse, so I got nailed for that one. It was a total crock, that was. Total setup." She smirked. "She got hers a little later on, that bitch. It was nothing to do with me."

Bree wasn't so sure. But she said, merely, "Did Mr. Jensen ever discover who had the duplicate set of keys?"

"Sure. The boss's kid. The one who stole that money from the cute little Girl Scout."

Bree gaped at her. "Lindsey Chandler?"

"That's the one." Tiffany giggled, a sharp, high sound like a bird cracking a nut. "Kid claimed somebody framed her. Yeah, right. You think she'd've come up with a better story than that."

⸻

"Oh, my God," Antonia said. "The whole thing sucks like a lemon."

Bree nodded glumly. She'd gone straight to the theater after hearing what Tiffany Burkhold had to say, in the hope of finding someone sane and lovable to talk to. Who better than her sister?

"Jeez." Antonia propped her knees against the seat in front of her and unwrapped the remaining half of Bree's BLT. "Poor kid. Isn't there anyone who gives a rat's behind about what's going to happen to her?"

Bree thought of Madison, who was sane, grounded, and focused, and Chad Martinelli, who wasn't. "Maybe. I hope so. I'm going up to rag on Lindsey this afternoon." She resisted the temptation to grind her teeth. "That kid! Are she and Chad mixed up in this robbery? And do the families know it? That goes a long way toward explaining why the Chandlers are keeping the lid on. Do you suppose it's some kind of revenge against their parents? *Why*, for God's sake?" She kicked Antonia's theater seat in frustration. "I can't, *won't*, believe that the two of them committed murder."

Antonia's silence was sympathetic. Then she said, "So what's going to happen now?"

"I'm going back to the office. I'm going to go through the file again. Maybe I'll make one of those charts on whiteboard. Except I don't have a whiteboard." Bree closed her eyes, suddenly sick of the whole investigation. Pseudoephedrine. Meth labs, probably. God help them. "You want to go out for a pizza after tonight's show?"

"Got a date. Sorry."

This was nice, normal, kid sister stuff. Bree gazed at Antonia with enormous affection. "No kidding? Sherlock or Watson?"

"Ew! Watson's got to be, like, forty-five if he's a day!"

"Sherlock, then," Bree said with approval. "Good looking, and a heck of an actor. He's was at the open house a few weeks ago, wasn't he? I'd forgotten about that. Lucky old you."

"Lucky old me," Antonia said with a happy sigh. Then, with obvious reluctance: "You can join us if you want. We're going dancing at Murphy's Law, that pub off of Franklin Square. Hunter dances, doesn't he? Bring him, too."

"Hunter, dance? Don't make me laugh."

"For Pete's sake, Bree. The guy moves like a boxer. I'll bet he's a wizard on the dance floor."

"I'm not about to find out." Bree eased herself out of the theater seat.

"Are you off?"

"I'm off."

"Are you going to tell Hunter about Lindsey and the keys?"

"I don't know." Bree stood in the theater aisle, thinking hard. She didn't want to make the drive back up to Cliff's Edge Academy, but she didn't see how she could avoid it. What she wanted to know from Lindsey, Lindsey didn't want to tell her. If she called, the kid could just hang up. And it was harder to lie when your interrogator was looking you straight in the eye. "What time is it?"

"Just quarter to one."

"I'm going to the office. Then . . . I don't know what I'm going to do."

"We'll probably end up at Huey's tonight, if you want to drop by late."

But Bree, halfway up the aisle, didn't have time to reply.

⁓

There wasn't anyone at home at 66 Angelus Street. Bree let herself into a darkened office. Outside, the wind was rising, and a slow roll of storm clouds headed into Savannah from the west. She fed the three dogs, and then, in response to Belli's imperative scratch at the back door in the kitchen, let them all out into the cemetery. Sasha relieved himself against the magnolia tree, then sniffed busily around the fence surrounding the graves. Miles and Belli went about their business in a more dignified way, then settled themselves down between the Pendergast graves. Tomb guardians, Bree thought.

She settled herself at her desk and began a methodical search through the Chandler file. A neatly lettered note from Ron was first.

I talked to Luis Chavez. To the best of his recollection, there have been three robberies at the warehouse. The first was in early June, the evening before PB's death. The other two occurred at ten-day intervals after that.

Then, from Petru:

Cell phone calls, day of client's demise:

Mr. Mel Jensen 6:00 a.m.
Dr. John Lindquist 6:07 a.m.
John Stubblefield 6:10 a.m.

Jensen, the store manager, must have discovered the robbery when he came on duty at six in the morning and called his boss. Then Chandler marshaled the troops, Lindquist and Stubblefield first. A long list of calls followed those. Bree skimmed through the phone calls—the man must have had the phone permanently implanted in his ear, from the number of them Petru listed. She stopped at the calls that must have occurred at the Miner's Club in the early evening. An *incoming* call from Chad Martinelli. An outgoing call to Peter Martinelli, his father. Another call from Probert to Chad, and then to Lindsey.

Bree sat back. So Chad called Probert first. Why? To make threats? She shook her head, puzzled. The kid didn't make sense to her. Not yet.

She moved on through the file, the witness statements, the accident report, the summary of her talks with the rest of the Chandler family. She read through the autopsy report again, noting, as she did, that Probert Chandler's blood type was OO.

That stopped her.

Bree was realistic enough to know that as a corporate tax lawyer—the area of law she'd specialized in before she'd been dragged into this loony defense work—the only real talent she had was a memory for minutiae. And something about that blood type bothered her.

She still had the lab report on Carrie-Alice's blood type crumpled in her pocket. She smoothed it out.

Carrie-Alice was OO, too.

And Lindsey . . .

Bree thumbed through the girl's medical history. There it was. AB−.

"Whoa," Bree said aloud. Lindsey wasn't Probert's daughter. She couldn't be. There was no way two double-O parents could have an AB− child. Bree remembered enough Mendel to know that.

Bree lifted her head and stared out the window, thinking hard, wondering why this bit of information seemed so critical. She reached for the phone. Carrie-Alice. Lindsey's mother was the place to start for answers.

A shout of thunder shook the house. Outside, the wind picked up with a shriek. Miles and Belli sat as if carved in stone. Dead leaves and dust whirled around them. Bree got to her feet—Sasha, at least, shouldn't be out if it was going to rain.

The swamplike mire that covered Josiah's grave opened up, slowly, a dread eclipse of movement across the ground. Miles whirled and faced the opening. Belli backed up slightly, head lowered, lips pulled back over those fearsome teeth, eyes glowing red.

A strange, furnace glow sprang to eerie life in the depths of the open grave. And then, with the sly, stealthy movement of a creeping snake, a path of filthy green light crept over the lip of the hole and onto the ground.

Bree discovered she'd backed up against the desk. A figure jerked horribly up the path. The shape was manlike, but distorted, as if she saw it through the shield of a scum-filled pond. It seemed to be made of flesh and bone, but a pallid, dead white flesh that crawled with corpse-mold. The man, Bree saw, or what had once been a man, raised his arms in a dreadful summons.

"Bree!"

Sasha appeared out of nowhere, tail thrashing furiously over his back, barking as if to raise the dead.

Which had been raised already.

Miles and Belli leaped forward. The ground caved under their feet. They fell, soundlessly, and disappeared from sight.

Sasha jumped backwards, avoiding the pit by a hairsbreadth. Josiah—who else could it be but Josiah?—lifted his head and stared directly at Bree. His eyes were a hideous, human blue in the ruins of his face. He grinned, horribly. Then he whirled and kicked. His boot caught Sasha under the chin. The dog screamed and flew backwards and hit the magnolia tree with a shattering thump.

Bree raced to the back door and flung it open. The wind smacked into her like a train. She staggered, got to her feet, and pushed herself against the roiling air like a swimmer coming out of the depths of the sea. Sasha shook himself, rolled to his feet, and raced to Bree's side.

She had nothing. No weapons. No way to fight him. Josiah shuffled over the dank and rotting grass. The stench of rotting flesh forced itself down her throat. Bree fought the fear that engulfed her, and sent up a wild, wordless prayer for the power that was her Company's gift to her and her kin.

Josiah's hands reached out to grab Bree. Sasha leaped full at him. Josiah fell back, flat onto the green miasma of the Bridge from the grave, and tumbled back, back, back to the ashy glow of the depths.

The grave closed in over itself, but not before Belli and Miles jumped out.

Bree was alone in the cemetery with her dogs. A gobbet of decayed flesh clung to her hands and the smell of the dead was in her hair.

"What I want to know," she said furiously into the phone, "is *where was everybody?*"

Professor Cianquino let a moment of silence pass before he responded. "The rules are fairly clear," he said, finally.

"Not to me, they aren't." Bree's hands were clenched tight on the steering wheel. She made a conscious effort to relax them. She was headed up to Cliff's Edge to confront Lindsey. Belli and Miles sat behind her in the back. Sasha sprawled in the passenger seat next to her.

"Like meets like."

"Like meets like?" Bree wasn't scared anymore. But as often happened when she'd been frightened out of a year's growth, she was angry. And that interfered with the ability to think clearly. So she said, as calmly as she could, "Does this mean I'm the temporal equivalent of a corpse?"

"Very good," Professor Cianquino said. His approval was a rare thing.

"No extras, then," she said. "I get it. The Pendergasts don't have any extra help, and neither do I."

"Precisely."

"So it's mano a mano?" She scrabbled around for her long-forgotten Latin and said, "Or *corpus a corpus*?"

"You would *not*," her professor said, "want it any other way. If you were able to call on the Company, they, in turn, would be able to call on . . ." He paused. "You would not like that. Not at all."

Bree rolled her eyes. *Says you,* she thought, but aloud she said, "Thank you. I guess."

"How is the case progressing?"

"Slowly. I don't have any real leads. And it's insane to try to solve this murder without any real communication from my client."

"But he has communicated with you," he said. "The paperweight, the keys, the blood test, and the photograph.

"The blood test has already led you to an essential key to the case, dear Bree. Listen to what else your client has to say."

---✦---

She made it to Cliff's Edge Academy in under two hours. The big wrought-iron gates to the school were closed. The fence surrounding the property was as firmly planted in the ground as ever. Bree drove past the grounds at a leisurely pace, as if looking for an address or admiring the Spanish moss that dropped from the live oak trees that dotted the landscape like so many sentinels.

"The thing is," she said aloud, to the attentive dogs, "I want to avoid Miss Violet Henry like the plague. The only hope I've got of getting Lindsey to Tell All is if I convince her no one knows for sure about the robberies but me—and as her attorney, I'm bound to keep my mouth shut about stuff that can put her in jail."

Sasha put his paw on her knee and yawned.

"As for you two"—Bree glanced in the rearview mirror, where Belli and Miles sat as immobile as a pair of temple dogs guarding a Chinese emperor's palace—"I just hope you'll come runnin' if I end up needing some help with nosy security guards. Ah. There we are."

There was a gap in the fence. More properly, there was a stile in the fence, which horses with the local hunt could jump over. There was a security camera perched on one of the fence posts. The camera would capture anything over five feet tall. Bree pulled up on the grass and parked the car. She got out, then released Miles and Belli. "Heel," she said to Belli, and pointed to her right. Belli stood at her right shoulder. If Bree bent over, she was concealed behind the big dog's shoulder. "Miles," she ordered, "heel!" She pointed to her left, and Miles took his position on her other side. She hitched her purse over her shoulder and took a deep breath.

"Up and over!" Bree commanded. She took off for the stile at a dead run, the two dogs running silently on either side. They scrambled over the stile in unison. Bree fell to the grass, rolled over, and lay there for a moment, to catch her breath. She got to her feet and ordered the two dogs back over the stile. They jumped back onto the grass verge by the road with ease, and stood looking at her doubtfully. From the safety of the front seat, Sasha cocked his head and looked on with interest.

"Stay," Bree said. All three of the dogs dropped to a stay position, and Bree took off across the lawn, toward the sprawling mass of the school building. With luck, she'd have twenty minutes or so before the guards who went out to check on the dogs thought to check on the owner of the car.

She found Lindsey in the dining hall. Cliff's Edge treated its students well. The room was large, sunny, and carpeted. The round tables, each seating eight, were draped in white cloth. Lindsey was slouched at a table in the corner. She was alone, picking listlessly at a hamburger. Bree threaded her way through the tables, nodding with confidence at the several teachers seated with the students. She reached Lindsey unchallenged, and paused and looked her over. Lindsey's color was good. Her skin was more pink and less gray. Her hair was washed. The circles under her eyes were less pronounced. The girl looked up at Bree in mild surprise, quickly replaced by her usual sullen, hostile sneer.

"I need to talk to you," Bree said without preamble. "And I don't want to do it here."

"There's grass stains on your skirt," Lindsey said.

"Yeah, well." Bree grinned. "My entry was a little unorthodox. Nobody knows I'm here."

"My brother didn't send you?"

"No. I came to talk to you. Come outside with me, will you?" She held her hand out, and added gently, "Please. It's about your father."

Lindsey shrugged. Then she shoved the hamburger aside and got to her feet. She followed Bree through the French doors to the terrace fronting the lawn outside.

"Let's sit here, shall we?" Bree pointed to a stone bench set under one of the ubiquitous live oaks. Lindsey perched on the very end, then drew her knees up to her chin and stared at Bree.

"Do you have a dollar?"

Lindsey blinked at her.

"I've quit my job as your brother's lawyer. I'm signing on with you. But I can't represent you unless you give me an official retainer."

Bree knew she desperately needed to gain the girl's confidence.

"I think you got a raw deal, Lindsey. I want to help you."

A peculiar smile flickered across her face. She shrugged—that shrug!—dug into the pocket of her jeans, and handed Bree a dollar.

"Good." Bree folded the dollar and tucked it away in her suit coat. Then she plunged her hand into her purse and brought out her set of car keys. She held them loosely in her hand, so that Lindsey couldn't see anything but the keys to the front and back doors of the town house. "Keys to the pharmacy and the warehouse at Marlowe's," she said gravely.

Lindsey sat up, her eyes wide.

"Your dad found out about the robberies."

"My dad?"

"Easy as pie, I suppose. Coming into the store, late at night, with a set of these." She jiggled the keys and they chimed faintly in the thick air.

"I don't know what you're talking about." She hunched over and rubbed her arms, as if she were cold.

"I'm on your side," Bree said. "I'm not turning any of this over to the police. I just need to know who else was in on it with you."

Lindsey looked frantically from side to side. "Nobody," she said. "Just fuck off, will you? Just fuck off."

Bree grasped Lindsey's hands and held them, hard. "Don't lie to me, Lindsey. If you lie to me, I can't help you at all."

"Leave me alone!" Lindsey screamed suddenly.

"This boyfriend of yours, Chad Martinelli . . ."

Lindsey sucked her teeth.

"I'm looking at him for some bad stuff, Lindsey. If he helped you with this, it's possible he was responsible for your dad's death. Possible that he killed poor Mrs. Chavez, too."

"Killed my dad?" Lindsey said. "Somebody killed my dad?"

"Miss Winston-Beaufort. Stop right there!"

Bree sighed. Less than twenty minutes. The security team was sharper than she'd thought. She stood up and waited for Miss Henry and the two burly guards trundling after her. "I'm going to see what I can do to fix this, Lindsey. I'm going to have to talk to Chad. You have any idea where he might be today?"

Violet Henry plowed to a heaving dusty halt in front of them, reminding Bree of the Road Runner in the cartoons. She stifled the impulse to say "beep beep."

"How did you get in here?" the headmistress demanded. She was furious. A very Southern Lady sort of furious. Her voice was low. Her smile was fixed. There wasn't a hair out of place. But she'd buttoned her suit jacket up starting with the wrong button, and a smear of gravy was on her chin. Clearly, she'd been interrupted while eating. Behind her, the two guards put their hands on their gun belts and looked menacing.

"She's my lawyer," Lindsey piped up. "She's my lawyer and I asked her here." She folded her arms defiantly. "So just fuck off, okay?"

Bree bit her lip. "I'm sure Lindsey's sorry for the language, Miss Henry. But I can't help but agree with the sentiment."

Lindsey rolled her eyes. "Talk to Madison, Bree. Okay? She'll tell you Chad didn't have a thing to do with it." She swallowed hard. "She's my best friend. She knows I didn't have anything to do with it, either. I know you won't believe me. But everybody believes her."

"Get out, Miss Beaufort," Miss Henry said between her teeth. "Right now."

So Bree got.

⌘

"She's not here," Andrea Bellamy said, when Bree got her on the cell phone twenty minutes later. "She didn't come straight home. She volunteers at the hospital on Wednesdays. She's a candy striper."

"Until what time?"

"Four thirty. Then she heads out to the Y to swim. She picks up Hartley first."

Bree sat in the driver's seat of her car. She'd made it back to Savannah around six, having been evicted from the Cliff's Edge premises in record time. Sasha yawned beside her. Behind her, Belli and Miles sat upright, staring at the street. She'd postponed the promise of the walk to blank looks from all three of them. She said, now, to Andrea, "Hartley Williams? The judge's daughter?"

Cordy'd backed off the whole Sophie Chavez mess with amazing speed, due, Bree had suspected, to a couple of discreet phone calls from that same eminent gentleman.

"Is her father a judge?" Andrea said, impressed. "You're kidding. I thought he ran a business of some kind. You know what? I'm a liar. It's her stepfather who runs the business. A judge. What do you know?"

"Does she live with her mother or her father?"

"Oh, her mom. I've met her. I can't believe Dorcas dumped a judge. 'Course, from what I hear, she's dumping this new husband, too."

Bree made an effort to control her impatience. "Do you have the address?"

"Sure. Hang on." Andrea put the handset down with a clatter, and then picked it up again. "It's a housing development out by the Oglethorpe Mall. Twenty-two Trail View. I've been there once. It's right off the main entrance. There's this pair of stone monuments with the name carved in them: Valley View. Trail View's the first right as you come in the front."

She'd rather talk to Madison in a venue less public than either the hospital or the Y. "May I have Madison's cell phone number? I'd like to meet her at Hartley's, if I could."

Andrea rattled it off. Bree scribbled it down, promised to let Hartley know her father was welcome at the Bellamy residence anytime, and phoned Madison. She went straight to voice mail. "It's important," she said. "I need to talk to you about Lindsey and the robberies at the warehouse. If you and Hartley know anything at all about this, Madison, I really need to talk to you. Lindsey needs your help."

Then she punched Hartley's address into her GPS. The trip time was less than twenty minutes. "So, you guys, we've got time for the walk after all."

Belli placed her huge head on the backrest and slob-bered gratefully in Bree's ear.

⸺∞⸺

By the time she reached the turnoff for Valley View—which had neither a valley nor a view of anything but the back end of the Oglethorpe Mall, Bree was running a little late, and the weather had worsened. It was going to storm again and storm hard.

Madison's little red Miata was already in the driveway. The housing development was new, and the landscaping was sparse. There seemed to be three different styles of houses. Twenty-two Trail View was at the more modest end of the scale. It was two stories, with a small front porch and an attached garage. A For Sale sign sat on the lawn. Bree parked at the curb, just past the mailbox, and got out of the car. The front door opened and Madison Bel-lamy waved at her. Bree waved back. Madison wore a bright pink T-shirt. The Savannah Sweethearts Social Club logo was picked out in sequins and the lowering sun struck metallic flashes off her chest. Bree squinted against the fractioned light; there was somebody behind Madison. Some guy, she thought. Hartley's stepfather, perhaps.

She reached into the rear seat for her briefcase, shov-ing aside Belli's huge forepaws to get it. As she backed out of the car, the briefcase awkwardly positioned under one arm, she collided with the mailbox.

"Watch it," Madison said in her ear.

Bree jumped. She shut the door. The dogs looked out at her. "Sorry," she said. "I didn't hear you come up. And it looks like I whacked the mailbox a good one. Sorry." The cheap wooden stake lurched to one side and the metal door to the mailbox gaped open. Bree gave the stake a firm shove to keep it upright, and palmed the door shut, idly noting the name as she did so.

The name on the mailbox was Hansen.

Bree froze.

Hartley's stepfather, Stephen, is a real asshole, Lindsey had said.

Marv Kleinmetz. Tiffany Burkhold. *Stephen Hansen.*

"Nice to meet you at last, Miss Beaufort," Stephen Hansen said.

"Oh, Madison," Bree said. She felt sick.

Hansen had a scar on his cheek.

Shirley: *He had a scar under one eye.*

Hansen was the third man in the old photograph in Probert Chandler's office.

Lindquist: *We were all chem majors . . . Steve Hansen was with us for a time.*

Madison stepped away from the car. The man behind her stepped forward. His hair was cropped close to his head. He had to be at least forty-eight, Bree thought, but he looked a lot younger.

Madison: *I prefer older guys myself.*

He was tall and rangy, with cold gray eyes. He draped one hand familiarly around Madison's shoulders. In the other, he held a gun. Madison glanced down. Bree didn't know as much about handguns as she did about shotguns, but it was a .38. "I thought you got rid of the damn thing," Madison said. "Damn it, Steve. That's just plain dumb."

"You're all in this," Bree said. Involuntarily, she glanced at the house. A third figure stood at the open door. Short, chunky, with that irritating giggle that cut through the heavy air like a squalling baby's. "And Hartley, too."

Madison snapped her fingers rhythmically and began to sway back and forth. *"Sweethearts send a sen-ti-mental sound to the guys to the chicks to the people all around. If you'd like another version that'll get you off the ground, it's the singin' Sweet Savannahs where the happy can be found."* She brought the back of her hand to her nose, sniffed heartily, and grinned.

Bree looked at the gun in Hansen's hand. She was furious. Coldly furious. "Lindsey said you knew all about it. I guess she was right."

Madison laughed. It was genuine, gleeful laughter. Bree didn't think she'd ever heard anything so chilling. "Lindsey, my ass. The only thing that little bitch is good for is the keys to her father's pharmacy."

"Hey!" Hansen said. "That's my kid you're talking about, here." He cuffed Madison on the ear, not too gently. Hansen was Lindsey's father.

The ninth circle. Treachery. Poor, friendless Lindsey.

"Probert discovered all of this that day at the Miner's Club," Bree said. "About the robberies, at least. Is that why you killed him?"

"I didn't have a damn thing to do with that. Bert never could handle his liquor. And he was worth more to us alive than dead. No way was he going to turn in his own kid. Not to mention my little meth lab and the kids here, who help me get the goods to the customer." He grinned at Madison.

"But if he'd just discovered that Lindsey *wasn't* his daughter . . ."

Hansen looked surprised. "He knew that?"

"You mean he didn't?"

Hansen shrugged. "Why cut off the source of the golden eggs?"

Bree frowned. "You mean you were blackmailing Mrs. Chandler?"

"You know," Hansen said, "I think this conversation is over." His eyes narrowed, and he looked meaner than any junkyard dog Bree had ever seen.

"And Shirley? What about Shirley?"

Hansen's eyes shifted away from hers.

"Got in the way." Madison shrugged. That all-purpose, in-your-face, so-what shrug. "And that was your fault, Miss Rich Bitch Beaufort. If you hadn't asked her that question about the store robberies, Shirley wouldn't have put two and two together. She tracked me down after you left, wanting to know if I thought Lindsey had anything to do with them. 'Cause Lindsey had the keys, see, from her dad."

Shirley's call to an unknown number. The keys. Bree wanted to punch something. She looked at Hansen. "So you shot her? Shirley Chavez?"

His face was stone. Flint.

"Maybe it's a good thing you did hold on to the gun, Stevie," Madison said. "I think you're going to have to shoot her, too."

Hansen cupped Madison's neck with a proprietary caress. "We'll ditch it after this," he said. "I told you it'd be dangerous to be in this kind of work without a weapon. I'm sure you'd agree, Miss Beaufort." He raised the gun to the level of Bree's forehead and aimed between her eyes. "Inside the house. Now!"

Sasha growled. Bree's hand tightened around her briefcase.

"The dogs!" Madison shouted. "Steve! The *dogs*!"

Bree swung the briefcase and knocked Madison sideways. Hansen leaped back and shot Sasha in the chest.

"Sasha!" Bree flung herself at her dog. She clamped her hands over the blood pumping out of Sasha's chest. Hansen leaned around Madison, crouched slightly, took aim through the backseat window, and pulled the trigger twice. One bullet for Miles. One bullet for Belli.

Behind the shattered glass, Belli and Miles roared in fury. Striker was a vast, silvery presence behind them.

Sasha's dying eyes locked onto hers.

Bree's rage burst its bounds.

She flung her hands wide, the dog's blood splattering the car, her hair, Madison's contorted face. The air around her began to spin with the ferocity of a rip tide. She grabbed it, held it between her spread hands and arms like a living animal, and molded it, directed it, spun it . . .

And she was at the top of a mountain, with the winds of Heaven at her command.

Nineteen

A deed of dreadful note.
—*Macbeth*, William Shakespeare

"How's Sasha?" Hunter shut the front door of the veterinary clinic behind him and paused uncertainly in the middle of the waiting room.

"Come and have a seat," Antonia said. "Bree, the lieutenant's here."

Bree looked up. Antonia had scrubbed Sasha's blood from her face and hands with a damp Kleenex but it hadn't helped much. Her skin was stiff and grainy. "He lost a lot of blood," she said. "Too much, they think. But he's going to make it." Hunter and Antonia exchanged looks. "He's alive," Bree said stubbornly. "And he's going to make it."

"They transfused him," Antonia said in a near whisper. "But he's got a different blood type than most dogs. They used a whatsit—a universal donor—but we're waiting to see if his system rejects it."

"Twenty-four hours," Bree said. "They'll know for sure after twenty-four hours."

Hunter looked at Bree, and then away.

"They'll let me sit with him as soon as they get the bullet out." Bree crossed her legs, and then uncrossed them. "They have a recovery room."

"Just like for people," Antonia said brightly. "Is that cool, or what?" She put the backs of her hands against her eyes to blot the tears.

Hunter rubbed his chin. His jaw was set tight. His eyes were narrowed. Anger? Frustration? Bree didn't really care. "We need to talk," he said.

"It can wait, can't it?" Other people had followed Hunter into the waiting room, Bree realized. The red-haired sergeant, Markham. And another uniform. *Taylor*, she thought. *His name is Taylor.*

"No," he said evenly. "It can't wait. We get a call that shots have been fired in a suburban area. We show up to find two terrified teenagers and a roughed-up adult being menaced by those two huge dogs of yours. Not to mention the blood all over the pavement outside this quiet suburban home. Not to mention the fact that you've taken off after firing two shots at these people—"

"Me!" Bree said indignantly. "You're crazy! Hansen shot my dog!"

"He claims you ordered the dogs to attack him."

"What?!"

"Hansen said if it weren't for some freak windstorm that swept through the neighborhood you would have shot him dead." Hunter leaned over her, his voice loaded with an emotion Bree couldn't identify. "This tornado, he says, kicked up such a windstorm of debris that you lost the gun. He picked it up. Then he claims you set those two monsters on him, took the gun back, and tore off down the street like a bat out of Hell."

"I don't own a gun," Bree said. "It's Hansen's gun." Her briefcase sat by her chair. She shoved it forward with her toe. "I picked it up off the lawn when this . . . windstorm spun it out of his hand."

Hunter looked into the briefcase. "God damn it." He jerked his head at Taylor. Taylor came forward, pulled an evidence bag from his hip pocket, and carefully loaded the gun into it.

Bree sighed. "You won't find my fingerprints on it, Hunter. You'll find Hansen's." She glared up at him. "And as soon as the veterinary surgeon gets the bullet out of Sasha's chest, you'll find it's the same gun that killed Shirley Chavez."

"Lieutenant!" Markham thrust her cell phone in the air. "I've got the captain and he's royally pissed. Are we going to get this woman downtown, or what?"

"Outside," Hunter ordered. His tone brooked no argument. Markham cast Bree a look of loathing. Hunter swung around and faced them, his jaw thrust forward. "Both of you." He waited until she and Taylor had retreated onto the front steps outside, and then turned to Bree. "Spill it."

"Drugs," Bree said. "It's all about drugs, this part of the case, anyway. The Savannah Sweethearts Social Club is a drug ring, with Hansen at the head. The girls acted as mules—that's the expression, right? Hansen booked the group into high schools, and Madison, Hartley, and Lindsey carried the drugs to contacts Hansen had established there. Pills, mostly. When Hansen's business was shut down, he lost his laboratory, too. The Marlowe's robberies were a stopgap until he got up and running again. That's my guess, at any rate."

"And the murders?"

"The gun, of course. I told you. The bullet that hit Sasha." Bree's cheeks were wet, and she blotted them with the back of her hand. "It's the same as the bullet that killed Shirley Chavez."

"This is bullshit. There's no evidence. None. This is all supposition." He shook his head in disgust. "*If*, and it's a very big if, your wild-assed guess turns out to be right and that is the same gun that fired the bullet that killed Shirley Chavez, what have we got?"

"We've got Hansen!" Bree said indignantly. "This is the only thing that makes any sense. I've just delivered the members of his little gang to you on a silver platter. Not to mention the fact that you now have a way to link the distribution of the drugs in the high schools. I'll bet your week's paycheck that there's a clear pattern between the Savannah Sweethearts concerts and drug activity in the schools where they sang."

"And if there isn't?"

"There's got to be. It's the only thing that makes any sense." She smiled, faintly. "You're one heck of an investigator, Hunter. I'll bet you a second week's paycheck that if you put Markham, there, on the computer for a couple of hours, you'll make those connections by tomorrow morning." She ran her hands over her hair. "Not to mention the confessions. Madison's going to be a tough nut to crack, but Hartley will talk as soon as you get her into one of those foul little rooms and threaten to cut off her supply of herbal shampoo."

"All three of them have lawyered up."

Bree dismissed this with a wave of her hand.

"Not only have all three of them lawyered up, but Hansen wants you and your license to practice law. He wants you arrested for assault, menacing, and intent to commit grievous bodily harm. Not to mention the charges *we* want to throw at you. Leaving the scene of a felony assault . . ."

"Just shut up," Bree said tiredly. "Please. And I'll come down to the station as soon as I see to Sasha. Please."

He shook his head. "No way, Bree. Sorry. I've got to take you in."

"You don't have to take me in right now. You have to wait for the bullet."

"The bullet?"

Bree looked at him. At her right, Antonia shifted uneasily in her seat. "Go ahead," Bree said. "Arrest me. I don't care. Just let me stay here until I see Sasha through this. Please."

Hunter rubbed his face with both hands and swore. He pointed his finger at her, his face grim. "Don't you leave this clinic. You understand me? You stay right here. I'll be back in five minutes."

He slammed out the front door. Bree let her breath out in a slow sag of relief. There was only one other client in the waiting room—a small, elderly lady with a cat in a blue plastic carrying case. She cast a scared look at Bree and scuttled after Hunter. The door closed gently behind her.

Bree leaned back in her chair. Antonia took her hand and patted it.

The Chatham County Small Animal Clinic was like most others of its kind; doors off the reception area led to the examination room and the operating theater. The door farthest from Bree opened, and a woman in green scrubs with a surgical mask hanging around her neck beckoned. Bree got to her feet. "I can go sit with him now."

"Breenie." Antonia stood up with her. "You want me to come with you?"

"Don't call me Breenie. I'll be fine. To tell you the truth, I'd sooner you were out of this and back at the show." Bree was moving toward the open door, and Sasha.

"Are you serious?"

"Deadly."

Antonia hesitated. "You want me to call Daddy?"

"You do that, I'll shave you bald, first chance I get. I can take care of myself, Tonia."

A brief giggle escaped her sister, then she said, rather fearfully, "Those dogs you set on Hansen and the girl . . ."

Bree did stop at that. She turned halfway round. "They kept it up until the police got there, didn't they?"

"That's part of the trouble, isn't it?" Antonia said with spirit. "Bella and Millis . . . ?"

"Belli and Miles," Bree said, giving the latter the correct pronunciation. "What about them?"

"They took off, God knows where, and I can't say I'm all that comfortable with the idea of those two roaming the streets of Savannah."

"They'll turn up," Bree said as Antonia left the clinic.

And of course, there they were, waiting for her, sitting outside the little recovery area where Sasha lay, perfectly whole and hearty. Belli greeted her with a snuffle. Miles raised his head, regarded her briefly, and got to his feet with a grunt. Bree sank to her knees and put her arms around their necks.

The veterinarian looked up as Bree came into the room, the dogs at her heels. Sasha lay flat out on a gurney. Someone had placed one of the hard plastic chairs from the waiting room next to it.

A shaved patch bisected Sasha's chest. The bullet wound itself was a small clean hole just over his heart. Bree sat down in the chair.

"I'm so glad your secretary thought to bring your other dogs by," Dr. Steiner said. "The female, Bella?" She nodded in Belli's direction.

Bree didn't correct her. She sank into the chair next to her comatose dog.

"She's a universal donor." Dr. Steiner was young, thin, and the kind of woman who would have looked totally unnatural in any kind of makeup. She pushed her spectacles up with one finger. "And we're equally lucky Bella's so big. Sasha lost at least thirty percent of his whole blood volume. He needed all the help that Bella could give." She fondled Bella's ears. The huge dog regarded her with a grave, unwinking stare.

"You saved the bullet?" Bree asked. She sat up and put her hand lightly on Sasha's flank. He felt cold. "It's evidence in a homicide."

"My assistant bagged it up. He's probably handed it over to the police out front already." Her glasses had slid partway down her nose again, and she pushed them up. "You're sure you want to stay?"

"I'm sure."

"We'll check on him from time to time. There's a bathroom right down the hall, if you need it. And the coffee machine out front. Is there anything I can get you?"

"My sister will bring a sandwich by in a bit," Bree said.

"If you notice any change at all, let one of us know, okay? The anesthesia's going to wear off in another hour or so. If he starts to thrash, give us a holler."

"That soon?" Bree said. Her heart beat faster. "You'll know that soon?"

"We don't expect him to regain consciousness for quite a while," the vet said kindly. "But yes, if the rejection is going to occur, the symptoms should start in a few hours. I'll be on call, if you need me. And, of course, we've got an all-night attendant on duty." She waited, awkwardly. Bree looked at her helplessly.

"We'll just have to see," she said, and then walked briskly out of the room.

"Well, Sasha." Bree put her cheek briefly against his furry face. He breathed in and out, in and out, with the sound of ocean waves.

There was a soft stirring of the air behind her.

"Hey, boss."

Bree turned around. Ron shimmered quietly in the corner, encased in a sphere of spinning light.

"This wasn't supposed to happen," Bree said in a fierce undertone. "How could it? How could it?!"

Lavinia stepped out from the other side of the gurney, her violet aura draped around her like a cocoon. She shook her head sadly. "Poor old boy," she said. "Poor old Sasha."

"I don't understand," Bree said. "Is Sasha going to die? He can't die, can he? He's one of you. He's a member of the Company!"

Lavinia reached across Sasha's body and brushed the tears from Bree's face. Her hands smelled of lavender. "It comes to all of us in the end, honey. One way or the other."

"There must be something we can do. Something *you* can do."

Sasha sighed, in his drugged sleep.

"Passing from one room to another," Ron said. "It's something like that. We have all the tools the temporal world can give us to save him, Bree. We'll just hope that it's enough."

Bree looked at them, her teeth clenched. She shook with helpless anger. "No. You didn't hear me. There has to be something else. Something . . ." She stopped, half afraid to ask—not even knowing the kind of question she *could* ask. She wasn't afraid to beg, if begging would save Sasha's life. "Can you? Can you help me? Can you help *him*? With . . ."

"Something extra?" Ron's voice was gentle. "No. No. I'm so sorry, dear Bree."

"I don't care *what* it costs," Bree began, recklessly, but they were gone, the two of them, and Miles and Belli, too, leaving her alone with Sasha's body, and the breath that barely stirred it. Bree bit back a shout. It wasn't fair! It wasn't *fair*!

It may have been hours later—it may have been minutes. Bree wasn't sure. Waiting, Bree had time to think. The motive for Probert's murder stuck out like a neon sign.

Suddenly, Sasha's golden body quivered. He began to pant, heavily, and tiny bubbles of foam appeared at the corners of his mouth. His right foreleg jerked in a spasm, then his left.

"Help!" Bree shouted. She put both hands on the now warm fur and pressed down, trying to keep his body still. "Hey! I need some help in here!"

"Help," said a smooth voice behind her. "We thought you'd never ask."

Bree whirled.

They looked like accountants. Or a Sinclair Lewis version of accountants, anyway. Medium height. Neat. Dressed in sober blue suits, white shirts, and nondescript ties. The taller one had a prim mouth; the shorter one was bald; both wore dark glasses.

The taller one took his glasses off and his eyes were a dark, dried-blood red with yellow pupils. He extended his hand. His nails were thick and manicured to blunt points. "Henry Beazley, at your service, Counselor. And this is Caldecott."

Caldecott smiled. His teeth seemed to be all canines, sharp and not quite clean.

"We represent the prosecution," Beazley said cordially.

Bree's chest got very tight.

"In the matter of Chandler v. The Celestial Courts," Caldecott added. The words "Celestial Courts" had a pronounced hiss—like the sound made by a fire doused with water. Or a large snake.

Sasha choked, gasped, and quivered. Beazley raised

his hand, in a "now, now" kind of gesture, and Sasha's breathing slowed to a peaceful tempo.

"T'cha," Beazley said, with patent insincerity. "Such a shame. Such an"—he paused, thoughtfully—"*ardent* soul, Sasha. Quite an asset to Beaufort & Company, I believe."

Bree bit her lip. She waited for the rise of the wind. She waited for the silvery shadow that was Striker. She felt nothing but fear for her dog and a gagging disgust for the burned-match smell that suffused the little room.

Beazley sat down in midair and crossed one leg over the other. Bree took a breath and gasped a little. "We thought it was time for a prehearing discussion," he said. "You've got a court date in . . . when is it, Caldecott?" He tipped his head in Caldecott's direction, but kept his red-yellow gaze on Bree.

"Fourteen hours," Caldecott said primly. "Two o'clock tomorrow afternoon."

"Petru filed the appeal yesterday!" Bree said indignantly. "I haven't had time to prepare my case!"

"Time," Caldecott mused, "is a mutable thing."

Beazley nodded. "Yesssss." The sibilance died away. He looked smug. "Our case looks good."

"Very strong," Caldecott said.

"But anytime prehearing negotiations can keep costs down . . ."

"The whole system benefits . . ."

"And we like to avoid cost overruns wherever possible . . ."

Bree folded her arms. "You're willing to withdraw your objections to a retrial for my client?"

"Not exactly, but we are willing to make some small concessions," Beazley said.

"Small," Caldecott echoed.

"We could reduce the eternal sentence to three or four millennia?" Beazley said.

"And perhaps move from the ninth circle—so cold, that lake! And Probert hates the cold—to perhaps the eighth?"

"Windy," Beazley said. "And quite warm, on occasion, but on the whole, much less discomfort."

"Thank you, gentlemen," Bree said. "But I'm becoming quite convinced there's been a true miscarriage of justice here. I'd like the evidence to be weighed again."

"We would be quite disappointed if you insisted on that." Caldecott held both his hands in the air in apparent dismay. Sasha stiffened, as if seized by the throat. Bree blinked back tears and held him. Caldecott dropped his hands, and the dog dropped back into his drugged sleep.

"Tricky thing, blood transfusions," Beazley observed coldly.

"It'll work," Bree said frantically. "It has to."

"Trusting in man, like your mother?" Caldecott sneered. "She trusted in the temporal, and look what happened to her."

Bree stopped herself from leaping forward and grabbing the opposing counsel by the neck. "Just what *did* . . ."

They were gone. Just like that.

Bree bit her lip hard, to keep the tears away, and forced herself to trust in God and man. And while she waited, she thought. About the paperweight she found that day by the scene of the crash. About the murder weapon. About the tracking system at Marlowe's, where every piece of merchandise sold in the store could be located at the press of a button.

And very soon after, when Sasha woke and yawned widely at her, her trust in man, at least, proved to be enough.

Twenty

One more devils'-triumph and sorrow for angels,
One wrong more to man.
—*The Lost Leader*, Robert Browning

Bree was arrested the minute she stepped out of the clinic doors. It was two o'clock in the morning. She didn't know if Hunter had waited outside for her all that time—it seemed unlikely—or if the vet assistant had called the police station the moment Sasha woke. Whatever. But she had had a lot of time to think. And she knew now who had killed Probert Chandler on that lonely bend of Skidaway Road. The syringe. The blood test. The keys. The Marlowe's paperweight. And the photograph from years ago.

Hunter was there, grim-faced and grouchy. Sergeant Markham read Bree her rights, handcuffed her, and pushed her into the backseat of the police car with a certain amount of purposeful glee. They drove off to the Chatham County Courthouse. Bree argued with Hunter all the way. Hunter grunted. She hoped he was listening. Markham set her jaw and muttered, "Bullshit bullshit bullshit" all nineteen miles back to town.

Bree spent five hours in the holding pen, dying for a toothbrush. She made one phone call, to Antonia, and made three requests. Her sister had no problem with the food and coffee—and too many questions about the second and third. "But where," she said, "am I supposed to find something like that?"

Bree told her.

"And you want it for what?"

"I've got a murderer to catch—and I've got to do it before two P.M. today."

When she was released on her own recognizance at nine thirty, Antonia waited outside the courthouse with hot coffee and a lox-and-cream-cheese-stuffed bagel.

"The other thing's all set up," she said. "Jeez. The guys at the garage think I'm nuts, by the way. But I gave them a hundred bucks each and a deposit on the thing-ummy . . ."

"Jackhammer," Bree said.

"In case it gets wrecked or whatever. And the one guy, Manny, wants to be sure you've got a court order to do this. Do you have an actual real court order, Bree? Or is that official piece of paper Ron dropped off for me a crock? I think it's a crock. I don't see how you could have gotten a judge to sign the thing at three o'clock in the morning, or whenever it was that you asked Ron to do this. I think," she said dramatically, "I just pulled a fast one on the guys who do our lube jobs. And I don't feel good about it."

"You'll get over it," Bree said unsympathetically. The hot coffee tasted wonderful. The bagel tasted even better. "How'd you get the car back from the clinic?"

"I took it back to the theater when I left the clinic. Hunter said you weren't going to need it for a long, long time. As I make it, it was only a couple of hours."

"He's mad at me," Bree said. "Or was. I think he's on his way to a little forgiveness, if things turn out all right this afternoon."

"You've got hope. I'm telling you, sister, you start

messing around with the guy's job, he's not going to feel
real good about it or you." Antonia pulled the car away
from the curb with a cheerful lack of interest in what the
rest of the traffic on Montgomery was doing. Since this
was Savannah, and not Manhattan, nobody honked or
swore or even made rude gestures out the driver-side
windows. "I'm taking you back to the town house."

"I really need to go to the office," Bree said. "I'll drop
you off."

"No, you *really* need to go to the town house." She
sniffed the air in a pointed way. Bree looked down at her
wrinkled suit and her filthy shoes. Her shirt felt like it
was glued to her shoulders. "Shower," she said wisely. "I
guess I need to clean up."

"I guess you do." The drive to Factor's Walk was
short. Antonia pulled up to the town house. "So how was
it? Jail, I mean. This is the first time any Beaufort's been
in the slam since the pirate Beaufort in 1763."

"The holding pen," Bree corrected her. "Not jail. And
it wasn't too bad, considering. Smelly, due to the unsettled stomachs of the lady drunks. Rowdy, due to the irri-
table tempers of those same lady drunks, who'd been
deprived of their gin. But not too bad." She heaved herself out of the car, wanting to sleep for a week. "To be
honest, I'd rather not do it again."

Antonia followed her into the house. In her room,
Bree stripped off her clothes and headed for the bathroom. She turned the shower water on, as hot as she
could stand it, and stepped in. She let the water run over
her for a long moment, without moving.

". . . back here!" Antonia called from the other side of
the door.

Bree dumped shampoo on her head. "What?!"

Antonia cracked the door. "I said I talked to Ron, and
he'll pick Sasha up as soon as the clinic's ready to let him

go. And he's *really* glad we seem to have solved the case."

Ron's picking up Sasha on his bicycle? Bree decided not to worry about how the carless Ron was going to retrieve the dog. Or why sometimes people could see him, and sometimes they couldn't. It appeared to be up to Ron.

"Those two monster dogs showed up at the Angelus office, he said."

"Ron said Miles and Belli are there?"

"Yes. And they've got to stay there, he said. Since the law wants to lock them up the way they just locked you up."

Bree scowled to herself. "They didn't bite anybody."

"They menaced, Ron said, which is enough to get them quarantined, these days, I guess. They scare me to bits, Bree, but I'd hate to see them end up in custody and then get put down, the way they do with those poor pit bulls."

"Fat chance." Bree would like to see those county officials brave enough to attempt to euthanize either one of the pair.

"Don't be too sure. And Ron said George Chandler has apparently called you about forty-two times."

Bree scrubbed herself down with the loofah, twisted the faucet handle from hot to cold, endured the spray of icy water for all of thirty seconds, and jumped out of the shower. She wrapped the first towel Antonia handed her around herself, and the second around her hair. "I'll have to get back to George later. One way or the other, he's not going to be happy with what I've found out. So I'd just as soon it was later."

"So now what?" Antonia said brightly. "You want some more breakfast? I think you should go to bed and sleep for the next twenty-four hours."

"Not yet." Bree looked at herself in the steamy mirror. She didn't look too bad, considering. Chandler's hearing

was today, which was totally outrageous. Petru had filed
the appeal the day before yesterday. She'd have to speak
to someone about the timing thing. It gave Beazley
and Caldecott a grossly unfair advantage. She couldn't
remember much about Einstein's theory of time as the
fourth dimension, but the Celestial Courts were on the
seventh floor of the six-floor Chatham County
Courthouse—not far enough away to make a significant
difference in the passage of time for Them, as opposed to
the temporal. She'd have to ask Goldstein about filing a
petition of some sort if days were going to be months
long instead of twenty-four hours.

"You're dead on your feet. Whatever you're planning
to do, you'll do better if you get some sleep."

"No time," Bree said, "no time." She looked at her
watch. Ten o'clock. She had less than four hours to get
enough evidence to reverse the judgment against Probert
Chandler.

She had one last chance.

She called Chad Martinelli at Marlowe's. And when
he found what she needed, she picked it up from the
store. Then she called Hunter.

The concrete mixer in front of Marlowe's research center
was gone and the base was smooth and dry. The day was
hot and sunny, unseasonably warm for November. Manny
and Gustavo stood at the base of the Marlowe's sculpture,
just as they'd promised. Manny leaned on the jackhammer, his forearms draped over the handle.

"Hey," Bree said, as she walked up to them.

"You got that warrant?" Manny said instantly. "You
don't know these guys, Miz Beaufort." He waved one
hand in the general direction of the Marlowe's building.
"I been checking around. They don't make a lot of noise

about it, but they carry some big weight around town. I
don't want no trouble."

Bree set her briefcase down on the concrete and pulled
out the document. It looked official. The signature looked
valid. It'd been notarized; there was Ron's signature next
to his notary seal. She didn't look too closely at the
judge's signature—it might have read Alvarez, who was a
circuit court judge for the surrounding area—and it might
have read Azreal. She wasn't sure. And she didn't want to
know. "Here it is, Manny. I thank you. And the citizens
of Chatham County will thank you."

Manny looked pleased. "So," he said expansively,
"where do you want us to dig?"

Bree walked around the base of the sculpture. The di-
ameter of the circle was perhaps twenty feet. The cir-
cumference, of course, over three times that. The concrete
was smooth and unmarked. She walked around it again.
Manny and Gustavo waited patiently in the sunshine.
Above them, faces appeared at the office windows on the
second and third floors. Bree walked around the circle
one more time, then stopped and sank her chin in one hand,
considering. The other held the warrant.

The glass doors at the front of the building burst open.
First out of the door was a harried security guard. John
Allen Lindquist was right on his heels. Lindquist was
white with anger. He grabbed Bree by the upper arm and
shook it. "What the hell do you think you're doing?"

Bree watched his eyes. They darted to the left, then
back again. She followed his gaze. She looked at Manny
and pointed. "Right there," she said. Then, as the noise of
the jackhammer cut through the air, she leaned close and
said into Lindquist's ear: "You, Chandler, and Hansen
were chemists at the University of Oregon together. Probert went on to found Marlowe's and took you with him.
Hansen was ruined and went on to seduce your sister.

You've been protecting her—and your own job—for years by paying Hansen off with money and drugs from the warehouse, so he wouldn't tell Probert that Lindsey wasn't his own child. Probert found out about it. You killed him. To protect yourself. To protect your sister. I don't think you gave a damn about Lindsey."

She pulled the sales receipt out of her briefcase. It was in an evidence bag.

"Your inventory system's just about perfect. You can track anything—anything—in those stores. Including the purchase of a two-hundred-watt searchlight. By you. And the dents in the metal, Mr. Lindquist, are going to match the dents in poor Probert Chandler's head."

Manny gave a shout of triumph. The concrete was only three inches thick. The flashlight was buried in a shallow pit. Manny reached into the dirt and held it up in one gloved hand.

Hunter, who'd just shown up with Markham, had told her once there were only three things a criminal could do when confronted with the evidence. Run. Lie. Or lawyer up. Lindquist ran. Hunter and Markham tackled him a hundred feet from his Lexus.

"If it was anything like the last time, I'll be back in time for a nice cup of tea." Bree shook the folds of her red velvet robe free of the box it was stored in and held it up against her. She, Petru, and Ron stood on the seventh floor of the six-floor Chatham County Courthouse.

"Ke-vite different, this Court of Appeal," Petru said glumly. "This is not traffic court, dear Bree."

Ron draped the robe around her and twitched a sleeve into place. Bree was getting quite fond of it. Lavinia had worked the lapels in fantastic gold embroidery. The velvet itself was whisper thin, and shimmered with sunset-light.

Ron folded the high collar into place. The wall that held
the great gold seal of the Celestial Courts reflected her
image back to her. She looked a stranger. Her silvery hair
was piled high in elaborate braids. The gold collar surrounded her face like a stiff halo. The robe flowed around
her feet. She looked eerily like the defending angels on
the stairs leading up to Lavinia's rooms in the office on
Angelus Street.

"Your pleadings," Petru said. He handed her a stack of
vellum, elaborately inscribed. "The case summary is ra-
tionally well argued, if I do say so myself. Mr. Probert
Chandler discovered Lindsey was Hansen's daughter and
his partner was allowing Hansen access to the drugs in
the warehouse. He confronted Lindquist, and intended to
stop him, even though it would mean the ruination of all
he'd built up. This should weight the scales in his favor.
He did not betray the child he raised. He was trying to
save her." He sighed heavily. "This case can go any way
at all. There's no hope of Heaven, I would say; I would
cross my fingers and hope for Purgatory."

Bree drew a deep breath, tapped at the bronze door
labeled NINTH CIRCUIT COURT OF APPEALS, and stepped
inside.

She froze.

She'd defended Benjamin Skinner in a quiet, cloud-
drenched room with no ceiling. There had only been one
angel present, a delightful, puckish old guy who'd har-
rumphed as she'd entered her pleadings, and dismissed
her with an avuncular wave of his hand.

This place was entirely different.

She stood in a gallery built around the top of a huge
expanse. The place was suffused with an indirect, blue-
tinged light. There was no ceiling above her—just a dark,
cloudy mass of roiling air. Below her was a large wood-
paneled expanse. Painted murals lined the wainscoted

walls. At first glance, the murals resembled the angels marching up Lavinia's stairs. But then Bree saw that the brightly painted figures moved, and that the scenes were of the cases cited in the documents she held in her hands.

The expanse below was set out in the familiar pattern of courtrooms everywhere. The prosecutor's dais was on the right; the defense was on the left. And on the judge's stand in front sat a huge pair of golden scales. The bowls tipped gently back and forth in the currents of air.

Caldecott and Beazley took their places on the right.

A broad staircase led down to the floor.

And Bree descended.

Epilogue

"You're working on a Saturday, Bree? Got a hot case?" Cordelia Eastburn wasn't a large woman, but she seemed to take up a lot of space in the elevator. She punched the Down button to head to the first floor of the courthouse.

"An appeal," Bree said. "Not your jurisdiction," she added, in case Cordy got a little nosy.

"Doesn't seem to be going all that well, from the look of you."

"Could be better," Bree admitted. "I don't think I'm going to get a reversal. I did get a review of the sentencing, though. I suppose that's something."

"Win some, you lose some," Cordy said. "All part of the great game of justice. But you did okay on the Lindsey Chandler case. Got the kid into therapy instead of a jail sentence. There's hope for that kid yet."

The elevator bumped to a stop. Cordy got out. So did Bree.

"I do believe there may be. She walked up to the theft charges, and that helped a lot."

"Ah, the rewards of plea bargaining."

"She wouldn't allow me to plea-bargain, Cordy. Just threw herself on the mercy of the court."

"Uh-*huh*."

Bree smiled a little. "But even cynical old you have to

feel good about this other thing, Cordy. You know the program Lindsey's in—it's good. Plus, if you keep your nose clean for the first six months, you can choose either to be released to your family on weekends or to stay in the center. Her mother asked her to come home, and Lindsey's agreed. So there's a step in the right direction there. And what's more, she's volunteered restitution of sorts. She's talked her brother into sharing the costs it'd take to fund a new rehab facility here in Savannah."

According to Ron, Carrie-Alice's confession about her affair with Hansen had not divided mother and daughter. Lindsey had given her mother a long, thoughtful look, and said: "So you're sort of a screwup, too?" And then did The Shrug, of course. But it was The Shrug accompanied by a reluctant smile.

"Maybe." Cordy snorted. "Your appeals case having the same kind of mixed result? Little teeny steps instead of a nice clear win? How much of a long shot was it?" She held the glass doors open, and Bree went through first. Outside, the sky was the crisp blue that heralds the advent of early winter in Savannah. Ron waved at her from her car. The sun glinted off the gold of Sasha's fur, as he poked his head out of the driver-side window. He barked when he saw her coming. Bree waved them on. She wanted to walk.

"How much of a long shot?" Bree repeated. She thought of Probert Chandler who betrayed his daughter. She thought of Josiah Pendergast—and the kind of eternity he faced; driven by hellish forces to haunt Bree until some final showdown. No neat resolutions for any of them. "Nine to one, going in. But I got the sentence reduced. And it's three to one that he'll feel it's fair." She faced Cordelia with a smile. "He did it, you see. The crime he was committed for. But like Lindsey, he threw himself on the mercy of the court, and he's attempted restitution.

And like Lindsey, he was pretty sorry about the way he'd lived. But we'll see."

She stopped at the corner of East Bay and Houston. They had walked all the way down to the turnoff for 66 Angelus Street. Cordy couldn't follow her there. But Sasha could.

"I guess you could say the whole thing's in Limbo, for the moment."

There was a newly dug grave in the cemetery surrounding 66 Angelus Street. It was empty, of course, but the tombstone awaited the arrival of the murderer. Justice would catch up with him. It always did.

STEPHEN HANSEN
TANT'È AMARA CHE POCO È PIÙ.
IT IS SO BITTER, DEATH IS HARDLY WORSE.

A Note on
the Celestial Spheres

The magic that drives Beaufort & Company in its quest
to redeem tormented souls evolves from old beliefs in the
Celestial Circle of Angels. The idea of the Celestial Circle itself arose from an amalgam of Christian, Jewish,
and Muslim theology in the early Middle Ages. Modern
sources describe the Circle as the hierarchy of angels that
form "an endlessly vast sphere of supernatural beings
that surround an unknowable center, called God." The
sphere is constructed of the Upper, Second, and Third
Triads. Within each Triad are ten Choirs, whose beings
include seraphim, serpent fires of love, cherubim, thrones,
dominations, virtues, powers, and the so-called Magnifi-
cent Seven, among others. I have added the concept of a
Shadow Circle of Dark Angels that parallels the Celestial
Circle.

Penguin Group (USA) Online

What will you be reading tomorrow?

Tom Clancy, Patricia Cornwell, W.E.B. Griffin,
Nora Roberts, William Gibson, Robin Cook,
Brian Jacques, Catherine Coulter, Stephen King,
Dean Koontz, Ken Follett, Clive Cussler,
Eric Jerome Dickey, John Sandford,
Terry McMillan, Sue Monk Kidd, Amy Tan,
John Berendt…

You'll find them all at
penguin.com

*Read excerpts and newsletters,
find tour schedules and reading group guides,
and enter contests.*

Subscribe to Penguin Group (USA) newsletters
and get an exclusive inside look
at exciting new titles and the authors you love
long before everyone else does.

PENGUIN GROUP (USA)
us.penguingroup.com